The Immortal

MacLeod

Kristy Pantin

DEDICATION

To my three precious girls; you are the reason I am.

~1~

*T*essa Anderson leaned against the 'Lost Baggage' counter at the Inverness Airport and cursed silently.

The past week had been horrible, and now to top it all off the airport had thoughtlessly lost her bags.

"Is there anything else you would like to throw my way while you are at it?" she grumbled quietly to no one in particular.

Maybe running off to Scotland on such short notice hadn't been the best plan of all, but in her defence, she wasn't exactly thinking straight at the time. Damn Aiden Gregory, somehow the whole baggage fiasco was his fault; when men like Aiden threw a bomb into the middle of your carefully organized life, the fallout just didn't stop. Granted, she had been having doubts about him anyway, but how dare he cheat on her.

The wedding was supposed to have been in a week, and it would have all gone off without her being any the wiser if she hadn't been fortunate enough to trip on a loose shoelace at their joint bachelor/bachelorette party at a friend's very expensive and very large beach house. This amazing feat of clumsiness resulted in her slamming into and through the door of the laundry room.

There she was, sprawled unceremoniously on the ground, looking up at her fiancé, who was in the midst of a very athletic move with an incredibly limber twenty one year old bleach dyed blonde. He even had the nerve to get angry and ask what the hell *she* was doing. Hurt and embarrassed, she hadn't bothered to dignify that with an answer and spent the rest of the night at home with a bottle of Captain Morgan's. The few things he had at her house mysteriously found their way into the pool in her back yard that night.

Tessa took a deep breath and focused once again on the man in front of her. A slight frown on his young face was the only sign anything was wrong as his fingers danced along the keyboard at a furious pace.

He finally looked up, regret evident in his green eyes as he brushed his shaggy hair out of his face. "I'm sorry lass," he said, his Scottish accent so strong it was a miracle she could understand him. "Your bags dinna get put aboard the plane on time and willna be arriving till tomorrow night. Is there a number and address we can reach you at when it arrives?"

Tessa sighed in surrender and gave him the requested information before turning and walking dejectedly out of the airport in search of a taxi to take her to Dunvegan Castle.

Being a famous author had its perks, but unfortunately it didn't seem to shield her from dating and almost marrying a complete loser - or having her bags misplaced at the airport. She shook her head sadly. How was it she hadn't even had the slightest idea that the man she had been with for two years was sleeping with another woman? How was that possible? It's not as if she trusted him completely or anything. Was she that clueless? It had apparently been going on for three months. How could she not have known?

She dragged herself into a silver, futuristic looking minivan kind of taxi that had pulled up in front of her. It seemed that she was the only person getting on, which suited her just fine since she wasn't exactly in a chatty mood at the moment. She told the driver her destination and laid her head back on the seat, eyes shut, willing herself not to cry. The silent tears came anyway. She tried to reassure herself that everything would be ok. In a month, when it was time to head back to Canada, she would be completely over what he'd done to her and ready to start a new life.

She thought about the look on her mother's face when she told her what Aiden had done. She had been heartbroken for her as any mother would be. Her father, a retired police officer, would have gleefully polished his glock and taken Aiden's head off if she hadn't quickly assured him that she wasn't really all that upset about it.

She told them that she was leaving for Scotland to get away for a bit and do some research on a new book. To their credit they took it well, understanding that it was just something she had to do to deal with what happened in her own way.

The taxi driver had been watching Tessa in his rear view mirror on and off for the past few miles as daylight faded and had noticed the tears leaking from her closed eyes. "Are you ok?" he asked softly, peaking into the mirror again.

Tessa jumped in surprise at the sound of his voice. She looked at his silvery eyes in the rear view mirror. Strange colour.

"I'm fine," she mumbled.

He turned to the mirror once again with a look of concern. "If there's trouble in your life, you might ask king Finvarra for help. You never know, he might be feeling overly benevolent."

Tessa opened her eyes again and stared at him with a frown. "I...I thought there was only the queen of England. There's a king too?" she asked, feeling rather stupid. And why on earth would a king want to take time away from running a country to fix her love life? She also briefly wondered why the driver didn't have a Scottish accent.

A deep chuckle floated back as the man looked at her in amusement. "No, that's not the kind of king I speak of, I mean the king of the faeries".

Oh good grief!

Tessa suddenly realized that she was in the middle of God knows where, at night, with a mad man. Her eyes went round with fear. What the hell was going to happen next in her life? Damn Aiden, damn him to hell, now she would be kidnapped and tortured mercilessly because of that stupid man! She was most definitely going to come back and haunt the bastard for this, she decided firmly. As her fingers gripped the door handle, she hesitated, wondering if it might be worse to give herself over to the mad man at the wheel or to open the door and hurtle to her death.

Before she could choose the second option, the driver spoke again, as if sensing her distress. "I don't mean to frighten you; you'll find these parts of Scotland are rich with legend and folklore. It is said these kinds of beliefs have a grain of truth to them. And besides, what would it hurt to make the request? I would think on that a bit if I were you."

Oh thank God, she wasn't going to die after all, she thought with relief as she blew out a huge breath she hadn't realized she had been holding, easing her death grip on the door handle at the same time. Taxi man isn't completely crazy!

The driver grinned at her relief that his sanity wasn't in question, and shook his head in obvious amusement.

They had been driving for just over three hours and during their short conversation, blackness had claimed the sky. The moon shone softly, as if unwilling to battle the darkness for its share of the sky. When they drove over the long narrow bridge leading to the castle, the lights of the taxi played with the shadows along the front of it, making them quiver and jump. The effect was slightly eerie, yet interesting at the same time.

After waving goodbye to the *maybe-only-a-little-crazy* taxi driver, Tessa stood in front of the castle, looking up at the battlements in the soft glow of lights. Everything was so magically beautiful, she thought in astonishment, imagining what it would have looked like back when it was newly built. She had been so focused on her bad luck that she supposed she didn't fully realize she was actually in Scotland until this moment.

Shaking her head in wonder, she hooked the strap of her carry-on bag on her shoulder, tore her gaze away from the towers, and headed up the steps to the huge, sturdily built front door. As she approached the door, it opened to reveal what could only be described as God in a kilt, complete with the surrounding halo of light. Good God these Scotsmen were gorgeous, she thought as she focused on breathing evenly.

Dragging in a long slow breath, she stared at the man's chest. It was a good place to start considering he was so tall that she would have had to crane her neck to see any higher.

His light, long sleeved shirt billowed slightly before coming to rest on an impeccably defined chest. The shirt was tucked into a kilt. Seriously? A kilt? Oh Lord, even in a dress the man looked manlier than a pirate. There was some sort of pouch tied around his waist, resting against his...well against something she was almost positive would be as huge as the rest of him. She blushed at the thought and continued her slow perusal of the God.

Below his kilt, two strongly muscled legs disappeared into soft looking black boots.

The boots suddenly shifted, reminding her that she was standing in the doorway of a castle ogling a man-god. She should have at least had the decency to say hello before treating herself to such delicious eye candy.

An incredibly deep, velvety voice spoke. "When you've have had your fill lass, I'm Cailean MacLeod, Chief of Dunvegan. I'd be more than happy to show you to your room." She could hear the smile in his words and groaned softly to herself.

Blushing furiously, her gaze darted up and locked with a pair of sinful blue eyes that were looking out from behind long, thick lashes. Didn't Scotsmen usually have green eyes?

She fully intended to apologize for her rudeness, but the look on his face stopped her. There was an arrogance about him, no doubt from years of having women fall over themselves around him. He had short black hair and a rugged, strong jaw that was covered with a light coating of stubble, and his sensual lips curved into a smile that promised the kind of passion that would make a woman swoon in delight. She also noticed a deep cleft in his chin which she had always thought sexy in men.

"Were you planning to shorten your visit lass?" he asked curiously.

Tessa looked up at him again with a confused look on her face and a trace of attitude in her voice. "What do you mean?"

"Normally when we have long term visitors, they doona show up with just a bag slung over their shoulder and a look of desire in their eyes," he teased with a grin. Damn him! Did he have to have such a sexy, lilting accent?

Tessa frowned and regarded the man blocking the front door. True she had been rudely ogling him, but did he really have to point that out? She should have realized that it was impossible to go anywhere in the world without encountering a man who thought he was God's gift to women...even though this one quite possibly could claim that title without even trying, but there was no bloody way she was ever going to tell *him* that.

Taking a deep breath, she tucked some errant strands of hair behind her ear and narrowed her eyes. "Is this what passes as hospitality in Scotland or do I actually get to come inside?"

He smiled mischievously, "You may come anywhere you'd like lass, I'd be more than happy to assist."

Tessa's eyes grew round and her jaw dropped in shock, not sure if to believe that the man she just met a few minutes ago had actually propositioned her.

Just when she was gearing up to lay into him, he motioned to her bag, "May I?" he asked, sliding the strap from her shoulder.

Tessa's jaw snapped shut and she did her best to regain her composure, not at all sure if she should be angry at his teasing or disappointed that he might have really been only asking if she wanted help with her bag. Well, whichever it was, it was still rude of him to keep her standing on the front step, she decided, desperately trying to work up some anger. Unfortunately, try as she might, she couldn't will herself to be angry at this sinfully gorgeous man.

"Look I just need to have a shower and get some sleep, it was a long flight and I'm exhausted," she said tiredly.

He chuckled and stood aside with a sweeping bow, indicating that she should enter.

*   *   *

Cailean led the way up the stone stairs of the castle to the second floor where the guest bedrooms were located. He smiled to himself at the disgruntled sigh behind him. Although he would never take the lovely lass in the intimate sense, for he knew by her aura that she was not for him, he had no problem teasing her. She looked too sad anyway, as if a distraction would do her well.

Hearing a muffled giggle behind him, he turned as he reached the top of the stairs. "Exactly what is it you find so amusing about my backside lass?"

She casually shrugged and muttered, "I just think it's strange for a man to wear a skirt that's all."

"'Tis a kilt," he growled, "and there are a great many groups and religions in this world where men wear some version of a dress or another and are considered manly."

"Oh really?" she snorted. "Name some."

"Name s....are you serious lass?" It was highly likely she had a sense of humour, but having only just met the lass he really had no idea.

"Sure, if you think it's so normal, name at least five groups or countries," she demanded, obviously confident he couldn't.

Growling in irritation because she had the gall to think his kilt unmanly, he snarled, "In Fiji men wear a skirt-like wrap called a Sulu. In Thailand and Malaysia they wear sarongs. In India, Pakistan and Arab countries they wear dresses called Caftans and Djellabas, and...," he reached out and gently lifted the crucifix that hung around her neck, almost pulling back in surprised at the small jolt of electricity he received when he touched her, "even your own Catholic monks, priests, cardinals and popes wear robes!"

Her eyebrows arched and her mouth dropped open, obviously surprised at both the amount of knowledgeable he had on the topic of men in dresses and the shock she got when he touched her.

When you've lived three hundred years, it was only normal to know a lot more than the average person, even about something as seemingly useless as men in dresses.

"How did you know that?" she demanded.

He snorted, "Doona underestimate me just because you think I'm wearing a dress, and I'll no' underestimate you just because you're a lass." With that he turned and stalked toward an open doorway, disappearing into the guest bedroom, leaving her staring after him with her mouth hanging open. He knew that comment would probably get her annoyed, but he was curious as to how she would react. So far she had failed to follow any semblance of normality when it came to female behaviour, except maybe ogling him when he'd first opened the door.

He had been amused at her apparent shock at seeing him. At a muscular six and a half feet, he was accustomed to being drooled over by the lasses, but none yet had managed to turn him on with a simple look as this woman had. When her gaze had traveled down his body, the air itself almost seemed to crackle with electricity and a strange heat had flowed through him, knocking him off guard for a moment.

She entered the bedroom behind him and he felt a moment of pride when he saw the look on her face. She took in the luxurious room with an amazed expression, obviously forgetting to be angry at him.

He and his brother Colin had worked hard to make the guest suites in the castle a thing of grandeur and ultimate luxury. From the thick, warm curtains and wall tapestries to the intricately carved wooden bedposts, the room had the feel of royalty.

She was standing about five feet from him and he smelled the same perfume he had noticed when she walked past him in the entrance. He had never been so tempted in his life to simply walk over to a woman he had just met and kiss her. How dare the wee lass think him any less than a man because he wore a kilt? And the longing way she was looking at the damn bed was giving him all kinds of ideas he shouldn't be having. He closed his eyes with a frown, cursing the Seelie king yet again for complicating his life.

His eyes flew open and he inhaled sharply when a delicate hand gently pressed against his chest, causing another bolt of electricity to knife through him. She was standing perilously close, looking up at him in concern.

"Are you ok?" she asked softly. "You look like you are in pain."

Saints alive how could such a light touch affect him so?

Tessa slowly slid her hand down a little before removing it, unaware of what that small movement did to him. She glanced at her hand before looking back at him as if also wondering at the shock she felt.

His jaw and hands were clenched with the willpower it was taking not to reach out and grab the beautiful lass. The surge of heat that went through him at her touch had focused itself on the one place she was guaranteed to notice if he didn't distract her, and himself. It was hard to focus his thoughts. All he wanted to do was pull her to him and plunge his tongue between those tempting lips. He suddenly ached to feel her writhing against him in ecstasy, begging for his touch.

He almost jumped back from her. Where had this sudden desire come from? He wanted to do things to her that would have shocked her speechless. God why did she have to be a blasted virgin, he could almost smell it on her, and what the hell had happened to his composure?

"Nay lass, I'm well," he replied in a husky voice as he stepped back to put some distance between them. "Just a wee headache."

She looked at him curiously before turning to examine the room once again.

"This room is just gorgeous," she sighed as she ran her hand up and down the bedpost. He groaned silently.

The bed had a thick, white, down-filled blanket covering twelve hundred thread count Egyptian cotton sheets, and there were enough fluffy pillows to get lost in.

The price of a stay at Dunvegan Castle wasn't something to be sneezed at, but for those who could afford it, they definitely got their money's worth. It worked out nicely that those who could afford to stay at the castle were not the type to party well into the night and cause unnecessary trouble for the brothers.

Cailean took advantage of her distraction to run his gaze down her body. She was wearing a grey blouse, and her slim, firm legs were encased in a pair of form fitting blue jeans. Black dress shoes completed the ensemble, giving her an air of casual elegance. As he moved his gaze back up her body, that strange heat ran through him again. His thoughts started to get fuzzy, and his body felt like it was vibrating. He shook his head, trying to clear it.

When she turned to face him, he looked up quickly and plastered a friendly smile on his face. Her green eyes sparkled as she gazed at him with a delighted smile on her face. She looked so happy at that moment that he wished he knew what pain she had suffered to cause her to come here alone and so suddenly.

"The bathroom is just down the hall," he said gently. "I'll leave you to get settled now, but if have need of anything, my room is the next one over."

"Thank you Cailean," she said when he turned to leave.

As he pulled the door shut, he heard her quietly tell herself that this vacation might just be exactly what she needed.

"I hope so lass," he murmured as he looked at the closed door.

He sighed and walked toward his room, wondering why he seemed to get zapped whenever he touched her. This wasn't something that had ever happened to him, and considering the length of time he had been alive, that was saying something. It wasn't even as if the castle had carpets to work up a static charge on.

Frowning in confusion he pushed through the door to his room and was immediately assaulted by a foul odour. He stiffened and looked around the gloom warily while sliding a dirk from his belt.

In the far corner, a being stood glaring at him with red, glowing eyes. It was a misshapen thing, obviously one of the Unseelie's war minions. Its head was a strange lumpy shape with long, lethal looking canines sticking out of its grotesque mouth from both the upper and lower jaws. Its grey skin was bumpy and covered in places with blood. The stench it carried with it was of death.

A low growl issued from its massive jaws seconds before it lunged at him, claws outstretched.

Armed only with a small dirk and unwilling to allow the beast out of the room for fear it might decide to make a meal out of his guest or one of the house maids, he slammed the door and vaulted over a chair toward the claymore hanging from the wall to his left. Yanking it off its hooks, he swung it toward the general direction of the monster. It jerked back and started coming at him again. He had no time to wonder how it had gotten past the wards placed at each corner of the castle before it swiped a huge hand at him, claws missing by mere inches.

Ducking under its massive arm, he came up on the other side of the swing and slid the sword deftly into its heaving side with a grunt. The monster looked stunned for a moment as glistening drool dripped in ribbons from its angry mouth. It looked Cailean in the eyes as it started to disappear. "It's not over yet human," it growled as a grey light surrounded it seconds before it blinked out of existence.

As suddenly as it started it was over, even the putrid odour he had first encountered upon entering the room was gone. He leaned forward bracing his hands on his knees, breathing heavily. What the hell was that all about? Those monsters were never normally sent out except during a war. Cailean straightened up. And how on earth had it had managed to get inside his bedroom? The castle was guarded by wards to prevent the uninvited fae and their minions from stepping foot inside. That thing, although definitely weakened, didn't show any signs of burns associated with trying to cross a magical ward.

He crossed over to the corner of the room where the monster had been standing. On the stone floor, glinting in the moonlight, lay the small silver ring he had found the day before when he was walking the grounds. It had been lying on the sand near the water, well outside the warded area.

Suddenly it hit him. The blasted Unseelie had put the monster's essence into the ring and dropped it where he would find it. He had picked it up and brought it inside the castle, placing it on his dresser for a closer look later. Because it had been touching his skin, and because it only had the essence of the monster in it, it was easily brought onto warded land. If it had been anyone other than he or Colin who picked it up, the wards would have blocked the ring's entrance like a solid wall. He would have to wear gloves from now if he was holding something while walking over that line so that nothing like this happened again. Having that ring in contact with his skin was as good as making it invisible. God he hoped he hadn't inadvertently brought anything else over. He'd have to keep his guard up just incase, and warn Colin to do the same.

He grabbed a washcloth from the night table and wiped the blood off the sword in disgust before stalking angrily over to the hooks to replace it.

Colin would be back the next evening which would give them time to discuss what had happened before the first day of their monthly battles.

Sighing wearily, he undressed until he was left with just his kilt. He was about to remove that too when he realized it might be better to have some clothing on incase the annoying Unseelie had anything else up their sleeves that night.

He lay down, sinking into the softness of the bed tiredly, and fought with images of Tessa pressing her hand against his chest and thought about how close he had come to kissing her.

Twenty minutes after finally falling into a disturbed sleep, a sudden noise had him flying of bed and ready for battle. He stood in a crouch in the dark room, dirk in hand, muscles tense – waiting - straining to hear any noise that might seem out of place.

After a few seconds, a tentative knock on his bedroom door caused relief to flood through him as he quickly realize what had woken him. He flipped on the light and opened the door to find Tessa looking sheepishly up at him, wearing nothing but pink and black silky pyjamas. He realized she had just finished having a shower because her hair was still damp and she smelled amazing.

Good Lord, this was not what he needed at one in the morning after waking up so quickly. The adrenaline rush alone was causing his hormones to scream at him, and he wasn't quite sure what to do about the fact that his damn kilt wasn't going to hide anything without the sporran on.

He cleared his throat, "Can I help you lass?"

"I'm so sorry to wake you up," she rushed, "but I just realized the time difference means that my mother is sitting by the phone, probably having a heart attack because I haven't called her to let her know I've arrived safely, and I don't know where to find a phone and my cell doesn't seem to work very well here."

So her mother was the reason for this middle of the night visit. He knew he would have been way off the mark had he thought for even a second that she had other plans. She probably didn't even realize that her shirt was damp.

Backing up so that he was partially hidden by the door, he motioned for her to enter. "The nearest phone is in my chamber, I'll give you some privacy."

Hesitantly she took a step forward, then seemed to decide that calling her mother was more important than being worried about walking into a half dressed strangers room and continued on, thanking him politely.

Closing the door behind him, he leaned against the wall outside the room and blew out a tense breath. He was either going to have to think twice about wearing a kilt around this woman or forgo his Scottish pride and invest in a pair of underwear. The way she affected him was something he had never dealt with, and the softest part of his body had decided that it should be happy to become the hardest.

He quickly realized that it would probably offend her innocence if he looked like a bull ready to rut when she opened the door, and took himself off to the bathroom to wait out his infernal erection, damning his ancestors for deciding there was no need for underwear under a kilt.

* * *

During her quick phone call, Tessa assured her mother that she was safe and secure in the most wonderful castle in all of Scotland. She mentioned the delayed baggage which had her mother off on a tangent about airlines and their lack of respect for other people's property.

While her mother was grumbling, she took the time to look around Cailean's room. It was pretty much the same as hers except for the fact that the bed had obviously been recently occupied. His sheets were a tangle as if he had fought with them and lost, and she could smell his delicious male scent on them.

His carelessly discarded shirt lay over a soft armchair along with the pouch he had been wearing around his waist. She wondered what would have been kept in a pouch like that back in medieval times and was just considering taking a quick peak to see what he had in it now when she was interrupted by her mother asking if she had gotten anything to eat when she arrived at the castle.

"It's the middle of the night here mom," she reminded her, deciding not to peak after all. "I'll eat in the morning." She grinned at the phone. Even half a world away she was still trying to take care of her.

After a few more minutes she politely insisted that she had to hang up so that she could get some sleep, not daring to mention that she was in her pj's in a bedroom that belonged to a half naked man that she had just met, and was even at that very moment sitting on his luxuriously soft bed, inhaling his scent. Her poor mother would no doubt have spent the rest of her day praying the rosary and begging God to forgive and guide her wayward child.

After the goodbyes and promises to call often, she walked to the door and opened it hesitantly. Stepping out, she looked around and realized that he was nowhere to be seen. This made her feel strangely disappointed but grateful at the same time. Walking to her room she remembered how incredibly sexy he had looked, all sleepy and half naked. Good God his chest and abs were enough to feed her daydreams for the entire month. Forget six-pack, the man owned the whole damn case.

Sighing happily, she looked forward to diving into pillow heaven. The desire she had to crawl into that fluffy bed almost trumped the desire she had felt to run her hands up and down Cailean's perfectly chiselled abs when he had opened his door....almost. Despite how turned on she was at that thought, fifteen minutes later she was soundly asleep, cocooned in a nest of feathery softness, exhausted from her long day.

~2~

*C*ailean was not happy.

Although he had managed to get a little sleep the previous night, his dream had been of a sexual nature. Naturally Tessa featured prominently in it which further annoyed him. What was the point of being immortal and having all this power if he couldn't get one wee brunette out of his thoughts? He shook his head, trying to clear the fogginess that the caffeine hadn't yet dealt with.

His dream had started off with he and Tessa kissing in the sunshine. Just thinking about it got him all worked up again and he shook his head in disgust, thankful that he'd opted for his soft leather pants today. This lack of control over his nether regions was really starting to annoy him.

In his dream, it had slowly gotten darker and darker, shadows blending into one another. Out of nowhere, one of the Unseelie grabbed Tessa and started dragging her off by her hair. Somehow there was blood everywhere. He could only watch helplessly as she disappeared into a faery mound beneath a tall tree that he knew for a fact was in the garden on the east side of the castle, just outside the wards.

Considering the very real possibly that this dream, like some of his others, was a true glimpse of future events, he had no idea how to proceed with the wee lass. It could be that if he just didn't ever sleep with her, he would be able to avoid it happening altogether. He'd found that the choices he made sometimes affected the outcome of those kinds of dreams. It would probably just be best to avoid temptation at all cost. He'd promised himself a long time ago that he would never again go through the pain of watching the woman he loved die. Keeping that promise this time had the added effect of potentially saving Tessa's life.

Satisfied that his decision was made, he just had to make sure he wasn't put in a position to be tempted by her again. Cailean dropped his head into his hands and groaned. The coffee definitely wasn't helping. His head screamed like a banshee.

As if the damned banshee had been calling to her, Tessa walked into the dining room and stopped behind him. The air sizzled and his hair stood on the back of his neck. What was it with this woman affecting the very air he breathed? He refused to move, hoping she would take the hint and leave.

"If your head is still hurting, a neck massage might help relieve some tension," she ventured. "I've been told I'm pretty good at it."

Almost jumping from the table in his haste to ensure no physical contact was made, which would no doubt cause that disconcerting spark of electricity he'd felt more than enough already, he quickly mumbled an excuse and strode out the door at a good clip, leaving her behind with what he was sure was a hurt expression on her face.

All he had to do was avoid contact with the lass for one month and then she would be on her way and things would be back to normal. That way there would be no chance of her being kidnapped by those pesky fae folk and no chance of that dratted "L" word messing up his life and causing another broken heart. How hard could it be to avoid her touch?

Walking toward the stable, he felt a soft breeze blow against his face and closed his eyes, deeply inhaling the calming air. So far so good. He strode into the stable and opened the stall door that housed his precious chestnut coloured mustang, Destiny. She came forward and nuzzled Cailean's hand, hoping for a treat.

Producing a lump of sugar from his sporran, he removed his shirt, picked up the rubber curry and started brushing her down. He loved these quiet moments with Destiny and often talked gently to her. Although one-sided, the conversation was usually interesting.

He had acquired her from Dejas Buckman, a friend from the States who owned a ranch somewhere out in the Mojave Desert. She had arrived one Christmas with a bow wrapped around her and a note.

Found her wandering around and thought of you!
Watch out, she has a wicked temper. Dejas.

Destiny did indeed have a temper and it took him a full month to convince her she should let him ride her. She proved herself to be a wonderful and loyal horse but refused to let anyone else get on her back. One of the stable boys was currently nursing a broken wrist after the last attempt that sent him flying into a fence.

He gently squeezed a fetlock and raised her leg to clean out the last hoof, taking the time to rub her leg to keep her accustomed to his touch.

Just as he was finishing up, he felt Tessa's presence on the other side of Destiny and stiffened. Was she doing her best to drive him insane? He put down Destiny's hoof and leaned his head against her belly, steeling himself. "Do you need something lass?" he asked from behind the horse.

"Ummm, yeah. I was talking to your maid and she said we should go tupping." It sounded more like a question than a statement. "So I was thinking maybe we could go for that ride that came with my stay here."

Cailean nearly fell over in his haste to rise, "She said *what?*" he roared incredulously, his voice sounding strangled.

She backed up at his explosion. "Well I'm not sure exactly what tupping means, being that it's not a normal Canadian word, but I assume, because of the context she used it, that it means to go for a ride, some sort of Scottish way of saying it," she replied hesitantly, completely unaware of the effect she was having on him with her innocent mistake.

He looked at her with a pained expression, and then sighed. "Aye lass, it does mean a ride of sorts." Good Lord this was going to be a long month. Keeping away from the lass was going to be more difficult than he had anticipated.

*   *   *

"Ok then. Can we?" she asked, not sure why the mood of the stable had suddenly shifted. It seemed almost dangerous now to be standing in front of Cailean with his shirtless body mere feet from her fingers. "It was included in the package," she reminded him,

22

"and I think your maid is already getting a picnic together. But if you're busy, we can do it another time."

She felt kind of bad now for springing it on him, but when she brought it up with the kitchen maid, the woman practically shoved her out the door in the direction of the barn mumbling something about the laird needing a good tupping anyway and promising to bring a picnic basket out immediately. Tessa realized how serious the maid had been when she showed up not two minutes later offering a satchel stuffed with enough food and drink for an army. She was about to thank the woman when Cailean spoke up.

"Lara my dear," he started, almost dangerously. "When the lass and I return from *tupping*, you'll need to instruct her on the meaning of a few Scottish words so that she will no' mistakenly ask someone whose no' as honourable as I am, to take her for a *tupping* and a picnic in the future."

The maids hand flew to her mouth and Tessa wasn't sure if she was shocked or trying not to laugh. Suddenly it dawned on her what *tupping* must mean, and she flushed in embarrassment. Oh good lord...I.Q. of one hundred and forty eight and she had just stupidly asked a relative stranger to screw her brains out and then have a delightful picnic with her after. For goodness sake why couldn't they just call it screwing or fucking? Tupping indeed!

She had to give the maid credit though, after muttering a quick apology, she managed to make it halfway back to the castle before stopping to bend over in a fit of laughter.

Cailean heard the maid and grinned while he shook his head at her antics. "Just canna find good help these days."

Tessa glared at him.

Apparently deciding that it would be wiser to pretend the whole tupping conversation hadn't happened, Cailean looked at Tessa. "Do you still want to go for the ride lass?"

She fought with herself for a moment, trying to decide if wounded pride was more important than the anticipated ride. After a few moments, the thought of a long pleasant ride along the shore convinced her that her wounded pride could heal itself. "Yes please," she replied stiffly.

How on earth could she have mistaken tupping for riding? Absolutely amazing! Her friend Laney would laugh herself silly when she told her. She was always telling Tessa that she took herself too seriously and this would just prove the point. Boy was she in for a ribbing when she got home. Oh well, maybe Laney was right. She would focus on just relaxing and going with the flow. She was in Scotland after all, the magical land of fairy kings. The jury was still undecided about the sanity of her taxi driver, but she allowed a small smile when she thought of how sincere he had been.

"Do you believe in a fairy king called Fin..something?" she demanded, deciding it would be best to decide on his sanity *before* trotting off alone with him.

Cailean, who had just been taking a gulp of water, choked and started coughing and spluttering.

When he had more or less coughed the water back out of his lungs, he looked at her in shock. "Where the bloody hell did that come from?"

Taken aback by his shock, she stammered, "I...ah...well the taxi driver said..."

"Taxi driver?"

"From last night. The one who drove me from the airport. He told me to talk to king Fin...something if I needed help. I was just wondering if all of you Scotsmen were insane or if it was just him."

Great, now he would think she was the insane one, suddenly sprouting questions about fairy kings and such. Why oh why couldn't she just have a normal conversation with this man? It was as if his just being near her provoked her into saying stupid things. It didn't help that he had his damn shirt off and those incredible muscles were screaming at her to touch them. God his chest was smooth and...muscley.

That's not even a real word, she thought in disgust.

"Oh forget it," she grumbled. "Can we just go for the ride?" This was just getting ridiculous. She came here to relax and so far had continuously found herself in situations where she was either embarrassing herself or making herself look stupid. It was definitely not conducive to peaceful relaxation.

She was so busy berating herself that she missed the look of relief on Cailean's face as he turned to grab Destiny's saddle.

Within ten minutes the horses were ready to go. She surprised herself by managing to mount her horse almost as smoothly as he did, and quietly basked in the surprised look of approval he shot her.

His horse was incredibly beautiful, and the way he rubbed her head and side showed that he truly cared for her. She wondered idly what those hands would feel like rubbing her then promptly discarded the thought. She focused instead on hanging on to the reins so that she wouldn't find another way of embarrassing herself by falling off the damn horse.

As she followed along behind Cailean, she took advantage of the opportunity to really take a good look at him and found that his black hair seemed to almost have a blue tint to it in the sunlight. His light shirt billowed in the small breeze, coming to rest often on a very muscular back. Her mouth almost dried up as she watched his lean hips moving forward and back with the movement of his horse. It was making her think thoughts she seriously shouldn't be thinking considering she had just ended a relationship two days ago.

He had not worn his kilt today and she wondered if it was because she had teased him about it the night before. She felt kind of bad and realized that she had unwittingly done herself a disservice because instead of his bare legs being available for her perusal, they were covered up in soft black leather pants of some kind. Still very sexy looking, she thought, as she noted his thigh muscles rippling under the thin fabric, but definitely not as good as his bare legs. She frowned in disgust. She had to stop ogling the man!

Looking up quickly when he suddenly turned around in his saddle, she noticed he had an amused look on his face. "Why do you no' ride beside me lass? Have you better things to look at back there."

Frowning, she nudged her horse a little faster and moved up to his side not saying anything. She promptly turned to look around, feigning fascination with the surrounding landscape. She had never worked so hard to ignore a person in her entire life.

*   *   *

Cailean grinned to himself as she looked away from him. He knew the lass had been looking at him. The raised hairs on the

26

back of his neck and the blush on her face proved it. While he had no problem with her fascination with his body, he couldn't help but tease her a bit. She looked so unhappy and tense all the time that it made him wondered what had happened to cause her to be so closed off. Of course it wasn't in his place to wonder such things, but he couldn't seem to help the pull she had on him. He supposed he could try being friendly. Friendship didn't automatically mean sex, after all. What harm was there? It would be a much better idea than trying to avoid her for an entire month. Even with Colin here to help it would be difficult because she would no doubt be wondering the grounds often.

Since she was pointedly refusing to look his way, he took the opportunity to gaze at her long brown curls. He could almost imagine the feel of those soft ringlets wrapped around his fingers, draped over his stomach as she... He shook his head, deciding that those kinds of thoughts were definitely not considered 'friendly', and moved on to her shirt. She had on a white shirt over a red tank top and her toned arms ended in delicate looking hands which had the reins in a deathlike grip. He wondered how many times she had ridden a horse. It couldn't have been many judging by the way she held her body so tensely, or maybe he was the one making her tense. A small smile lifted the corner of his mouth. He shifted his gaze to her blue jeans. They seemed to fit her like a second skin, and her legs looked firm as they gripped the sides of her horse tightly.

He shifted uncomfortably in his saddle. He was definitely not having a 'friendly' reaction to her, especially after thinking about her legs wrapped around him instead of the damn horse. What was it with the lass that she could turn him on without even trying?

Hell she was even doing her best to ignore him. At least he wasn't wearing the damn kilt this time, he thought grumpily.

Deciding to distract himself, he cleared his throat and forced his gaze to her face. "So what brings you to Dunvegan Tessa?"

She turned slowly, as if she was consciously forcing herself to make eye contact with him, and seemed to consider her answer before speaking.

"I had a disagreement with my fiancé and needed a break from everything for a while," she said, the words tumbling out as if rehearsed.

Cailean almost stopped his horse in shock. He quickly shot a look at her left ring finger, noting that she wasn't wearing an engagement ring, not that that meant much, and then looked back at her. Her faced had taken on a strange expression, almost like sadness mixed with anger.

This revelation certainly reaffirmed his decision to treat her like a friend. He couldn't exactly be any more than friendly to a lass about to be married.

He suddenly realized that he was more disappointed than he rightly should have been at this news. Knowing that she was off limits for reasons other than his own chafed him. Stupid idiot, he thought glumly. It's not as if you planned on being involved with her anyway.

"I'm sorry," he offered, in a strained voice, not entirely sure what he was expected to say at that point. "I hope things work out."

"They will," she answered confidently, not realizing that they weren't talking about the same thing, then turned back to her perusal of the water, which effectively ended their conversation.

After continuing on quietly for another hour, he suggested that they stop for their picnic. Since he had run out of the dining room this morning to escape her, he had forgotten completely about breakfast and was starting to get hungry. He also decided that he had enough of staring at her legs and needed a break from the uncomfortable saddle.

They stopped near a small pond. The sun danced on its surface, bringing to mind sparkling diamonds, and the fresh ocean breeze wound its way gently through their clothes, smelling of heather, lavender and salt. He slid off of Destiny and proceeded to unstrap the bag that contained their meal. He was about to lay it on the ground when he glanced over and found Tessa still astride her horse looking embarrassed.

"What's wrong lass? Why are you still on your horse?"

Taking a deep breath she looked at him so helplessly that he immediately stopped what he was doing and went over to her.

"Are you ok lass?" he asked as he put his hand on her leg, suddenly worried that she was ill.

Tessa fidgeted on the horse's back and went red.

"Ummm, I'm scared to get off," she mumbled.

"What?" he exclaimed. Surly he must have misheard her.

"I've only ridden once before," she started hesitantly. "The ride went fine, but when I tried to get off, the horse moved suddenly and I fell with my foot still in the stirrup. I broke my ankle. I guess I'm not as over it as I thought."

Cailean laughed with relief, "Is that all? Good grief lass."

Tessa stiffened.

"It's not funny," she snapped.

Stifling his laugh, he cleared his throat, "Of course not, my apologies."

Tessa frowned down at him as he reached his arms up to her.

"Just swing your right leg over his neck and slide down. I'll catch you. You doona even have to put your foot in the stirrup."

He was just thinking she might stay up there all day when she suddenly seemed to decide he made sense and started moving. If he had realized that she was scared of getting off the damn horse, he would have picked a shorter one. As it was, although Beauty was the gentlest one he owned, she was also one of the taller ones in his stable so he really had to reach up in order to hang on to her waist. The moment they touched, that blasted electricity ran through them again and Beauty fidgeted, making Tessa tense up.

She braced her hands on his shoulders as she slid forward and he eased her down his body so as not to bring her down too fast.

In hindsight, this was probably the worst move he could have made since it caused her to press against him every damned inch of the way down.

His arms tightened unconsciously, pressing her even more firmly against him. Time seemed to stand still and she stopped sliding altogether when her lips were inches from his. He could feel her heart beating wildly and tried to reason with himself, saying that it was only her fear of falling that caused it to pound in her chest. The same chest that was currently pressed against his own. Her lips were parted slightly and her breathing quickened. He slowly let her continue sliding down; his own breathing suddenly ragged as she pressed against the part of him that ached for her touch. He was painfully hard and tried to convince himself that he should just let her go quickly, that he had no right to her. She was promised to another man and he shouldn't be pulling her hips toward his, shouldn't be pressing her against him as he was doing right now. God he had to stop this insanity. He heard her intake of breath when she felt his hardness pressed against her. He expected to see anger in her eyes. Instead, he saw a torrent of emotion and felt her legs wrap around his waist.

He inhaled sharply at the contact, and almost against his will, took her mouth in his own, dragging a moan from her as he slid his tongue inside, sweeping along her velvety heat. He couldn't think straight. Her mouth tasted minty and he vaguely remembered she had been chewing gum while they rode. What the hell was he doing? He was just about to pull away when he felt her tongue tentatively probing his. Every good intention he had evaporated with that touch and he pressed against her again as their heated kiss took on a life of its own, and groaned as she tightened her arms around his neck and angled her head to deepen the kiss.

Her fingers slid up the back of his head, nails scraping softly at his scalp, driving him wild. She tightened her legs around his hips just like he had imagined she would when he saw her on her horse, and pressed against him with a soft moan.

He was just considering lying on the grass with her in his arms when Beauty suddenly reared up on her hind legs, making a strange noise.

Almost dropping Tessa in his haste to move her away from the scared horse, he forced himself to let her go and quickly turned back to see what had caused his normally calm horse to startle.

Beauty's agitation abruptly disappeared and she landed back on four legs, standing as calmly as if nothing had ever happened. Cailean had never witnessed anything like this before and stared at his horse in amazement. What had just happened? He reached out and touched her jaw, looking into her eyes. She just looked back at him as if everything was fine.

Turning, he caught sight of Destiny. She was looking in Beauty's direction as if wondering what the horse was up to, but she also looked calm.

"What is wrong with your horse?" asked Tessa breathlessly.

He turned his attention back to the woman who had been mere minutes away from finding out what it was like to have sex with an immortal in the middle of a field. By the saints, he had almost lost control. That never happened to him. He had been about to strip off her clothes and take her, virginity be damned. What the hell had he been thinking?

He started to say something, then thought better of it and turned abruptly, grabbing Beauty's bridle without a word and walking off with the horse toward the pond that lay about one hundred feet away. He needed to be alone for a moment to figure out what was going on.

When he reached the pond, he sat down at the edge and gazed into the clear water. He had never felt so confused before, had never been so mindlessly turned on by a woman that he just threw common sense to the wind. He prided himself on self control, but with Tessa that ability seemed like a foreign concept. There had to be something going on here. Something not normal! Anger swept over him. If king Finvarra was messing with him again he was going to kill him. He would have to be on his guard around Tessa because it seemed that something or someone was trying to make him break his own rules.

*   *   *

Tessa stared at Cailean's back as he led his horse to the small pond. Good God, had she really just wrapped her legs around the man like a wanton little hussy? That was just not like her. Maybe she had been drugged somehow. Yeah right! By the gum she had today since she missed breakfast completely. Oh God how embarrassing. It wasn't even as if she could just run and hide...he had her damn horse.

She looked up at the sky in prayer. Oh Lord, she prayed quietly, if you could see fit to rewind what just happened, I promise I will start going to church every Sunday, I'll even put money in the stupid collection plate. Please, please give me a mulligan on this one.

As much as she tried to feel disgusted at herself, her traitorous body kept remembering the feel of him pushing into her at such a perfect spot that she was positive she had been just mere seconds away from her very first orgasm. Oh how could a man feel so good? Even though she had been attracted to Aidan, there was absolutely no way she could ever compare how she had felt when Cailean slid his tongue into her mouth. He tasted like sugar and was so hot she was sure she would have melted if he had continued his glorious assault on her mouth.

Tessa raised her hand to her lips and closed her eyes for a moment. When she opened them, Cailean was sitting beside the pond with his back to her. What was he thinking? He had obviously been turned on. Very obviously! His leather pants were soft enough that she felt every amazing inch of him as he pressed against her. She was pretty damn sure it was a sin or something to be having these thoughts two days after ending her engagement.

She could just imagine how Laney would react if she knew. Her crazy friend would probably organize a party to celebrate.

Shaking her head with a little smile, she looked down and found the picnic bag by her foot. Well the least she could do is get it all set up and ready. She was hungry...for the incredibly sexy man sitting by the pond. Stop it! There is no way she was getting involved in a relationship or a one month stand. It's completely ridiculous to even think about it. Geez she had just left Aiden TWO DAYS AGO, did she really feel so little for him that taking up with a man this soon didn't even faze her? What did it say about her that she was going to marry him? Ok that's it! She was officially swearing off men until she could get her act together and understand what love really was about, because obviously she had no clue.

With this decision firmly in hand, she set out the wine bottle that the maid...what was her name again? Oh yes, that *Lara* had so thoughtfully packed. Silly woman! Shaking her head she put two plastic cups next to the bottle and jumped when Cailean suddenly sat down behind her.

"Oh good, I'm starved."

Arching her brows in surprise, she realized that he had apparently also decided that what happened was a mistake and not worth discussing.

Tessa carefully schooled her expression before turning to look at him. "Me too," she agreed as she moved to sit as far away from him as possible.

They had their picnic in a slightly strained silence while looking out over the cliffs. It was a beautiful day and the saltiness of the ocean mixed with the sweet smell of the highland heather.

For all that she had imagined Scotland would be, in all of her daydreams while growing up, this moment far exceeded what she could have ever hoped to experience. It was so utterly peaceful here and so incredibly beautiful. If she closed her eyes she could imagine being happy living here, lying on the cliffs day after day, breathing in the smell of the ocean. She inhaled deeply. What a life it could be.

"What are you thinking about lass?" asked Cailean curiously.

She opened her eyes and looked over at him lying on his back; legs stretched out and crossed at the ankles. It really wasn't fair that he could effortlessly look so delicious.

"I was imagining what it must feel like to have no worries and live in such a peaceful place," she answered truthfully.

He considered her words a moment.

"Lass, those who say they doona have worries are no' telling the truth. But as for the peace...aye 'tis definitely peaceful here," he agreed, sitting up, "but we should get back. I'm expecting my brother Colin to return this afternoon and have much to discuss with him."

He groaned and stood up, stretching with a feline grace that caused her mouth to go dry.

Wishing she could stay longer, Tessa sighed and slowly made her way to her knees to start putting away what was left of their picnic. Cailean went off to gather the horses. The man was dangerous, she thought. All she had to do was look at him and she got wet.

After about five minutes, Cailean returned with Destiny and a strange look on his face.

"Beauty's gone," he stated bluntly as if it were to be expected.

Tessa looked at him in surprise, "Gone? Where?"

"If I knew that lass, we'd no' be in this situation," he remarked as he frowned at Destiny's saddle.

She was confused. What kind of situation were they in? And how on earth was she going to get back without Beauty?

Oh God! Suddenly she looked up at him, understanding dawning on her face. They were going to have to ride together...on the same horse...touching.

Sighing heavily, he reached over and started unbuckling Destiny's saddle, grumbling under his breath.

"What are you doing?" she asked, thoroughly confused.

"We'll no' be able to ride together on one saddle so I'll have to leave it and send a stable boy back for it later," he replied as he dragged the saddle off of the patient horse and lay it on the grass beside them.

Tessa took one last hopeful look around, praying that Beauty would suddenly materialize, but quickly realized that there was little hope of that considering she could see no animals of any kind around except for Destiny. She sighed unhappily and watched him get up onto Destiny's bare back.

He leaned over and put his hands under her arms, lifting her effortlessly and placing her in front of him.

Sliding one arm around her waist, he pulled her securely against him as he picked up the reins with the other. Tessa sucked in her breath and did her best to try to ignore the feel of his hard body pressed against her back.

He softly nudged Destiny's side, causing her to move forward at a slow trot which made Tessa gasp and grabbed both of his thighs in a death grip. Horses were definitely not her thing.

After about ten minutes, and a lot of tense movements to keep herself sitting firmly on the horses back, Cailean suddenly leaned over and growled into her ear.

"Lass you'd do well to stop squirming before you find yourself on the ground."

Tessa froze. He had breathed into her ear when he growled at her, causing her breath to catch as her heart hammered mercilessly. Oh God this just wasn't fair. She could feel him hard against her bottom now, pressing against her with each step the horse took. The feeling was as close as it could get to him thrusting against her without actually doing it on purpose. Oh this ride was going to definitely be torture. She quickly thought that if God could just allow her to get back in one piece, she promised... Her well intentioned prayer was cut short as Cailean suddenly pulled her more firmly against him and lowered his head. His lips grazed her neck softly, causing goosebumps to run down her body and heat to pool where she wished it hadn't. She involuntarily leaned her head back against his chest, giving him more access to her neck.

His breathing became ragged as he ran his tongue along the sensitive area of her neck, tasting her. He nipped at her softly and immediately soothed her neck with kisses.

Tessa felt him drop the reins and slide his other hand toward her breast, gently cupping and squeezing while the other hand continued to pull her against him with each step Destiny took. The movement was so erotic that she couldn't seem to see straight and everything went fuzzy. He let go of her breast and a desperate noise escaped her. His hand slid under her tank top and he continued his exploration, almost causing her to scream in pleasure when he brushed her bare nipple with his thumb. She couldn't understand why she was having such a powerful reaction to this man. It wasn't like her to act this way.

She arched back against him, making him groan. God why the hell hadn't he worn his kilt today? She ached to touch him, to caress him as he did her.

Sliding both hands up along the inside of his thighs, she reached behind her and found what she was looking for. God but he was huge. He throbbed hotly through the leather of his pants, straining the laces that held it shut against her.

Cailean growled at her touch and pushed himself against her soft hands, biting softly on her neck at the same time.

"Tessa," he gasped. "How do you bewitch me so lass?"

He moved his hand away from her aching breast and somehow managed to unbutton her pants while holding her firmly against him with his other hand.

Her hands stopped their explorations and she gripped his thighs tightly as he slid his hand slowly downward. There was no returning from this point. Say something! Tell him to stop! She knew somewhere in the back of her mind that they had crossed that invisible line and were now headed into dangerous territory, but she was helpless. Her traitorous body burned with the need to feel his hand on her and she arched toward it, begging silently.

She almost exploded when his finger found her clitoris. He pressed gently against her most sensitive part, moving slowly. Reaching up with his other hand, he turned her head toward him and covered her mouth with his, taking her tongue into his mouth at the same time his finger pressed against her and started moving in quick circles. Pressure built inside her almost immediately and she came in a blinding fury against his hand as he captured her yell of release with his mouth. Her orgasm went on for what seemed like an eternity and it painted everything in her vision in blackness and stars. Her underwear was soaked with the force of her orgasm, yet it continued.

This is amazing, she thought almost mindlessly as her stomach clenched and she pressed against his circling fingers. She heard moaning and realized it was her own voice, but couldn't stop. How had she gone so long without feeling this? Her thoughts were a jumble and she wondered if her brain had short circuited from the intensity of it all. He had continued kissing her passionately throughout the entire orgasm even though she could do nothing more than just accept the kiss while her fingers bit into his thighs almost painfully.

She had never had an orgasm before and was amazed at the intensity of it. Her whole body throbbed with pleasure. His hand felt so good against her. She could feel him still rock hard against her bottom, pressing into her with each step the horse took. She wanted him. She wanted him inside her so badly.

Just as her orgasm started to subside, causing her a moment of disappointment that it was over, pleasure suddenly ripped through her again as he slid two fingers shallowly into her silky depths, careful not to go too deep. She jerked against him when he started moving his thumb on her clitoris. God she was dying. How could this kind of pleasure exist? She strained against his hand as he moved his fingers, willing him to push them further in, feeling strangely empty when she came hard against him for the second time, whimpering in pleasure. He pulled her to him as he thrust from both in front and behind her with the rhythm of the horse's steps as she spasmed continuously around his fingers.

After a few minutes, when her spasming had stopped and her breathing started slowing down, he gently pulled his fingers out and buttoned her jeans. With one arm around her stomach, he picked the reins up with the other and guided Destiny toward the stables.

She hadn't even realized they were near the castle. How had the ride ended so quickly? She felt like wet spaghetti and was not sure how she was going to stand on her rubbery legs.

What on earth did you say to the man who had just given you your very first, absolutely amazing orgasm? And second for that matter. Oh Lord how was she supposed to look him in the eyes now?

They reached the stable and she heard him take a deep breath in and let it out slowly through gritted teeth before easing himself off the horse. She wondered if he was uncomfortable. She knew he was still hard.

"Come down lass," he said huskily in his deep burr, which was even thicker now from emotion. His voice sounded strained, like he was in pain.

She slowly swung her leg over Destiny's neck, not trusting her coordination at that point, and looked down to see him gazing up at her with pure desire in his hooded eyes. His jaw was clenched and he reached up and grabbed her hips, lifting her down quickly so that she didn't touch his body. He looked almost angry.

"What happened during the ride will no' happen again. Twas a mistake I'll no' be repeating." With that he turned back toward Destiny and grabbed her reins, leading her into the stable.

Tessa looked at his tense back, flushing in embarrassment. Was it something she had done? What on earth would make the man take her to heaven one minute and throw her into hell the next?

Anger started to build inside her. How dare he violate such a private place and then tell her it was a mistake, as if she wasn't good enough. How dare he insult her that way? Well two could play at that game she decided, burning with barely controlled anger. Turning, she stomped off toward the castle as a tear rolled down her cheek, refusing to give him the satisfaction of seeing how much he'd hurt her.

~3~

*C*ailean led Destiny into her stall, stopping to glare at Beauty who had beat them back. "You'll be the death of me Beauty," he grumbled before continuing on.

When he had Destiny in her stall, he slid down the wall next to her and sat in the hay, resting his head on his palms. He was still shaking.

Remembering the feel of her clenching against his fingers as she came, he leaned his head against the wall and groaned. It was almost ridiculous how hard it was for him to control himself around her.

What on earth was he going to do with the lass? He couldn't seem to touch her without wanting to jump on her, which is exactly what he promised himself he wouldn't do. He had never felt an attraction as powerful as this and it disturbed him to no end. There was no way he was going to make it through the month at this rate. It was all he could do to let her go after he took her off the horse when they arrived. He knew that if he had given in for even half a second that he would have ended up tupping her right there outside the stable for all to see. He wanted her so badly that he was in actual physical pain. He glared at the stall door and silently dared her to come back into the stable. He wished it. God he hurt.

Destiny leaned her head down to Cailean and nuzzled his face. He reached up and rubbed her jaw, taking comfort from her soft, warm cheek.

"What do you think girl, is Finvarra behind all this?" he asked softly.

Destiny nodded her head and he laughed. "Yeah you're probably right, this stinks of fae magic."

He sat there among the sweet smelling hay for so long that time ceased to have meaning to him. Long ago he had learned the futility of wishing. As a young boy he had wished his parents would allow him to go to the grand balls. It had so fascinated him to think of the men all dressed up in their fancy clothes and the lasses in huge beautiful ball gowns swinging around, dancing and laughing. He had wanted to be a part of that so badly that in a fit of anger, he had sworn to them that one day he would attend those balls with his wife, and let his children go too. He had been half-a-score at the time and his parents smiled knowingly and lovingly at their determined son. What would they say now if they knew that three hundred years later, their beloved little boy still hadn't been able to follow through on that angry promise, that he would never have children for fear of having to watch them grow old and die while he lived on alone.

His wife, Leah, had gotten pregnant early on in their marriage. He had still been a mortal at that time, having not yet been visited by the treacherous fae.

They had celebrated the pregnancy and anticipated the birth of their first child with joy. They were crushed beyond belief when, in her sixth month, Leah had tripped on the hem of her gown while descending the castle staircase one day, causing her to lose the baby and almost her own life in the bloody birth that night.

Little Catharine had lived for a few minutes, trying desperately to drag a breath into her tiny undeveloped lungs. Cailean held her struggling little body cupped in one hand. She had been so incredibly tiny and her impossibly small mouth had been open, searching for air that refused to come. He'd felt so helpless as he looked down at his precious daughter, unable to help her, unable to ease her pain and fear, unable to force her lungs to accept the air he had tried so desperately to breath into her. Tears rolled down his cheeks and splashed his babe, mixing with the blood. He dropped to his knees, begging the Gods to help his child as he pulled her to him and cradled her into his warmth.

His chest had heaved with pain and sorrow when he finally looked down at her and saw that she was quiet. She had looked so peaceful at that moment that he could almost fool himself into believing that she was asleep, her tiny body curled up within his large hand, her cheek pressed against his chest as if seeking comfort. He stayed that way for a long time, afraid to move, afraid to admit to himself that she was truly gone. His heart shattered that night, and she held every piece in her tiny fists.

They buried baby Catharine in the courtyard the next day in a small willow basket. She lay on a bed of soft silk with a tiny blanket of down to keep her warm on her journey, a small cloth bunny tucked beside her for comfort. Her tiny face an image of perfection frozen in time.

44

Leah had not been the same after that, always weak and ill. It was as if the loss of her child had drained her of the will to live. They had not been able to conceive another child after that and the doctors claimed that the fall had damaged her uterus too badly for it to be able to support one.

Leah had lived out the rest of her life in a dark place filled with pain, sorrow and regret. She blamed herself daily for what happened, and when she finally lay on her deathbed as an old woman, looking up at a husband who still looked as if he were a score and ten, her last words to him were, "I shall finally be able to tell her how sorry I am."

He'd shaken his head sadly as he looked down at his wife through a haze of tears, "She already knows my darling, she always has. It was no' your fault."

When Leah died that night, he felt as if his heart had been ripped from his chest. The pain of knowing she had spent so much of her life suffering such guilt was so overwhelming that after her funeral he left the castle in a daze, returning a year later a changed man. During his absence he fought many battles, letting his frustration and pain out little by little as each man died beneath his sword. He'd cursed the faeries over and over, begging them to allow him to die, to allow him oblivion.

They never answered.

Cailean pushed up from the hay and closed Destiny's stall door as he left. Thinking about his past life was not something he did often. It caused too much pain and the weight on his heart was too heavy. The only good that came from it was that it strengthened his resolve not to become deeply involved with a woman again. The remembered pain was like a wall he had built around himself to keep him sane. It was a wall he had no intention of ever letting another woman topple.

He felt badly about what had happened with Tessa. It was cruel of him to turn her away so abruptly after what he had done, but it was the only thing he could think of to get her to leave quickly before he gave in to his painful desire.

She had looked so beautiful sitting in front of him in the midst of her orgasm. Her face was pure rapture. He had been so very close at that moment to grabbing her off of Destiny and pressing her to the ground beneath him. He wanted to bury himself inside her silky warmth so badly that it took all of his control to keep riding. He could just imagine the feel of her wrapped around his shaft, pulsing as she had around his fingers.

He groaned. Thinking that way definitely wasn't helping the issue.

He was just about to head toward the castle in search of a bucket of cold water to pour over himself when Colin came sauntering through the door with his beautiful black and brown Arabian. The stable boy who entered with him took the horse's reins, leading her off to get watered and fed.

"Good day brother," said Colin jauntily, obviously in good spirits.

Cailean grinned at him.

It was hard to stay upset around Colin. He had the type of personality that caused others to smile against their will. A genuinely happy soul despite the hand fate had dealt him. It was no wonder the rogue had women crawling over themselves to get to him. Of course his blue eyes and long silky black hair combined with a six foot three inch warriors body didn't hurt.

46

Although there had been a few special women in his life, he had married only one, having three children with her and subsequently living to watch them all die; his wife Katie and daughter Isobel of old age, and his two sons Calum and Angus in battle. Luckily Isobel had married and born five children of her own. He looked at this as a good thing because he was able to meet his descendents and ensure the continuation of the MacLeod line through the years. He continuously told Cailean that he was doing the MacLeods a disservice by not having children of his own, which caused Cailean to laugh since it was clear that Colin's descendents suffered no virility problems whatsoever. In fact there were so many that Colin himself was barely able to keep up with them.

Cailean grabbed him in a bear hug and pounded him on the back.

"'Tis good to see you back brother, how was your trip?"

"All in good time. I've barely eaten in a week and am apt to fall down from hunger if I doona get some meat fast," he grinned. "And wine too," he added for good measure.

"Ah Colin you're always hungry," Cailean grinned, shaking his head in amusement.

"Well I've got to keep this body strong or I'll no' be able to keep up with my adoring companions," he laughed.

Cailean shoved him playfully and they laughed as they made their way toward the castle.

* * *

Tessa had stomped up the castle stairs to her room and had been sitting on her bed for almost half an hour trying to control the tears that threatened. Even though he hadn't taken anything for himself, and in fact bestowed upon her the most amazing gift of her first...and second orgasm, she felt used and betrayed.

She was angry at herself for letting him touch her so intimately. No one had ever gotten that close, not even Aidan whom she had been with for two years. Their encounters had always ended with him being frustrated and upset. He told her that it was because he loved her so much that he wanted every part of her. She didn't once consider the fact that he may have been getting satisfaction somewhere else and that his frustration was because he couldn't convince her to hand her virginity over on a silver platter. He had apparently looked at sex with her as a conquest, and it must have frustrated him to no end that he wasn't good enough to make her give it up voluntarily.

She groaned and lay back on the bed, pressing her hands to her eyes as if that might stem the flow that was threatening. She couldn't believe she had been in Scotland for not even twenty four hours and was already trying to throw her virginity to the first Scottish hunk to show interest. Good grief, what was it about this country? She felt as if she were a dog in heat. Every time she got near the man she felt this overwhelming urge to touch him. What was her problem?

Well she wouldn't be touching him anymore, she decided with conviction. After that rude dismissal at the stables she wasn't about to put herself in that situation ever again. She had good reason to stay in her room and write now, but decided that if she wanted to go outdoors to do it, she would find a place where he wasn't and completely ignore him from now on. Horrible man.

She went to her bag and pulled out her laptop, thankful that she had been smart enough to put it in there instead of the bigger, lost one.

She really hoped she would get the rest of her bags back tonight like the baggage claim guy said. If not, she was going to have to figure out a way to get to a mall or something because she only had two pairs of underwear; the first she had been wearing on the plane and had changed out of last night when she showered, and the other was currently soaked thanks to the big oaf outside.

She took a frustrated breath and removed her underwear. Oh well, it wasn't as if she had never gone commando before, and it's not as if anyone here cares. Or will ever know, she amended hastily.

She sat down at her laptop after plugging it in using the weird plug adapter the man from The Source had given her. Why Scotland had such weird outlets was beyond her. She opened her laptop and frowned at it for a few minutes while it loaded up. Finally, after checking her email, her Facebook account, and updating her website, she started writing, managing to get about four hours in before her stomach started to complain. She hated stopping when she was on a roll and was starting to get very annoyed about the fact that she needed to eat to survive.

Sighing in impatience, she closed her laptop and grumbled a bit before heading down to the kitchen for something to eat.

She walked into the kitchen to find Lara standing over a boiling pot that smelled simply delicious, and decided at that moment that she would forgive her for the whole *tupping* incident if she would allow her to eat whatever she was cooking.

Just as she was about to ask, a man almost as good looking as Cailean walked into the kitchen and greeted Lara who giggled with pleasure. Seriously...what was it with Scotland and gorgeous men? Did they breed them differently here? Maybe it was the food, or something in the air. Whatever it was, Tessa thought she would be wonderfully happy to live in Scotland for the rest of her life if she got to ogle men like him all the time.

The man stopped his inspection of the pot Lara was diligently stirring when he realized that someone else was in the room.

Straightening up, he looked at Tessa with an incredibly sexy grin and moved toward her.

"Good day lass, I'm Colin MacLeod. Did you just arrive at Dunvegan?" he asked with a husky voice that was just as deep as Cailean's.

"Um yes." Wonderful...another MacLeod.

"How long will you be staying with us?" He was smiling from ear to ear, causing her to smile against her will.

His obvious happiness at her presence raised her mood quite a bit and was making her feel better than she had all afternoon.

"I'll be here for a month...writing."

"A writer? Are you a famous then?"

"Well I've written a few books, but I doubt you've read any as they are all romances," she laughed, suddenly feeling self-conscious.

"Ah luv, how else is a man to know what a woman wants without reading those romances they all go crazy over?" he asked her with such a genuinely serious voice that she couldn't decide if he was teasing or not.

"Umm...well...I suppose," was all she could think to say.

50

Colin laughed and took her right hand. She tensed immediately, expecting to feel the shock Cailean kept giving her.

"There's also another way I know of to find out what a lass wants," he said seductively as he stroked her open palm. She looked at him warily.

What the heck was this gorgeous man up to, she wondered, incredibly thankful that there were no sparks or electric shocks with him as there were with Cailean.

*   *   *

Cailean walked into the kitchen to see his brother holding Tessa's hand in his own while he slowly caressed her palm. Colin looked up and grinned at him, but didn't let her hand go.

"Why have you no' told me of this beautiful lass you were hiding in here Cailean?" he asked mischievously.

Cailean cleared his throat, definitely not liking the feelings he got as he watched his brother continue to caress Tessa's hand. "I had no' thought about it brother, do I bring up every guest that stays here?"

Colin raised his eyebrows at the tone of annoyance he caught in his brother's voice. It wasn't like Cailean to be rude and it had Colin wondering what had gotten his back up. The lass?

Cailean could see his brother was curious about his reaction and cursed himself for not hiding his annoyance better. It wouldn't do to let Colin think the woman affected him at all because that would lead to weeks of him trying to convince him to finally give in and love someone. Definitely not something he wanted to go through again. The last time Colin tried that, Cailean had thrown him out of the castle for a fortnight...during a winter storm. His amorous brother didn't suffer outdoors for as long as Cailean had wished though. He had a great number of willing bedmates that were only too happy to provide accommodations for him during his time of suffering.

Colin turned to Tessa with a look of sympathy. "I'm sorry lass, my brother seems to have a wee problem with manners today. He's normally a gentleman, I assure you."

Tessa gave a snort of disgust as she pulled her hand slowly away from Colin's caress. "I have yet to see the gentleman part. He's been nothing but an ass to me."

Colin looked stunned for a second before he suddenly roared with laughter and looked over at his brother who was staring at the ground, looking for all intents and purposes as if he were sulking.

"Good Lord Cailean, what did you do to the lass to get her in such a fankle?" he asked in amusement.

"I did naught but take her for a trail ride and picnic," he said stubbornly, looking at Tessa, silently challenging her to contradict him.

"It was how you acted at the end of the ride that made you an ass Cailean MacLeod," she gritted out, shoving past him to leave the room.

He grabbed her by the arms as she pushed past him and swung her around to face him, growling, "You would thank me if you knew the truth of why I treated you so lass."

"I would never thank a man for hurting me the way you did," she retorted before yanking out of his grip and leaving the castle through the front door.

Cailean stared after her retreating figure and felt an acute pain in his heart. He had hurt her more than he'd thought.

Guilt washed over him and coloured his cheeks. He was angry at himself for his lack of willpower. If he had been in control, none of this would have happened and he wouldn't have had to hurt the lass. If he gave into his lust, she had more of a chance of being abducted by the Unseelie. He refused to be responsible for that.

Cailean felt his brother's hand on his shoulder and turned slowly toward him.

"What did you do to the lass Cailean?"

Cailean sighed unhappily. "I doona wish to discuss it brother. Let's just say she's right and I was an ass, but it was for her own good."

"I find it hard to imagine a situation where hurting a lass would be for her own good," said Colin seriously, his smile gone.

"Just leave it Colin," he growled as he stalked out of the castle in the opposite direction from Tessa.

*   *   *

Colin sat at the dining room table alone, wondering what had gone on between the two to cause such hostile emotions. Considering the lass had only arrived the night before he was at a loss to explain how she had gotten under Cailean's skin so quickly. He was normally very even tempered and Colin found it disconcerting that his brother was acting so strangely.

The longer Colin sat there thinking, the more convinced he became that his decision to force a reaction from Cailean was a good one. If Cailean didn't care for the lass, then Colin's advances would be welcomed. She was quite a beauty after all. On the other hand, if there was something between them, provoking jealousy in his brother might be all that was needed to finally get Cailean to give up his insane oath not to fall in love again. He would love to see his brother happy after so long.

He'd either force Cailean to admit he wanted Tessa, or keep her for himself if he was wrong and find another woman for him.

Colin pushed up from the table, the wooden chair scraping noisily on the floor. He left the castle in search of Tessa.

* * *

"I come with news of Teluth," said Onagh as he bowed in front of king Finvarra who was at the moment amusing himself by making the air in front of him shimmer and sparkle in wondrous shades of blue and purple.

The king looked down at Onagh and noticed that he looked pale. "Are you well?" he asked kindly.

Onagh looked at his king and grimaced, "The trip was not fun for me my King, but Oberon succeeded in getting the information our queen requested."

Onagh and the queen's companion, Oberon, had just returned from the Black Hills where they went to gather information about king Teluth's plans to take over the Seelie.

Finvarra smiled sympathetically. It was obvious that poor Onagh had been the one affected by the Kaitol spell and was still suffering some after effects. Teluth had been feeling particularly mischievous the day he wove that spell around the Black Hills. It made its victim incapable of thinking of anything other than having sex. Luckily it was only strong enough to affect one fae at a time.

"Well then, what have you found out?"

"Teluth's army is growing my King. It numbers in the hundreds now and they plan to attack soon."

Finvarra frowned in concern. He was still waiting for the council to find another MacLeod descendent with the traits they needed. If they didn't hurry, it would be too late. Unfortunately, Cailean's stubbornness on the matter of having a wife and children meant much less chance of finding a suitable addition to their little group.

Fae and humans survival were intricately intertwined. If the Seelie females didn't mate with human males, their ability to reproduce would end. The release of human sperm into their reproductive tract was the only thing that made their eggs receptive to fae sperm. While the closing of the gates to the human world wouldn't cause a problem for them for a long time, losing their only means of continuing the fae species wasn't a risk they were willing to take.

All of the humans with a sixth sense and other such powers were the result of male fae mating with the human females. The half-fae that resulted from that union were purposely left in the human realm because of the important part they played in the survival of the human race.

Although regarded as fakes by most of the humans, and even scoffed at, the gift of second sight, advanced intelligence, and anything to do with what humans term 'the sixth sense', are sure signs that those particular humans are direct offspring of a fae-human union. Unfortunately, those humans who are mentally damaged in any way are the ones who got too high a dose of fae DNA which damaged their own beyond repair. Sadly, even with all their knowledge, the fae haven't figured out how to stop that from happening. But what is known, is that without these half-fae, human blood would be diluted so much that humans would lose the ability to foretell future events and try to alter it for the better. Their intelligence would dwindle, causing chaos and the return of the cave-man era.

By closing the gate between the two worlds, they would also doom the humans to certain death because it was the Seelie who intervened in the event of a serious disaster, making it more manageable and reducing the death count drastically. Separating themselves from humans was not a decision to be taken lightly.

One of the most famous half-fae was named Nostradamus. It was his prediction that warned the Seelie of the impending attack from king Teluth.

Some of those most lettered in the celestial facts
Will be condemned by illiterate princes:
Punished by Edict, hunted like criminals,
And put to death wherever they will be found.

There were only two ways to kill fae. One was by using a special sword or knife forged of a rare material called Senk from their home world, Basteerus. The other was for fae to have prolonged contact with a magic ward.

King Teluth and his army had been scouring Basteerus for millennia trying to locate as many pieces of Senk as they could. They finally found enough to break into hundreds of pieces, each just long enough to form short blades to be used as knives.

By using senk, the only thing fae, or humans, needed to do was cut a main artery in order to cause the fae to bleed out since it made their wounds heal as slowly as a humans.

This is where the other problem of closing the gate to the human realm came in. If that gate was closed to protect the humans, they would be unavailable to help the fae reproduce should their numbers be significantly reduced by king Teluth's single-minded plan to rule Basteerus and the human world. It was highly possible for the Seelie to become extinct due to this war.

Though Nostradamus predicted the war on the Seelie, it was well known that his prediction could be averted if the situation leading up to the war was changed drastically enough. It was up to the Seelie king to find a way to do this without destroying the human and fae realms in the process.

Finvarra dismissed Onagh with a distracted wave. The time was near for him to make the decision he had tried so hard to avoid.

~4~

*T*essa woke up the next day to the sound of an argument.

Jumping out of bed, she moved to the window and peered out, shading her eyes against the sun's glare.

Cailean and Colin were standing across from each other at the edge of the loch, gesturing angrily. She couldn't hear what they were saying because they were too far away, but the wind carried the tone of the argument to her.

She wondered what they were going on about as she admired their physiques. Cailean was a couple inches taller than Colin and just as muscular. They both had silky black hair, and as she stood looking out of the castle window, she thought that Colin's waist long hair made him look like a warrior. She was sure that if he untied it from its band, it would blow about in the wind quite sexily.

Cailean suddenly looked up with a frown as if hearing her thoughts.

For a few moments, the urge to hide behind the wall was strong, but she stood firm, fighting with herself. She decided that she wasn't going to be intimidated by the man and just kept looking at him. Colin looked up too and waved with a smile so she waved back with a grin, making sure Cailean understood that he was not invited to be the recipient of her friendliness.

Cailean turned toward his brother, shook his head and walked off. She laughed silently as Colin shrugged his shoulders at her and shook his head. She was just about to turn from the window when she noticed a car coming over the bridge toward the castle. She jumped for joy when she saw the Inverness Airport logo on the car and threw her clothes on hastily, brushed her teeth and took the steps two at a time in her haste to get to her long awaited clothes.

She burst out the front door and ran smack into what felt like a wall. It took her a few seconds to realize Cailean had turned and was holding on to her arm.

"Slow down lass," he snapped. "Why did you no' tell me you were leaving?"

"No I.." she started, only to be cut off by the driver who had stepped out and was dragging her luggage out of the trunk while looking curiously at them. "Tessa Anderson?" he asked.

She nodded to the driver and could have sworn that for a second, before Cailean saw the luggage, there was a look of regret in his eyes. She was almost sure that's what it was, but it was gone in a heartbeat, only to be replaced by that infernal frown of his.

The taxi driver brought the bags to the steps and put them down at her feet. She noticed right away that he was not the same driver from before.

"Thank you so much for bringing my bags."

"No problem lass," he said tiredly. "I hope you enjoy the rest of your trip."

"Oh I will thank you."

Cailean reached into his sporran and pulled out a wad of bills that he handed over to the driver.

"Thank you sir, have a good day," he said happily. The amount of money Cailean had handed him obviously did much to cheer him up.

Cailean replied to that with a sort of grunt before picking her bags up and starting into the castle.

She looked at his retreating back with a frown.

"I'm perfectly capable of carrying them myself Cailean," she said grumpily.

He ignored her as he continued up the stairs to her room and placed the luggage beside the bed. She followed him in hesitantly.

"Will you be needing anything else lass?" he asked quietly, looking into her eyes.

"N..no thank you," she stuttered. Goodness if looks could melt she'd be liquid honey right now. It wasn't that he was trying to be sensual or anything, probably the opposite, but he seemed to be looking right into her soul and it made her stomach do a fluttery butterfly thing. She wondered what he was thinking about at that moment but had no time to ask before he abruptly walked around her and left, closing the door firmly.

"And men say women are impossible to read," she muttered as she unzipped her bags. She cheered up immediately when she saw her long lost clothes and personal items. It felt almost like Christmas and she spun around the room with a pair of clean underwear in her hands.

Fifteen minutes later she was showered, dressed – including underwear – and ready for the day. She had originally wanted to get a bit of writing in before breakfast but the excitement of getting her clothes back distracted her, so she opted for breakfast first and happily forged her way toward the dining room with a smile.

Colin didn't so much walk into her, as slam her into oblivion. Apparently this was her day of walking into human walls.

"Oh good Lord lass, are you ok?" he asked in concern as he grabbed her arms to stop her from flying backwards. "I should think it would be hard to miss someone my size, but you seem to have done a fine job of it," he teased.

She laughed and looked up at him. "I'm ok Colin, thanks for catching me."

"Anytime luv," he answered softly, looking down at her with a smile.

His tone of voice had alarm bells going off in her head and her smile faltered.

He glanced over her head for a second before turning his gaze back to her, lowering his head is if to kiss her.

She was about to stop him when Cailean scared her witless by yelling behind her, making her jump violently. "Just what the hell do you think you're doing?"

Looking over her head as slowly and calmly as if his brother had asked a polite question, Colin answered him. "The lass ran into me. I was merely making sure she dinna fall."

"With your lips?" Cailean gritted from between clenched teeth.

Colin looked innocently from Tessa back to Cailean, "Whatever do you mean brother?"

She swore she could hear a hint of amusement in his voice and hoped that he would be kind enough to put her aside before Cailean barrelled into him. Although she wasn't facing him, she could feel the anger emanating from behind her in steady waves.

And was that jealousy she heard in his voice? It couldn't be. He hated her. What was going on between the brothers today?

"Would you like to take this outside Cailean?" asked his brother calmly.

"Damn right I would," he replied angrily, before turning and stomping outside to wait for his brother.

"Colin, you're not going to fight him are you?" she asked worriedly, pulling at his shirt as he walked past her.

"Lass, sometimes men need to blow off a little steam to help them think clearly. If Cailean needs to fight to do that, then as his brother I'm bound to help him work through his anger. Doona worry yourself luv, we heal fast." With that, he turned and calmly followed his brother outside.

Oh God they were going to fight over her! What an utterly barbarian thing to do. Things had happened so quickly that she felt like the world had just tipped over and wasn't making sense. She struggled to figure out what to do.

Nothing! She wasn't going to do a damn thing! She was going to get breakfast, go upstairs, put in her ear plugs and write for a few hours, completely ignoring the insanity going on outside. Crazy men! Bound to fight indeed! Why do men think fighting is going to fix anything?

* * *

Cailean paced back and forth, waiting for Colin to come outside. Just this morning he had told him to stay away from Tessa.

He ended up listening angrily while Colin came up with reason after reason why that was a stupid request.

Cailean had explained to him about the dream and the possibility of her being put in danger. Colin replied that since Cailean was the one in the dream, it didn't apply to him.

He had then told him that she was a virgin. Colin's response to that was a yawn.

It ended with Colin waving to her as she looked out the window at them, and Tessa waving merrily back, studiously ignoring him.

The silky pyjamas she had on as she stood framed in the window, were the same from the previous night, and her hair had been messed up from sleeping, making her look incredibly sexy. Lord this was not going well. He had been suffering from a God awful erection since the moment he met her and it was starting to wear on him.

He stopped pacing and looked up as Colin walked down the steps and straight toward him. When he reached him and stopped, Cailean swung out and knocked him clear off his feet, watching in satisfaction as he landed with a thud ten feet away.

Colin rubbed his jaw. "Do you feel better now?"

"Nay!" Cailean growled as he started toward him.

When he reached him, he leaned down to yank him up and was taken by surprise when Colin kicked his feet out from under him, causing him to fall flat on his back with a grunt.

They lay in the dust and looked at each other for a second before grabbing the others shirt. The fight started in earnest then, with punching and swearing and dust flying.

After a while, some of the staff gathered around the brothers and egged them on, laughing and taking bets, thoroughly enjoying the show.

It was a good fifteen minutes later before Cailean finally started to feel more human again and eased up on the choke hold he had Colin in, dropping to the ground in exhaustion. This elicited a groan of disappointment from the crowd and they walked off muttering about the fights always ending in a tie.

Lying on his back, Cailean looked over at Colin who was grinning at him happily, blood trickling down his chin from a split lip.

"Now I feel better," he said.

Colin's grin got wider. "Good," he replied, gasping for breath. "Have we settled things then?"

"That depends. Are you going to stay away from Tessa?"

"I promise I'll no' try to seduce the lass Cailean, besides 'tis clearly you she desires anyway."

Cailean looked over, searching for signs of a lie.

Not finding any, he sighed and rolled over, forcing himself to stand upright. He groaned and stretched before pulling Colin up too.

He looked at his brother and wondered what he would have done if the fae hadn't thought to make him immortal too. How lonely he would have been all these years. He was pretty sure that the only reason he stayed sane was because of him. Colin who would never die and leave him alone to face the world. Colin who had such an upbeat personality that he could make you smile on the darkest of days. Colin who would agree to a fist fight just because. He loved his brother more than life itself and as long as

64

they had each other, he could do this job of defending the world against the Unseelie, he could wake up, day after day, knowing that his brother was the only person he would never have to watch die.

"Are you ready for tonight?" he asked Colin with a sigh.

After this long, it got to be a bore having to fight the Unseelie every month. It wouldn't be so bad except that they were useless for the next two days because they were so drained from using magic and muscle to protect the Unseelie's latest victims. The weakness grated on him. He wished he and Colin could find a way to fix that problem so that they were always ready to fight. It seemed stupid to keep doing the same thing every month for three hundred years. When would it end? There had to be a better solution than this.

Colin nodded and stretched his arms out to relieve some of the kinks. "As ready as always."

When Cailean entered the front hall, he noted that Tessa wasn't around. Probably back in her room writing.

Relieved that he didn't have to face her yet, he poured himself some cereal and milk and sat with Colin in the dining room for a while.

*   *   *

Tessa had spent a relatively relaxing day at her laptop, and had gotten quite a lot of writing in. She had finally stopped thinking about the brothers and their childish way of dealing with anger, and was trying to decide if she was going to get the female character in her story in bed with the Peruvian prince who was currently dating her sister.

Although she wrote mainly romances, she had also tried her hand at mysteries, which she thought she preferred. They sold reasonably well, but nowhere near as well as the romances. After a lot of soul searching she finally came to accept the fact that romance was what she was destined to write, and started to pour her heart and soul into them. Considering she was a twenty eight year old virgin, it said a lot about her writing that twelve of her books had been best sellers.

She humbly accepted the praise and compliments from family and fans alike but could definitely do without that part of the writing business. She hated being the center of attention. It was originally for that reason that she took up writing. It was a solitary hobby. Solitary that is, until you made it big and became a millionaire practically overnight due to the huge response to your books. Oh well, it would be pretty stupid to complain about fame if it gave you a nice house and car that were completely paid for, and enabled you to take expensive month long trips like this on the spur of the moment. Yes fame definitely had its perks, so she supposed she would just deal with the bad parts and be thankful for the good.

She had her mother to thank for her determination. All through her childhood, she'd drilled it into her that she could do anything, and with enough effort could be the best at whatever it was she had chosen to do. The biggest thing she could ever do to disappoint her mother was not to give everything she had in something she did, no matter how insignificant the task seemed. She'd told her repeatedly as she grew up that even if she got fifty percent in a test, but had studied and tried her best, she would be proud of her. Likewise, if she got ninety five percent on a test that she didn't study for, she would be disappointed knowing that she hadn't tried her best.

It had taken her years to understand that her mother really meant what she said, and from that moment on she made sure that she tackled any task assigned to her, no matter how boring, with everything she had. Over time, she found that this way of thinking became part of her personality and it felt good knowing that people felt they could count on her because of her track record. Everyone knew that if they assigned a job to her, it would get done and the results would be amazing. It was wonderful to feel that sense of accomplishment and respect.

Her mother had always encouraged her with her writing because she understood that it was her dream, and believed that she could succeed at it if she really wanted to. Through the years it had taken her many tries and many failed attempts before she finally succeeded in finishing a book. She had learned valuable lessons from each aborted attempt. Her mother had positively beamed with pride when she came over one day to tell her that the publisher loved her book and had offered her a contract to write another, as well as quite a sizable amount of money due to a bidding war that had taken place.

She would always remember the words her mother said that day: "I've always believed in you my darling."

To this day, those words echoed though her head whenever she sent a new manuscript in to her publisher. Her mother had taught her to believe in herself, and that was the most amazing gift a person could ever receive.

Tessa jumped when she heard a knock on the door.

Taking a breath first to fortify herself incase it was Cailean, she opened the door to find one of the house maids standing there.

Knowing it was stupid for her heart to fall at the sight of the maid, and determined not to let the maid see her disappointment, she greeted her almost too happily. "Hi Angie."

Angie gave her a friendly smile. "Supper's ready lass."

She was just about to refuse, knowing she still had a lot of writing to do, when her stomach made the decision for her.

Angie looked at her with a smile, "I think you'd best be coming down lass, it might get awfully hard to hear your own thoughts over that racket."

Giving in with a grin, she followed the maid down and entered the dining room to find Cailean sitting at the large table. He stood as she sat, then took his seat again and resumed eating his delicious smelling Sheppard's pie.

"Where's Colin?" she asked curiously.

"He's in his chamber," he mumbled over a bite of potato.

"Will he be joining us for supper?"

"No lass, he's no' feeling too good just now. Angie already took his supper up to him."

"It's because of the fight isn't it?" she asked, getting angry. How could the man hurt his own brother so badly that he couldn't even make it down the stairs for supper? Utterly barbaric and childish! "How could you be so horrible to your own brother?"

Cailean sighed heavily and stopped eating. "Lass...there's a great many things you doona understand about us, but be assured, I love my brother more than my own life."

What a curious thing to say. He really did look upset, but it just didn't make sense to her that he could beat his brother up so badly when he claimed to love him so much.

There was pain in his eyes when he looked over at her and she could almost believe he meant it.

He pushed his half eaten meal away with a sigh and walked out, leaving her alone to consider what had just happened.

Maybe he accidentally hurt Colin more than he had planned and was feeling guilty about it. She really couldn't think of any other reason for him to be acting that way. He had looked so genuinely upset that a piece of her was softening toward him. Maybe there was more to this than she was seeing. It was possible. Or maybe she wanted to forgive him so much that she was seeing things that weren't there. She liked that idea better because it made it easier to stay angry at him.

She finished her supper quickly, not realizing she had been quite so hungry. After picking through a wonderful assortment of decadent desserts, she decided to go for a walk before retiring for the night so that she could work off the extra calories she had practically inhaled.

Walking down the path to the water, she gazed at the incredible beauty that lay around her.

Swimming in the loch, not twenty feet away from her was a beautiful duck type bird. It had a black head and there was a white band around its neck. It had dark grey feathers on its back that were spotted with white. As she approached, it looked at her curiously for a second before continuing on its way.

Hearing a noise above her, she looked up and caught sight of bird that had her staring in amazement. It was a bright, reddish-orange colour, almost the same as fire. It was so adorably round and chubby that it was a wonder it could even fly.

She sighed happily as she closed her eyes and breathed in the smells around her. She could hear the birds talking to each other in the trees and the soft sound of the water lapping against the shore. It was all so fresh and clean and so incredibly peaceful.

As she listened to the beautiful noises around her she realized that one of those noises wasn't exactly a nature kind of sound and opened her eyes to look around.

After taking a few steps to her left, she was able to make out a movement through the trees and walked slowly toward it, stopping in her tracks when she saw Cailean standing about twenty feet away from her in a small clearing, wearing nothing but his kilt and boots. He was doing slow movements with a sword, as if practicing for a battle. Sweat glistened across his chest, trailing its way down his stomach to the dark whisper of hair below his navel that disappeared into his kilt. The back of his hair was plastered against his neck, and his broad, glistening back tapered to a narrow firm waist.

Each torturously slow movement had his muscles bunching and rippling, which made her swallow as heat started to pool in unwanted spots. The man definitely had abs of steel, you could do ramps off those things.

When she was finally able to tear her gaze away from his stomach, she realized that he had stopped and was looking at her with such a heated gaze that she was sure her clothes would catch fire.

He was frozen in position, his sword held in front of him in both hands at an angle, with one leg bent in front of the other as if he were doing a short lunge. Sweat dripped down the sides of his face and he looked so positively sexy that she had this insane urge to walk right up to him and push him over so that she could straddle him and have her way.

That thought shocked her to no end, causing her to suddenly regain her senses. She turned and moved away swiftly, almost running back to the castle. Her body felt superheated from the intensity of his gaze. It was as if he had been thinking the exact same thing she had.

He was definitely dangerous, and she seriously needed to make sure she was never alone with him again or she could wave a cheery goodbye to her virginity. She was pretty damn positive her little eggs were sulking, but they would just have to deal with it.

She didn't stop moving until she got to her room and shut the door with a thud, leaning her back against it as if that would somehow help keep the thoughts she shouldn't be having out. She realized she was almost hyperventilating and focused on drawing in deep slow breaths to calm herself.

Ok, so apparently she was never going to be able to walk outside again because every time she saw the damn man she wanted to lay her virginity at his feet on a beautiful welcome mat complete with little pink flowers and a bold sign that said "Please take me!" She was slowly starting to think that her strange taxi driver might have actually been saner that she was.

That thought was so disconcerting that she discarded it immediately. It had to be the thrill of being in Scotland, coupled with the beauty of the place that had her acting all funny and made her insides do strange things.

She leaned her head back against the door and sighed. What was she going to do about this whole Cailean situation? How could one man be so completely confusing?

*T*he next day, Tessa came down for breakfast and noticed

Colin sitting at the table alone with a huge plate of bacon and eggs in front of him. He didn't seem to look too bad and only had a few cuts and bruises here and there.

"Are you doing better this morning?" she asked in concern.

"Aye luv, I'm fine. A few bumps and bruises will no' keep me down for long."

"Do you guys always fight like this?"

Colin sat looking thoughtful for so long that she started to think he hadn't heard her.

"Lass...'tis sometimes hard for a woman to understand the ways of men, and what makes sense to a man may seem like nonsense to a woman. There's also the possibility that the man thinks he's doing the right thing for all involved but is actually making a huge mistake."

Tessa sat back in her chair and stared at Colin open mouthed. He certainly didn't seem like the happy-go-lucky man from yesterday, and what was with him having such deep thoughts all of a sudden? What the hell had really happened to him yesterday?

"What I'm saying lass, is that Cailean is a good man. He's just a wee bit confused at the moment."

"Ummm okay."

Tessa looked down at the plate that had mysteriously appeared in front of her and realized that in addition to being confused, she was ravenously hungry. She decided that it would be best to eat breakfast first and ponder the mystery of Colin later.

Ignoring him for the moment, she tucked into a delicious piece of omlet, savouring it as she chewed. She wondered if she might be able to convince the cook to give her the recipe to take back to Canada. Her mother just loved to collect recipes from all corners of the world and had amassed quite a collection that she was now entering into a recipe program on her computer.

She idly wondered what her parents were up to as she started on her second piece of toast. Her mom was probably puttering around in the garden while her dad worked on their car. Nothing was ever wrong with the thing but he kept telling her that the reason for that was because he was always working on it. It seemed to make sense to him anyway.

Colin spoke suddenly, jolting her out of her reverie. "Lass, Cailean asked me to see if you would no' mind coming to his chamber this eve so he could apologize for his behaviour. He'll be out till about ten tonight on an errand."

She frowned and thought about that for a few minutes before answering. It seemed like an odd request. Why not just meet in the dining room, or outside for that matter. Why his bedroom?

"Well I suppose I can think about it," she replied without committing to an answer.

Colin nodded and finished his breakfast before rising carefully and hobbling back to his room.

She wondered what she should do about Cailean's strange request. She had two options, go or don't go. Unfortunately, fate had blessed her with a ridiculously curious mind and the 'don't go' option didn't seem very likely. At the same time, the 'go' option seemed stupid considering what seemed to happen whenever they were alone together. She sighed in frustration and decided that she would have the rest of the day to think about it so wasn't going to worry herself too much at the moment. She also decided that since one of her hosts would probably be in his room recuperating for the foreseeable future and the other was supposedly out on an errand all day, she would go explore the grounds by herself to get a better lay of the land for her novel.

After breakfast, she made a detour to her bedroom to grab a notebook and pen before leaving the castle in search of inspiration.

As she walked around the castle, she looked at the heather and birds, and at one point even sat to watch a family of ducks swimming around. The air was absolutely wonderful and the view breathtaking. It was a shame the rest of the world couldn't see what she was seeing.

Lying back with her hands behind her head, she looked up through a tree into the sky and sighed happily.

Stress seemed to flow out of her like water as she relaxed in the warm heather, and she sleepily wondered if she should move to Scotland permanently. It wasn't as if her job was one that would keep her stuck in one place. One of the best parts of being a writer was that it could be done anywhere.

A couple hours later she awoke with a start to find Colin standing over her with a grin.

"You're going to burn if you continue to lay there like that all day lass," he laughed, plopping down on the ground beside her.

Tessa stretched and yawned, "Mmmmmm I know, but it's just so peaceful here."

"Aye 'tis. I've loved this place forever. As young lads, Cailean and I used to play out here every day, pretending to be brave warriors protecting our parents from invaders."

"Oh it must have been wonderful to grow up here," said Tessa enviously.

"It was for sure. Luckily there were no great wars while we were very young."

"Wars?" she laughed. "There haven't been any wars in Scotland for over a hundred years."

Colin stiffened slightly. "Of course, that's why we were lucky."

She looked at him thoughtfully, "I guess so."

Colin stood up abruptly and reached his hand down to her, "I was told to come get you for lunch lass. We'd best be off before we get a scolding for letting the food cool."

Tessa laughed and let herself be pulled up by him. She gathered her notes and they made their way back into the castle, following the tantalizing aroma of chicken soup and fresh bread that was wafting from the kitchen.

* * *

It took Tessa a good fifteen minutes after her watch announced ten o'clock to finally decide that she just couldn't force herself to ignore Cailean's request, no matter how hard she tried. For some reason she needed to know what he could possibly say that would make things better. What excuse he had come up with for the way he treated her.

Grumbling at her complete lack of willpower, she dragged herself off the bed and slowly walked out of her room, hoping she would suddenly be able to fight the urge to know what the blasted man had to say. Sadly she made it all the way to his door. Still grumbling to herself, she hesitantly raised her hand to knock quietly, telling herself that if he didn't hear the knock it would be just too bad for him and she would return to her room.

Groaning when she heard a faint "Come in!" from the other side, she steeled herself, took a deep breath, and let herself in.

What she saw in the dim room shocked her to the core.

Forgetting her anger in an instant, she immediately shut the door and went to his side. There was a bloody rag in his hand that he was squeezing into a bowl that sat on a table beside his chair. His arms were cut and scraped and he had a blood smeared bandage wrapped around one calf.

"What the hell happened to you?" she yelled in surprise, causing him to wince and hold his head with his free hand.

"God lass, keep it down. My head feels like 'tis about to split open," he grumbled softly.

Tessa put a hand over her mouth and looked at him in pity. "I'm sorry. What happened?" she whispered.

"Got into a fight. I won."

"Oh good Lord, the other guy must be dead if you look like this."

He looked up at her with a trace of humour in his eyes, "Thanks."

"Sorry. That's not what I meant. Well maybe it is. You do look pretty horrible. Is there anything I can do?"

"Leave."

He looked up as he said and must have seen the look of hurt that briefly flashed on her face before she had a chance to cover it.

"I dinna mean it that way lass," he sighed, holding his head again. "'Tis just too much for me to have you here right now. I need to be alone."

Tessa stood firmly, and despite the hurt she felt at his dismissal, resolved to help him since he was obviously in a lot of pain and not thinking straight.

Taking the bloody rag almost effortlessly from his weak grip, she dropped it into the bowl and took it to the sink to rinse it out and refill with fresh warm water. She could hear him groan behind her and brought the bowl back over to the table.

"I'll be ok lass, I'm used to looking after myself. Besides 'tis really not as bad as it looks."

"I'm just going to clean you up a little and then I'll leave," she told him firmly. "Complaining isn't going to change my mind so you may as well save your breath."

Cailean shook his head and leaned back, letting her wipe the blood off his arms revealing deep scratches underneath. His eyes closed part way through her ministrations and his breathing became deep and regular. It scared her how weak he seemed, and she hoped that he wasn't too badly hurt. Should she call a doctor? His brother?

She washed out the rag again and started on his bloody calf after removing the cloth that was wrapped around it. There was a long slice and she gritted her teeth at the amount of pain he must be in and cleaned the wound as gently as possible. After she deemed it clean enough, she moved up to his right thigh which also had a large amount of dried blood on it. As she wiped the blood off she realized that it had hidden a large nasty looking gash. She gasped and looked at him in pity. That really must have hurt. She got to work on cleaning that one too and bandaged both of them up at the same time. After that she refilled the bowl again and cleaned off as much dried blood from his legs as she could. She had to move his kilt aside a little to get at it all and couldn't help admiring the strength and size of his thighs. Lord the man was built like Hercules. She rinsed out the rag for the third time and went back to scrubbing lightly, not realizing that his breathing had gotten ragged and shallow until he spoke in a strained, husky voice.

"Tessa...stop."

Tessa jumped at his sudden request, sure she had hurt him.

"Oh I'm so sorry, was I rubbing too hard?"

"Nay lass," he said with his eyes closed, "I just canna...please...doona touch me right now."

Tessa looked at him curiously, confused. Well if she wasn't hurting him, then....OH! Suddenly she realized that he must be turned on but too weak to stop her from touching him himself. Helpless almost.

The idea intrigued her immensely and she felt a strange power swell up within her. She could pretty much do whatever she wanted to him. A payback of sorts for what he did earlier. The more she thought about it, the more intrigued she became at the idea.

Smiling slyly, she decided that payback was definitely in order. And what better time than now?

Reaching into the warm water again, she squeezed out the rag and returned to rub softly at his inner thigh.

Cailean's breath caught and his hands weakly gripped the arms of the chair.

"Please Tessa, you doona understand," he gasped softly, raising his head to look at her with a dangerous glint in his eyes.

She gently slid the rag under his kilt a little further each time, causing Cailean to groan and tense up. His breathing was becoming faster and he lay his head back on the chair, too exhausted to keep it raised.

"Please," he mumbled softly.

She wasn't sure anymore if he was asking her to stop or begging for her to continue. She decided he meant the latter and slid his sporran to the side so that she could slide the rag further under. As soon as she moved it she was able to see the full effect of her touch on him. She let the rag graze against his straining cock and he moved his hips upwards slightly at the contact and groaned. He opened his eyes to look down at her kneeling in front of him. They looked glazed and his mouth was partially open as he struggled to control his breathing.

"What are you doing lass?" he gasped, moving his right hand off the arm of the chair to capture her roving hand. His grip, however, was too weak to be effective and she pulled her hand away, placing the rag back in the bowl in favour of her own hands.

She put his hand back on the arm of his chair and placed her hands on each of his knees.

"Just relax," she said softly, looking into his eyes as she slowly slid them upward, toward the only part of him that didn't seem weak at all.

When she wrapped her hand around his shaft, his hips lifted once again and he groaned in pleasure, still looking into her eyes. His chest rose and fell erratically with each breath when she started to stroke him up and down.

"Tessa," he warned.

"I want you to feel what I felt yesterday on the horse. I want you to know what you did to me before you hurt me."

"I'm sorry...," he panted. "I dinna mean to hurt you."

"Then why did you touch me in the first place?" she asked quietly, as she kept stroking him...tormenting him.

"I could no' stop myself," he gritted out.

"Neither can I," she whispered.

Her hand started moving faster and his body tensed more and more with each stroke.

What she hadn't foreseen, was that doing this to him while he was so helpless would turn her on so unbelievably. She hadn't realized that his moans of pleasure would make her want to rip her clothes off and sit on him, press him against her, slide him into her. She obviously hadn't thought this whole scenario out properly.

She suddenly wondered what he would taste like. That was something she had done before with Aiden so she was confident she would be able to do it to him too, despite how huge he felt under his kilt. Oh Lord! Now that the idea had entered her head, it was extremely difficult not to think about it and about how it would feel as she slid him into her mouth. She wanted to taste him so badly now.

*   *   *

Cailean bit back a groan of disappointment when Tessa stopped stroking him, and dropped his head back against the chair while trying to get his breathing back under control. God he wanted her so badly. He cursed the fact that he was so bloody helpless. Why did she have to come to his room tonight of all nights? He was just trying to convince himself that he was glad she had stopped that wonderful stroking when he felt his kilt being lifted as she moved forward and realized that he was in even more trouble now than before.

"Oh God...Tessa," he begged as he felt cum start to bead on the tip of his shaft at the thought of what she was about to do to him.

His mind went blank for a second when he felt her tongue lick the small drops of cum off. "Tessa," he panted, as he grasped her shoulders with his hands. His half hearted attempt to stop her worked against him as she suddenly slid him completely into her mouth, right up to the base, dragging a soft yell of pleasure from him as he mindlessly shoved his hips upward to meet her, tangling his hands in her hair.

Not giving him any time to come to his senses, she continued her assault on him. He couldn't even think straight anymore. His only feeling was intense pleasure as her warm mouth slid up and down, bringing him closer and closer to the edge far faster than he had ever experienced before. Everything was happening so quickly that in his weakened state he was absolutely incapable of stopping her. He wanted her so badly now that if he had the strength, there would have been no stopping him from savagely ripping her clothes off and plunging into her, over and over until they both came together in a surreal explosion.

In his dazed state, he started thinking that he was indeed sliding into her the way he wanted. As soon as that thought entered his mind he exploded into her mouth with a guttural yell, gripping her shoulders almost painfully as he pushed up into her mouth. He could feel his seed pumping into her for what seemed like forever. She swallowed every drop.

When it was over, he collapsed back into the chair in a heap, passing out almost immediately from exhaustion.

*　　*　　*

Tessa leaned back and smiled at his unconscious form. He truly was a gorgeous man. His firm, sensual lips just begged to be kissed, and after watching him sleep for a minute or so she finally gave in and bent over, kissing him softly. She was so turned on that it was all she could do to straighten his kilt, stand up, and walk out of the room without jumping on him. Part of her couldn't believe what she had just done and the other part was wishing she had straddled him as he sat in the chair and had her way with him. What a hussy she was becoming.

She went to her room and changed into her pyjamas, but as she had expected, she found it extremely difficult to fall asleep as turned on as she was, and ended up lying awake replaying everything for hours before finally submitting to sheer exhaustion.

~6~

*C*ailean's first thought when he woke the next afternoon,

having slept straight through the morning from the previous night,
was that his mouth felt like a desert.

Opening his eyes was not high up on his priority list, so he
concentrated instead on trying to swallow. Lord what he would
give for a glass of water.

As if the Gods heard his wish, he felt a glass being placed to
his lips and drank greedily, not even bothering to see who his
saviour was.

"I hate the thirst too. 'Tis always the worst part," said Colin
matter of factly.

Cailean rubbed his eyes and yawned.

"Did you sleep well?" asked his brother, innocently.

Suddenly the night before came back to him in a flash and he
jerked upright in his chair and looked at Colin in anger.

"'Twas you who told her to come to my chamber last night,"
he accused angrily. "Damn it Colin, why?"

84

Cocking his head sideways, Colin looked at him a moment before answering. "You know very well why brother. You canna go through the rest of your life alone."

Cailean angrily threw a cushion at his persistent brother. "'Tis no' up to you to decide my future Colin!" he yelled. "What about Tessa? Would you so callously damn her to watch me stay this way as she grew old? Would you damn me by making me once again watch another person I love grow old and die without me?"

"Cailean," started Colin quietly. "Everyone has to watch the people they love die at one time or another. Would you damn yourself by living alone forever, never knowing love again? To me, 'tis the worst punishment I could ever think of, and I would no' wish that on my own brother."

Colin's declaration took all the wind out of Cailean's sails, and he sat back in the chair with a flop.

"Instead of fighting it every step of the way, why would you no' consider yourself blessed that you have another chance to find true love. Life's no' worth living if you're purposely closing yourself off to every lass you meet."

Cailean looked up at his brother with a frown, "What of all those women you've been with? None ever get further than your bed."

"Tupping is a joy for me," laughed Colin dryly. "Love, however, is a gift I've only known once and fear may never know again. But what I tell you is the truth Cailean, 'tis no' because I'm purposely hiding from it, it just hasn't found me yet."

He took in his brother's now serious expression and suddenly realized that although Colin was forever surrounded by women, they meant no more to him than a way to pass the time until he found the one he was meant to be with. This surprised Cailean so much that he was at a loss for words. For the first time he saw loneliness in his brothers eyes.

"I had no idea."

"Yeah well, does no good to dwell on the sadness in life when surrounded by so much good. I choose to look at it as a quest. I know one day I'll find that special lass. After all, I do have forever."

"Time is definitely no' a problem for us. Doona think this means I agree with your thoughts about Tessa though, and I'm still annoyed with you about last night, but you've given me something to think about. That's all I can promise."

Colin jumped off the bed with a grin, "'Tis all I ask brother. Oh! And one last thing...is there any particular reason you think that by no' tupping the lass, you'll no' fall in love with her?" he asked as he happily left the room, slamming the door behind him, making Cailean wince as his aching head complained about the noise.

Sitting in the chair dumbfounded, he realized that his brother did have a good point. Did he not already think about her constantly? As he pondered that question, he started remembering bits and pieces of the previous night. It was hard for him to believe that Tessa had done what she had. What did virgins know of that kind of thing? Obviously a lot, he thought as he started getting hard at the memory of her hot mouth sliding up and down on him. And did she actually have sex with him? That part was a bit fuzzy, and try as he might he could not remember for sure, but judging from the lack of virginal blood on him, he guessed not. Then again it was possible he was wrong about the virgin part. In the hundreds of years he had been alive, no woman had ever taken advantage of him in the way Tessa did last night. Although, since she didn't get anything out of it...probably, because he was almost ninety nine percent positive that her mouth was the only thing she used on him...was it really taking advantage of *him* to give him pleasure so selflessly? And God forgive him but the thought of being taken advantage of like that turned him on immensely, even though it chafed him at the same time that he was so helpless.

Well the one good thing about being so turned on at the moment is that less blood pounding through his brain meant his headache wasn't so intense, he thought wryly. Good Lord the things she did with her mouth. He groaned at the memory.

It took a good fifteen minutes to convince himself that a cold shower would be the best thing to alleviate his suffering, so after shivering under the cold needle-like spray for what felt like forever, he finally decided he would be able to handle seeing Tessa again without dragging her off to bed the very moment he laid eyes on her. He still was unsure what to do about the lass but decided that for the moment he would be better off being angry at her. If anything, it would prevent him from dragging her off like a caveman.

Believing this was the best plan of action, he left his room prepared for an argument. He was still quite weak from the fight with the Unseelie the previous night but was able to make his way downstairs for something to eat.

Tessa was nowhere to be seen which suited him just fine, and he sat and demolished a huge sandwich, half an apple pie and three glasses of milk before dragging himself back to his room for more rest.

*   *   *

Tessa watched Cailean eat through the window behind him, feeling absolutely mortified about what she had done to him yesterday. There was no way she would be talking to him any time soon and had decided that hiding from him for as long as she could was the best bet.

Definitely a hussy! What kind of woman takes advantage of a man who is weak and in pain? God what must he think of her now? She may just have to leave Dunvegan after last night because she honestly didn't see herself ever being able to look him in the eyes again.

Miserable with regret, and angry at herself, Tessa turned and found herself muttering into Colin's massive chest.

"What ails you luv?" laughed Colin, grabbing her arms to steady her.

She blushed a very unhealthy shade of red as she tried to extricate herself from Colin's grasp. "Uh...nothing, why do you ask?"

"Well," he began, smiling down at her, "Normally people doona stare at others through a window muttering to themselves unless there's something to mutter about."

"I wasn't staring!" she began indignantly. "I was just making sure he was ok. He was in pretty bad shape when I saw him yesterday."

"Aye, well he's been in worse scrapes before and came through them ok. Did he apologize to you?"

Tessa almost stumbled as she tried to get away from Colin's stare. "Not...exactly. He was too hurt to do much of anything."

"Mmmm I see. Did you fix him up then?" He raised his brows innocently.

Apparently it was actually possible for her to turn a brighter shade of red than she thought. Struggling to find a way out of the conversation, she answered quickly, "I have to get some writing in. I'm sure he will be fine."

Colin chuckled, "Oh aye lass, he's doing very well today. I talked to him just this morning."

Tessa's eyes went wide in horror. Oh God did he tell him? No! There's no way he would do something like that.....is there? Colin grabbed her arm just as she tripped over a stone and stood her upright, watching with a grin as she turned and practically ran inside.

She headed straight for her room, trying desperately to convince herself that Cailean did *not* tell his brother what she had done to him last night. What would Colin think of her? Oh please oh please, she begged God. She just wanted to curl up into a ball and disappear before she embarrassed herself any more. She might just be the first person to literally die of embarrassment.

Slamming the door behind her, she realized she was almost hyperventilating again. She had to calm down. She was going to lie in bed, calm down, and forget anything ever happened. Yeah that sounded good.

She promptly climbed into the pillow-strewn bed, pulled the covers up to her chin, and concentrated on taking deep breaths in and out. Besides, she reasoned, she was only paying him back for the way he had treated her before. She had walked away and ignored him after just like he had done. Yes he had been asleep, but that didn't change the fact that she *did* walk away and hadn't talked to him today.

She was slowly starting to feel a little better, and after a while she had even managed to convince herself that she was the one in control and that now he knew exactly what it felt like to be used and ignored. She had actually come full circle and was now angry at him again for doing what he did in the first place. She could deal with this, she decided. She had every right to be angry and refused to let him intimidate her!

Deciding that this was the right way to be feeling, and happy that she wasn't quite so mortified anymore, she got up and decided to do some writing. She did, after all, have a new experience to write about. She kind of liked the idea of the woman taking control while the strong but helpless man just sat there, unable to stop her from touching him yet not sure if he wanted her to stop. Wow did that feel good! She wondered what he thought of that. Probably sulking about it and too embarrassed to show his face. That thought made her feel a little better and she put her earplugs in to drown out any distractions and settled down in front of her laptop.

*   *   *

Cailean lay in bed unable to sleep. He couldn't get the picture of her taking him into her mouth out of his head. He could almost feel her hair dragging along his stomach as she moved up and down. "This is absolutely pathetic," he grumbled to himself. "How's a man supposed to get to sleep if he canna stop thinking about one wee lass?"

Getting up, he pulled on his shirt and decided to go for a walk since he couldn't sleep. One way or another he would get that woman out of his head. He and Colin had to make sure the castle wards were still in place and strong anyway.

Tonight the Unseelie would be able to get their victims through without worrying about fighting the brothers as they were still both too weak to do much damage to the powerful fae, even if they fought together. They had tried it in the past, and apart from annoying the Unseelie into beating them senseless, nothing had been gained. They had then spent the next week in bed, unable to do anything but groan in pain with each movement. Although they were immortal and healed much faster than mortal men, they still felt pain like a mortal, and fighting the Unseelie that soon after their initial fight had drained them so badly that Finvarra himself had shown up to scold them for their stupidity. It was not a mistake they would make again.

He slowed as he passed her doorway.

He had decided that there would be time to deal with her when he had more control over his wayward thoughts, and although this made a lot of sense, he still had to force himself to continue walking past the big wooden door that separated him from the very intriguing woman. He could hear the tapping of keys as he passed, which assured him that she was indeed inside and working on her book. This meant he wouldn't bump into her during his rounds.

Damnation! He refused to act like a hormonal teenager over the woman. When he talked to her later, he would set her straight on a few things, especially how wrong it was to take advantage of a full grown man in a time of weakness. No matter how amazing it felt. And Lord did it feel amazing.

He got to the bottom of the staircase just in time to see Colin ease himself gingerly out of a chair.

He looked at him curiously. "Were you waiting for me?"

When Colin turned, a flicker of alarm went through him. There was fresh blood on his face and hair, and his shirt had rips in it. "What the hell happened to you?"

"Apparently one of the wards was disturbed last night."

Anger and guilt raced through Cailean. "But I checked! I'm sure I checked them all."

"Calm yourself brother. I checked last night as well and they were all fine, the fault is not your own. Somehow the fae were able to send more through before the gates closed for the night and were able to dislodge the east ward. That particular fae is dead of course because he had to touch it to move it, but another was sent along with him who attacked me when I did a check an hour ago. I was unconscious until a few moments ago and on my way to tell you, but I had to sit and rest for a minute."

Cailean moved to his brother's side in concern and motioned for him to sit. He felt as if he'd been struck by lightning. "What does this mean?"

"I'd hazard a guess that they're trying something new. Maybe hoping that if they attacked us enough when we were this weak that they might maim us for good, or at least put us out of commission for a while. Teluth must be getting desperate."

"Damn," said Cailean quietly. He had never even considered that the Unseelie would try something like this. It was entirely possibly to hurt them enough in this condition to cause them to need more than a few days to recuperate. The possibility of their demise was also increased, especially now that the Unseelie had taken to fighting with senk daggers.

"Oh my God!" came a yell from the stairs. "What is with the two of you? Is fighting a hobby for you guys?" Tessa stomped toward them, anger and concern all over her pretty face.

"It almost seems so lately," muttered Colin dejectedly.

That comment caused Tessa to stop her tirade and look at him curiously. "You didn't do this to each other this time did you?"

Cailean looked at her, choosing his words carefully. "Nay. It seems that we have made a few enemies somehow."

He got to his feet and walked toward her. "Can you promise me you'll stay inside until we say 'tis safe to leave the castle?"

She frowned, looking from one brother to the other. "Is it really that bad?"

"Aye, it could be much worse than that even," said Colin ominously, rubbing at his bruised wrist.

"I'll stay inside," she promised quietly.

"Thank you lass," said Cailean with relief. He touched her upper arm for a second before pulling his hand back as if he'd been burned. He turned back toward Colin quickly, masking the desire on his face with a frown.

"Would you like me to help get the blood off of you?" Tessa asked Colin.

"Nay!" growled Cailean abruptly, a little more firmly than he'd intended. "He can do it himself or get one of the maids to help."

Tessa and Colin both raised their eyebrows at him before looked at each other, Tessa in confusion and Colin with an eyebrow raised and a grin on his battered face. He shrugged carelessly after a second and turned away, probably with the aim of finding a cute maid to help him.

Tessa went beet red when she realized why Cailean was against her helping his brother. "I uh have to go back to work anyway," she stammered, turning quickly and all but running up the stairs.

Cailean left as soon as she got to the top of the staircase, stomping out of the castle, gritting his teeth in anger. What on earth was that woman up to offering to clean his brother up? Was she trying to make him jealous...crazy? He had no right to be jealous! So why the hell was he?

When he approached the spot where the east ward used to be, he found the stone that used to sit there gone and a small trail of blood leading to the lake. Following it, he finally came upon the remains of the fae who had dared touch the ward. All that was left of it was a small pool of blood and some shredded, burnt skin.

Teluth must have decided that this new tactic was worth voluntarily giving up one of his limited warriors, otherwise he never would have allowed one to die needlessly before the actual war he was planning. This concerned Cailean greatly. If Teluth was willing to go this far, there was no telling what else he might do and how far he would go. They would have to be constantly on guard.

He put his hand on his hips, sighing as he looked over at the faery mound, wondering what to do.

Suddenly, the peace was shattered by a piercing scream that ended as suddenly as it began. Tessa!

Cailean turned and raced back toward the castle with his heart hammering in his throat.

*   *   *

"I really have to stop blushing about last night," mumbled Tessa.

As she walked down the hall, glancing briefly at Cailean's closed bedroom door, she remembered the previous night and shook her head in disgust. Who was that woman anyway, she asked herself as she walked into her room and closed the door firmly behind her.

Before she knew what was happening, she was thrown across the room by someone incredibly strong. Her head slammed into the wall with a thud before she slid to the floor in a daze.

After her vision cleared, she looked around and saw that there was no one in the room with her. Her heart sped up as she started to wonder if it had been the work of a poltergeist. After all, the castle was hundreds, or even thousands of years old.

She had just decided to try standing up and running from the room, when she was picked up by unseen hands. She screamed in terror as she was again thrown across the room. Hitting hit the wall with a bone crunching thud, she had only a second to feel the pain before her world went black.

~7~

Both brothers burst into Tessa's room at the same time. Colin held on to her door for support and looked around, still weak from his recent attack. Cailean quickly searched the room and found blood on the far wall and the floor in front of it, but saw no sign of Tessa.

He stood still, heart pounding, staring down at the blood. His face was white. If the Unseelie took her - which was very likely - then she was either dead or would be used as bait. Both options terrified him and his hand shook as he grabbed the bedpost for support, struggling to remain calm.

A few moments later he felt Colin's hand on his shoulder, but was too frozen to turn. "Cailean, there's a message."

Looking up, Cailean realized that his brother meant the words that were written on the wall. When he first entered and searched the room, his brain must have refused to acknowledge it, probably because it was written in blood...her blood.

COME FOR GIRL

It was clear that the writer of the note meant to exchange Tessa for either he or Colin...or both. By getting them into the fae realm, they would be able to either imprison the brothers to keep them out of the way or even kill them.

He stood there for a few minutes just staring at the blood streaked wall before he managed calm down enough to talk. "God 'tis my nightmare and I dinna even tup the lass."

The room was eerily quiet.

He looked around. "Colin? Where the hell did you go?"

The moment he realized what Colin must be doing, he whipped around and started running down the stairs as if every demon in hell were after him. "Colin!" he yelled, as he ran out of the castle, praying he would make it in time to stop him.

He ran around the side of the castle just in time to see one of the Unseelie dragging Colin into the mound. Tessa was lying unconscious...or dead...in front of it.

Torn between saving Colin and protecting Tessa, he ignored the ache in his heart and ran to her, knowing Colin stood a better chance of surviving than she did. When he determined she could be moved without making her worse, he lifted her into his arms and walked back toward the castle, careful not to jostle her too much. He carried her upstairs and lay her on his bed.

Cailean moved her hair off of her face gently, letting his hand rest on her cheek. When he saw that she was breathing steadily, he fought the urge to sag against the bed in relief and propelled himself into action, grabbing a fresh rag and bowl from the bathroom and filling it with warm water before setting it on the table beside her. Before he started to clean her wound, he called their personal doctor who assured him that he would be right over.

Not wanting to hurt her, he gingerly started to clean the nasty cut on her head. He worried about the amount of blood he was seeing in the bowl after each squeeze of the rag but knew head wounds bled a lot and often looked worse than they were. That knowledge didn't ease his mind one bit though, and his heart pounded with the effort it was taking to stay calm.

When he was finished, he sat on the edge of the bed, staring down at her. She was colourless against the stark white sheets. His heart ached when he realized that she might never have known how he felt about her, that he may never have given her a chance to find out. His brother had not even thought twice about potentially giving his life for this woman, because he knew without being told that Cailean was in love with her. Knew it before he himself had even figured it out. He groaned at his own stupidity. Now he might have lost them both if Tessa didn't wake up soon and if he couldn't figure out a way to get Colin back from the blasted Unseelie.

Not wanting to leave her side, but aware that the castle needed more wards, he bandaged her head and called one of the maids to keep an eye on her, leaving strict instructions for her to yell for him if anything unusual happened, or if Tessa took a turn for the worse. The maid frowned warily at the first part but nodded at the second and stood guard over her unconscious patient.

He left the room reluctantly and moved around the exterior of the castle as quickly as he could, forging new wards as he went and checking the old ones.

When that was finished, he did a complete sweep of the interior of the castle, looking for any fae that may have made it in during the time the east ward had been missing.

Finding nothing unusual, he returned to Tessa and was immediately relieved to find her awake, though a little groggy.

"How's your head feeling lass?" he asked gently, motioning for the maid to leave them.

Tessa blinked a few times before raising her hand to touch the bandage that he had tied around her head. "I'm pretty sure it's cracked in half," she said, wincing.

He fished in his pocket until he found the bottle of painkillers he had put there earlier. She put two in her mouth and he lifted a glass of water to her lips, encouraging her to drink. "Those should do the trick."

"What happened?" she asked, after gagging slightly.

Cailean studied her, trying to figure out how much to tell her.

"You were attacked by someone who was hiding in your room."

"One of the enemies you talked about?"

"Aye," he hesitated. "They got Colin."

"What?" she yelled, then immediately grimaced and grabbed her head in pain.

"Calm down lass, you'll only do more damage," he admonished, pressing her firmly but gently back against the pillows.

"Do you know where he is? Did you call the police?"

"Nay!"

"Why haven't you called the police?" she demanded, looking thunderstruck. "What are you waiting for?"

"'Tis complicated lass."

"What's complicated about calling the police to report the fact that your brother was kidnapped?" she asked bewildered.

Cailean leaned forward and rubbed his eyes tiredly. He sighed, knowing he would have to tell her the truth before she pushed further for police involvement.

"They canna help us lass. Colin wasn't taken by a man."

He took a deep breath and let it out. "He was taken by faeries."

Tessa stopped trying to get up and lay looking at him, one eyebrow cocked, clearly convinced that he was the one who had hit his head. "Are all you Scotsmen mad?"

He sighed, fully expecting her disbelief.

"I'm no' mad lass."

He paused. Well...what the hell, she would either believe him or not...there weren't exactly a plethora of options.

"I'm immortal!"

"Oh Lord you *are* crazy," she said in a dismayed voice.

Cailean let out a breath of frustration and got up and started pacing the room.

How the hell was he going to explain this to her without making her think he was insane? What proof could he give her?

He tried again. "Lass, every month Colin and I fight the bad fae, who are called the Unseelie. They canna reproduce, so they take humans as prisoners to build their army. An army they intend to use to kill off the good fae, the Seelie. If they succeed, that would leave humans alone and vulnerable. The Seelie protect us from them. Colin and I were made immortal to stop the Unseelie from increasing the size of their army, to give the Seelie time to figure out what to do."

His eyes lit up suddenly. "Do you remember the gash that was on my leg yesterday?" he asked, knowing now how he could prove it to her.

"Yes," she answered hesitantly.

He raised his kilt enough to show her that the gash was almost completely gone already. All that remained was a silvery line.

He then showed her his arms that had deep scratches on it the previous night. Those were completely gone, not a trace of a scrape or anything marred his perfect, golden skin.

Tessa frowned and looked into his eyes. She looked scared.

"That's impossible," she said weakly. "People don't heal that fast."

"No' unless they're immortal."

He stood looking down at her, knowing she had to process what she'd just seen. Hoping she could.

"Wh...what you are asking me to believe is...well...impossible! How can I believe something like that?"

"I know 'tis difficult to fathom, but I swear 'tis true lass. I swear it on my own brother's life."

Tessa raised her hands to her face and rubbed at her eyes.

"God help me, I believe you."

Cailean heaved a sigh of relief at her answer and took her hand in his, to brace her for what he had to say next.

"Colin might have given his life for yours to get you back from the fae who took you," he said gently. "I have to talk to the king of the good fae to find out what I can do, and I technically canna do that until next month because the gates between our worlds are only supposed to be open for three days each month, for a short time each day."

Tessa put her hand over her mouth. "Oh Cailean, why would he do that?"

He looked down at his kilt and frowned, not wanting to admit what he didn't believe yet.

"Because he's a good lad. And a loyal brother."

*   *   *

Tears slipped down her cheeks as she saw the pain flicker across Cailean face. How could he even look at her knowing that his brother may be dead because of her? Oh God why would Colin even do this? It's not like he knew her that well.

"I'm so sorry Cailean," she sobbed.

He took her hand in his gently. "Doona be sorry lass, he's a strong lad. Have faith."

She sniffed and nodded, forcing confidence she didn't feel. "Ok, you're right. He'll be ok."

Cailean nodded and rose abruptly from the bed. "I must go re-check the wards again. I'll return soon. I'll send someone in to keep you company."

"Wards?"

"Ah...they're protection spells that are placed around the castle so that the Unseelie canna get through."

"Ummm...then how did they?"

Cailean sighed unhappily. "They're no' fool proof. If an Unseelie is willing to end his life, and can move the ward far enough away...that invisible chain breaks, allowing them through."

"Oh."

Tessa watched him turn and walk out of the room. *His* room, she realized. Why was she in his room instead of hers? As she tried to figure that out, severe exhaustion suddenly overwhelmed her and she lay back on his pillow, inhaling his scent. Her eyes fluttered and within seconds she had drifted into a pain free oblivion.

The next time she woke, there was a maid she didn't know sitting in a chair next to the bed reading a book. She looked up and asked Tessa if she needed anything, but she must have fallen back asleep immediately because when she opened her eyes again Cailean was lying beside her and the maid was nowhere to be seen. They were both covered in a blanket, but she could see that he was shirtless. It was dark in the room so she assumed that she had been asleep for some time. Her head felt remarkably better, probably thanks to the incredibly strong painkillers he'd forced down her earlier.

She turned her head to look at Cailean sleeping next to her. The moonlight shone softly through the open windows, giving off enough light so that she was able to see the steady rise and fall of his chest. His face was a mix of shadow and light and for the first time, she really studied his features, filing each crease and crevice away in her mind. He had thick, black eyebrows that lay in an almost straight line over his closed eyes, and his eyelashes were long and thick and ridiculously sexy looking. He had a straight nose, and lips that were neither too thick nor too thin, and his stubborn chin jutted out slightly with a deep cleft in the centre that was half hidden in shadows. He seemed to have a permanent blue shadow to his jaw, evidence that he probably had to shave daily. She lifted her hand toward him, wanting to run her it over his smooth jaw, wanting to slide her fingers against his lips, along the length of his face the way a blind person would to memorize a lover's face.

She hesitated and let her hand fall back to her chest, not wanting to wake him. He looked so peaceful.

She was distracted from her daydreams by her stomach growling and an empty feeling of hunger.

Deciding that she should probably get something to eat before her noisy stomach woke Cailean, she started to get up.

As she tried to rise, Cailean's arm swept across her, effectively pinning her to the bed. "I'm guessing by the yelling coming from your stomach that you're hungry lass," he said in a husky, sleepy voice as he pushed the blanket aside. "I'll go get you something, just wait here."

She was relieved to note he had his kilt on, not that it was much better than him being naked, considering he wore nothing under it. Her hand itched to reach out and touch his bare back, but she resisted, unsure of how he would react to her touch after last night.

While he was gone, she managed to make it to the bathroom and back without incident, and her mouth felt better now that she had brushed her teeth to get rid of that cottony feel. She had also jumped into the shower to freshen herself up a bit and managed to find a clean shirt of his in the bathroom. It hung to the middle of her thighs.

Because she was feeling weak and shaky from hunger, she decided she would find some underwear after she ate so that she didn't pass out on the way to her room and embarrass herself yet again.

Cailean walked into the room just as she pulled the blanket up again, and laid a tray on her lap, filled with a mouth watering muffin, sliced oranges, and some kind of meat, along with some orange juice.

"I dinna know what you'd be hungry for but I knew you'd be starving since you've slept away a full two days."

"Two days?" she asked in shock.

"Aye, I was starting to get a little worried," he said as he got back under the blankets beside her, sniffing appreciatively at her freshly washed scent.

She eyed him warily before turning back to the delicious meal in front of her. After about five minutes nearly everything was eaten and she was finally starting to feel a little more human.

"Do you need me to get you anything else lass?" he asked with a yawn.

She looked over at him, wondering how much sleep he'd had in the last couple days. "Ummm no, I'm ok now. I think I'll just go back to my own room."

For the second time that night she felt his arm prevent her from getting up.

"The doctor came to take a look at your head and suggested that for a couple days twould be best if you are watched constantly. You have a concussion."

"Oh, ummm ok." She tried scooching away a bit. "I can sleep on the chair so you can have your bed back."

Again that familiar arm pressed across her, pulling her down while he rose above her, gazing down with half lidded eyes. "What's wrong lass? Are you scared of touching me now that I'm no' helpless?"

Tessa's mouth opened and closed like a fish as she tried to think of something to say to that. What finally came out was an indignant "No!" Oh wonderful...that was convincing.

"Good," he said as he lay back down. "Then I'd like to get some sleep."

"Wait...what do you mean 'good'?" she asked, a second before her mind told her it was a trap and that she should keep her mouth shut. Damn it! This was going to lead to some kind of embarrassing situation...she just knew it.

He lazily rose on to his elbow again, leaning over her with a sly smile, inches from her mouth. His voice was soft and sensual. "Good...because you turn me on like no woman ever has, and since the minute I met you I've had an eternal hard on that's really starting to get annoying. So since you're no' scared of touching me lass, there's hope that maybe one day soon...you will."

She trembled as she felt his breath on her mouth. He was so close that all she had to do was lift her head a couple inches and she could kiss him.

"Uhhhh." She wasn't sure what the sound coming from her mouth was supposed to mean, but it seemed to make sense at the time.

He leaned closer, his breath whispering against her lips. "I'll give you fair warning lass, I won't be waiting forever for you to make the first move," he said seductively.Tessa gulped and automatically licked her lips before kicking herself for doing something so suggestive.

He took that as an invitation and slid his lips gently across hers.

Her breath stuttered at the contact and electricity shot through her. God he felt so good! What could a tiny kiss hurt? Just for a few seconds?

With her willpower effectively shoved to the back of her mind for a moment, she turned her head slightly to find a better angle and raised her head enough to touch his wonderfully sensual lips again.

He sucked in a quick breath and pulled away slightly, looking at her with a frown, obviously not expecting her to kiss him willingly.

His breathing quickened as she softly touched her tongue to his lips, and he hesitated for half a second before claiming her mouth so suddenly and completely that all thoughts of how tiny the kiss was supposed to be flew from her mind.

Her head pressed back against the pillow as he assaulted her mouth, probing with his tongue in the most fantastic way. It almost felt like he was making love to her mouth. And man was he good. Her insides melted like butter and she slid her arms around his neck, pulling him closer. Without hesitating, he moved over her, pressing her body beneath his. She could feel him through the material of his kilt. A half naked man was lying on top of her and all she had on was his shirt and a serious lack of willpower. Her little eggs cheered happily.

For about two seconds she considered pulling away, but then she felt him press against her most sensitive part and moaned in pleasure, immediately forgetting that thought. Her legs opened as if by some invisible force and wrapped themselves around his lean hips, causing him to groan and press into her even harder. What the hell are you doing, a petulant voice yelled at her. Virginity isn't something you can get back if you decide you made a mistake. Are you seriously going to throw it away for a man who has annoyed you from the first moment you met him.

Ignoring the annoying voice, she suddenly realized that the movement he was making with his hips was sure to make her come any second, and groaned in complaint when he suddenly pulled away from her, knowing how damn close she was.

She was about to ask him what he was doing when she felt him lift her borrowed shirt over her head. He looked at her for a moment as she lay naked beneath him, then leaned down and drew her nipple into his heated mouth. She gasped, arching toward him in pleasure as sensations she never knew cascaded through her, rippling right down to her toes. Any nagging complaints and warnings that the little voice in her head had, died an instant death.

His hand slid slowly down her stomach while he sucked her other nipple into his mouth. She was sure she would explode when his hand eventually reached the part of her that she knew would made her completely forget what the word 'willpower' even meant.

Arching toward him, silently begging for his touch, she pulled his head to her mouth and kissed him passionately. When his fingers found her clitoris she shuddered and pressed against them. His breathing was harsh and she could sense that he was only barely managing to control himself as he slid his finger into her wetness. She heard a soft, urgent sound and knew it was coming from her but was helpless to stop. A deep aching pressure started building inside her and she moaned and lifted her hips toward his hand, demanding, pleading. He slid a second finger inside her while he used his thumb to rub her clitoris, driving her insane with need and bringing her so close she felt like she was melting from the heat. "Oh God Cailean. I can't stand it...please." Every nerve ending in her body was humming, and she felt as if she were going to explode.

He moved his thumb faster and plunged deeper, causing her to come in a blinding fury. He bent his head to capture her yell with his mouth, kissing her tenderly. Her world shattered into a rainbow of colours as wave after wave of pleasure ripped through her. She was almost sure she would die from it and grabbed on to him, fingers digging into his rock hard arms.

When she finally felt as if she could think again, she pulled back and smiled shyly at him. He looked at her with such passion that she almost forgot how to breathe.

He pulled away to undo his kilt and she slid her hand down and wrapped it around him, eliciting a groan from him.

"Tessa, doona do that or I'll come right here lass," he moaned, lying on his back as he pulled off his kilt. His voice was deep and husky and his Scottish burr much stronger in the heat of passion. It was incredibly sexy.

She decided that she could do a little teasing on her part as well and started sliding her hand up and down. His breathing was ragged and he suddenly wrapped his hand around hers, forcing her to stop.

* * *

"Doona move," he said urgently, holding her hand tightly around his cock. "You doona know what you do to me lass." She stubbornly kept trying to move her hand. With every squeeze and every minute movement, pleasure jolted through him in a way he'd never experienced. He was helpless to explain what she did to him.

"But I want to make you feel the way you make me feel."

"I know lass, the difference is that if I come now 'tis all over, but if you let me go...and stop squeezing," he gritted out, "I can make you come in ways you've only dreamed of. I can slide into you and show you what pleasure truly is."

She appeared to think about that for a moment while looking at him lying on his back, trying to control his breathing while keeping a death grip on her wayward hand.

He relaxed slightly when she slowly released her grip on him, but tensed again when she slid her fingers against him as she moved them away. He shuddered and grunted. "God lass, you do enjoy playing with fire."

Smiling, she leaned over to kiss him.

Knowing his control was iffy at best around the lass, he quickly flipped her over.

Startled, she let out a small yelp as she landed on her back, but it was quickly replaced by a moan as he slid his tongue into her mouth and began to kiss her into oblivion. She started to wrap her hands around his neck but he pulled away and started kissing his way down her body, stopping everywhere he could think of to taste her.

Eventually, he reached the soft folds that he had been dying to taste. He closed his eyes and slid his tongue along her softness, making her buck against him as soft sounds of pleasure escaped her. Her reaction almost undid him, but he pressed himself against the bed as he licked her hard nub, forcing himself to be patient while he brought her to new heights of pleasure. He hadn't felt like a hormonal teenager in so long that he was both surprised and taken aback that she could do this to him with so little effort.

When he slid his tongue inside her, she bucked against him again and came in a rush, yelling in pleasure as she pulsed against his mouth. He drank her in and lapped at her until her hips stopped jerking. She was the most amazing woman he had ever known. So alive and vibrant. Just looking at her made him want her in every way. Somehow, without him even realizing, she had not only gotten through his walls, but completely destroyed them in the process.

He dragged himself up along her sweat slicked, shuddering body and groaned when the head of his cock touched the spot he had just been licking. She felt so hot and wet against him, and he pressed softly, testing. She moaned and suddenly pushed against him, sliding him into her slightly. It was all he could do to force himself to move slowly so that he didn't hurt her too much. With each inch he gained, he lost half of that pulling out again. She squirmed beneath him, her fingers threaded through his hair, begging him to go faster. His willpower was quickly depleted as she moved and bucked beneath him, causing him to slide in faster and deeper each time.

"Cailean...oh...you feel so good," she panted, bucking against his straining cock, driving him crazy.

He grunted as he pushed all the way, breaking her barrier.

She gasped in pain and tensed under him, making him stop immediately.

"Are you ok?" he managed to ask between breaths, hating that he had to hurt her.

"Yes...I'll be ok in a minute."

They both lay still for about a short time until little by little she started moving her hips against his, silently demanding he follow. He kept himself still, letting her go at her own pace, but after a few seconds she wrapped her legs around him and pulled him hard against her, destroying his good intentions completely.

He gave in with a groan and started thrusting in and out, faster and faster until they were both completely unaware of anything but each other. He could feel his orgasm building as he thrust, and forced himself to hold back, the need to satisfy her foremost in his mind. "Christ, you truly are magnificent Tessa."

Just when he thought he wouldn't be able to hold out any longer under the sweet torture of her hips rising to meet his with each stroke, Tessa suddenly arched toward him and he felt her muscles contracting around his cock while she panted in his ear. That was all it took to make him explode inside her with a groan. His body was wracked with shudders as he came, the force of his orgasm shocking him to the core. He felt a strange kind of power flow through him unlike anything he had ever felt before. He came for what seemed like eternity, and knew without a doubt that if he were to die at that moment, he would have no regrets.

When his orgasm finally subsided, he rolled off of her and pulled her to him tightly, closing his eyes and breathing in the scent of her freshly washed skin.

He couldn't remember sex ever feeling like this...being this incredibly intense. When he was finally able to get his breathing under control, he opened his eyes and looked at her. She was looking back at him, eyes wide in wonder, sweat glistening on her skin.

"Is it always that amazing?" she asked in a stunned whisper.

He cupped her jaw with his hand. "I've honestly never felt anything like that in my life lass." He leaned over and kissed her gently.

When he pulled away, she looked at him with a shy smile. "I could definitely get used to that."

"Me too," he sighed happily, as he pulled her close and looked up at the ceiling in the darkness. He wondered about the strange feeling that had shot through him at the end? He felt stronger somehow. Stronger than he'd ever felt before.

As the night crept on, he held her in his embrace, thankful that he had finally given it to what he had been feeling for so long. They made love two more times before he eventually fell into a fitful sleep as his brain tried to make sense of what had happened and how he was going to save his brother. Tessa slept deeply, cuddled in his strong arms, unaware of the nightmare that was haunting his sleep.

~**8**~

$\mathcal{T}$essa woke up at noon the next day and stretched lazily in bed. His bed! Her sleep fogged brain cleared instantly and she shot up and looked around the empty room. Was it all a dream, she wondered curiously. Maybe she had hit her head harder than she'd thought. She lifted the sheets and looked down at herself. Naked!

She yanked the sheet back against her, eyes wide. She was sure she had put his shirt on after her shower last night, but it was entirely possible that she had pulled it off during the night because she had gotten hot. She lifted the sheets again and looked at the bed between her legs and saw that the white sheet she was sitting on had streaks of blood on it. Oh God! She yanked the sheet back against her again and took a deep breath, exhaling with a puff. Her period? Possible. Unlikely, since the last one had finished not even two weeks ago...but possible.

The door to the room opened suddenly and she shrieked and slid down into the blankets with the sheet at her chin.

Cailean stopped in his tracks and grinned at her.

"Good morning lass. Did you sleep well?"

Oh Lord how do I answer that, she asked herself, mortified. Just answer 'yes', replied the exasperated voice in her head that had tried to warn her the night before about throwing things away frivolously. You've already crossed the line, jumped the log, crossed over the bridge. *Ok, ok, you don't need to go on*, she growled at the inane little voice. She really had to stop talking to herself, she was sure it was an unhealthy thing for one to be doing all the time.

She took a deep breath and squeaked out, "Yes." It sounded more like a question than a confirmation.

He just stood there smiling at her. Was he expecting her to say something else? About last night maybe?

"Are you ok lass?" he asked with a trace of humour in his voice.

She looked up at him again and glanced away quickly. "Ummm yeah...fine." *Wow, and I'm a writer? I can't even get more than three bloody words out...and ummm isn't exactly a word. Think you idiot. Say something to get him out of here so you can go clean up and burn the damn sheets.*

"I'm hungry." *Oh my Lord! There's a Pulitzer winner if there ever was one. I'm hungry? Why not just announce that sex has turned you into a brainless cavewoman and you've lost the ability to string more than three words together...or two if we've decided for sure that 'ummm' isn't a real word.*

He chuckled softly and walked over to her in that insanely sexy, masculine way that only he could. When he reached her side, he leaned down and kissed her lips softly before pulling away. "Then breakfast is what I'll get you lass...or lunch anyway, since 'tis noon already." With that he turned and walked out of the room, shutting the door firmly behind him.

Geez now the man is probably wondering if she'd broken her brain. If turning into a simpleton is the result of insanely amazing sex...well...well...she actually wasn't quite sure how to end that sentence. Oh no! Did she just admit to herself that she *did* have sex with that incredibly sexy man last night? *Ok just breathe. Calm down and think. He wouldn't have just come up to you and kissed you all casually if he didn't have sex with you, you idiot. So...if that theory is correct, then...she had sex last night! With him! In his bed! Naked!*

The door suddenly opened again and she screamed in surprise and yanked the sheets up again.

He looked at her in amusement, a smile spreading over his handsome face. "I was going to ask you if you wanted coffee too, but you seem a little too jumpy already."

Blushing furiously she couldn't seem to look him in the eye. "Coffee...yes!" she agreed. *OH MY GOD! What the hell brain?* "I mean, I would definitely like some coffee please," she said, rephrasing her previous cavewoman-like answer.

"Ok," he said simply and shut the door again.

She was just about to relax when he stuck his head in again. "One sugar or two?"

"One."

"Milk?"

"Yes."

He shut the door again and she glared at it...daring it to re-open.

116

When nothing happened for a full two minutes, she decided that now would be as good a time as any to race to her room for clothes and have a shower.

She gingerly got out of bed, convinced even more about having sex the previous night when she felt the soreness between her thighs. Wrapping the sheet around her like a mummy, she quickly whipped the blood stained bottom sheet off his bed and raced to her room with it, dumping it unceremoniously into her laundry basket.

What on earth was she supposed to say to him at breakfast, she asked herself while the hot shower sprayed over her. What does one say to the man they've just lost their virginity to? How about that virginity huh? *Oh my God I'm officially insane. Who thinks of things like that anyway?*

She dragged in a deep breath and succeeded in inhaling just enough of the shower spray to cause her to go into a hacking fit for a good two minutes. When it was finally over, she leaned her head against the tiled shower wall in defeat. It was obvious that sex had not only killed her brain cells, but managed to turn her into a complete klutz as well. Imagine choking to death while *standing* in a shower. Good grief.

When she decided that she had hidden in the shower long enough that her skin was going to stay permanently prune-like, she forced herself to dry off and get dressed. Making it out the bathroom door without bumping into him was another matter altogether, and the more she thought about it, the more she liked the idea of hiding out in her room all day. She could just use the excuse that she was writing.

Firmly deciding that the writing plan was a far better option than the alternative, she left the bathroom and went straight to her room, shutting the door firmly behind her with a relieved sigh at not encountering Cailean on the short trip. She was leaning with her forehead against the cool wood of the door when she suddenly felt a prickling awareness on the back of her neck and spun around, gasping in surprise when she saw Cailean standing two feet from her, arms crossed, grinning from ear to ear.

"You know lass, I'm almost getting the feeling that you're trying to hide from me after last night," he said in a deep, sensual voice as he uncrossed his hands and moved toward her.

"Wha...wha." *Oh great, here I go again with the cavewoman brain. Come on Tessa, never let the predator see fear...or stupidity for that matter.*

She cleared her throat and tried again. "I have no idea what you are talking about."

"Nay?"

She shook her head a little too enthusiastically. "I was just coming to my room to get some writing done."

"Really?"

"Uh huh," she said as he got closer, not quite sure if to nod or shake her head and managing a mixture of both. She could smell his masculine scent now, shower fresh and utterly male, unencumbered by cologne or aftershave. For some reason he was the best thing she could ever remember smelling. Her brain stalled for half a second before she reminded it that it was working for her and there were no coffee breaks allowed.

"I...I haven't been able to write for a while and I thought of some ideas when I was in the shower." *There...that should do it.*

"Mm hmm. What kind of things did you think about in the shower?"

Her mouth went dry and her brain once again got stuck. "Uhhh about the writing," she managed, not quite sure if that made any sense at all.

He bent down to her neck and inhaled. "Mmmm you smell good lass."

"Huh...ahhh." *Would you look at that...another Pulitzer*, she dimly thought as her brain went all fuzzy.

He bent his head and drew his lips slowly across hers, teasing. She was sure she would melt into a puddle if he did anything even nearly that erotic again. The man was simply desire on legs. How could she possibly have entertained the idea that she stood a chance against him?

"Tessa lass, you're enough to drive a man insane with desire."

Her? Drive *him* crazy? Ok the man was officially on drugs, she decided about three seconds before any and all thoughts were completely wiped from her mind when he thrust his tongue into her mouth and dragged her against him with a growl. His hands seemed to be everywhere at once and her shirt was whipped from her body in a heartbeat. He undid her bra with a practised hand and one breast found its way into his hot, demanding mouth, causing her knees to buckle. He effortlessly lifted her up and carried her to the bed. She could feel his rigid flesh against her hip, hard, straining against the material of his soft leather pants. He wasn't wearing his sporran this time and she was ever so thankful of that.

He sat her on the edge of the bed and made her lie down so that he could pull her jeans and underwear off. After they were flung across the room, he lay half on top of her with her legs dangling off the bed and continued his meal of her left breast. She was extremely glad that she was lying down this time because her knees seemed to think that once his mouth touched her breast they were off duty.

He moved up from her breast to her neck and slid his tongue deliciously along the side of it on his way up to her ear, where he did things that made goose bumps break out all over her body, causing her to shiver in delight. He pressed against her with a groan, causing an entirely different type of shiver as she prayed his pants would suddenly do her the favour of jumping off his body. He continued the assault on her neck and ear and she slid her hands down his naked back, vaguely wondering when he had taken his shirt off, but deciding she didn't care as long as it was off. His back was broad and his muscles rippled as he continued to thrust gently against her, making her breath come in gasps.

Sliding her hands further down his back and around his waist toward the ties that held his pants on, she heard him grunt softly when she grazed his swollen flesh, and somehow she managed to find the end of the ties on her first try and opened his pants with one tug, freeing him somewhat.

He gasped against her ear when she slid her hand into the front of his pants and wrapped her fingers around him. God he was huge, she thought in amazement as she moved her hand slowly up and down his shaft.

Shifting slightly, he claimed her mouth again and positioned himself a little better so that she was able to direct him toward the ache she was feeling between her thighs.

When the head of his cock hit home, his breath caught and he pushed into her slowly, as if drawing out the pleasure of it. She let

120

go of him and grabbed his firm, muscular backside, pulling him into her as she wrapped her legs around him. He slid his hands around her back and somehow managed to stand up with her still joined to him.

Pressing her against the wall beside the bed, he pushed into her over and over until she was sure she would die of pleasure. His tongue caressed hers in a kind of mating dance, melting her from the inside. God how could anything possibly feel so good? She heard soft grunting noises as he thrust into her and it took a while to realize that they were coming from her. She couldn't even make herself stop, it was as if her body was in a different world from her brain and refused to be controlled. He felt so good sliding in and out of her that nothing else in the world mattered to her at that moment. Her legs tightened around his hips as she felt the pressure building inside her. Again and again he slid into her, kissing her as if he would die without her. With each thrust she could feel his power pressing into her, forcing the pressure inside her to expand until it was a tight ball ready to explode. Again he thrust, and this time she exploded with a cry. Pleasure ripped its way throughout her entire body as she pulsed around his shaft, dragging a harsh growl from him and causing him to exploded inside her at the same time, pressing her hard against the wall.

Just like last night, she felt a strange feeling flow through her, and when he tensed and thrust one more time, she knew he had felt it too. She held on to him with a deathlike grip, sure that if he put her down she would crumple to the floor in a sodden heap. Instead of making her stand, he pushed them away from the wall and carried her over to her bed. He lay her down across the bed, still inside her and slowly slid into her two more times before pulling himself out and raising his head to look at her.

"I doona understand why it feels the way it does with you, but 'tis like a drug, and it makes me want you even more now than I did before," he said in a husky voice before leaning close to kiss her again.

Not quite sure how to reply to that, or that she could even talk at that point, she pulled him down again for another kiss.

*   *   *

Cailean could feel his himself starting to respond already to that last kiss, but not wanting to make her too sore, he let her go and stood up.

Without looking at her, he re-tied his pants with some difficulty and looked back up in time to see her wrap a sheet shyly around herself. He wanted to tell her to leave it off, but realized that it was better for his own self control to have all those delicious body parts hidden from view.

Reaching for the breakfast tray he had put on her bedside table while she was in the shower, he placed it on her lap. "You need to eat."

She looked down at her food and back up at him. He swore she was searching him for answers to some unasked question and was just about to ask her what it was when she raised her hand and handed him his shirt. She hadn't talked much since this morning and he was pretty sure she just didn't know what to say to him after last night.

He took the shirt from her hand and slid it on, and when he looked at her again she almost looked disappointed. Was it something he had done? Said? He fought with the idea of asking

122

but decided that he would just let it go for now since she seemed a bit overwhelmed. He knew she was probably feeling a fair bit of guilt over her fiancé and that was somewhere he didn't want to go just yet. Maybe later, after the confusion inside him settled somewhat, but not now.

The thought of her fiancé suddenly got him angry and he turned abruptly and walked out of the room, shutting the door behind him. He wasn't sure if he was angry at the man or at himself for letting it go this far with Tessa knowing that at the end of her month's stay she would fly back to Canada, back to her life and marry someone else, never giving him another thought.

He stopped in shock and leaned against the stone wall of the hallway. He had only known the woman a few days and he was jealous? What the hell was happening to him? And while he was on that topic, what the hell was that surge of power that went through him after he came? He wasn't lying when he told her it was like a drug. That was why he stayed in her room after dropping off her breakfast. Why he waited for her. It was almost as if he couldn't force himself to leave. He needed her.

"I need her?" he asked himself softly, confused. "Since when have I ever needed a woman, or anyone for that matter?"

He pushed away from the wall and walked toward the stairs. "And since when do I talk aloud to myself?" he said, shaking his head in disgust.

He reached the bottom of the stairs in no better mood than the top and stalked out the door toward the stables. He needed to go for a ride so that he could calm down and put things in perspective. He was worried about Colin. He wished there was some way he could find out if he was ok or not. Would he be killed by the fae?

Would his brother, who had been with him through so much, be gone forever? It was too hard to comprehend. How did he face eternity without Colin? It was hard enough doing it after his wife and child died, but to go on without Colin who had been with him since the beginning of this whole nightmare? There were no words to even describe how much it scared him to think of losing his only brother and having to go on alone...forever.

He walked into the stables and Destiny raised her head and whinnied. She could always sense when he was upset. It was almost like some kind of connection she had to him. She kept her head raised, looking at him as he approached.

Reaching down to get a piece of sugar from his sporran, he realized he hadn't put it on that morning and was surprised at his forgetfulness. He had never forgotten to wear it before, especially when coming to visit Destiny. It was like forgetting to put on pants, it just didn't happen. He frowned and reached out to rub his hand down her neck. "Sorry girl, I seem to be a wee bit forgetful today." She rubbed her head against his in forgiveness.

"Want to go for a ride?"

Destiny whinnied and snorted in response.

He put on her saddle that the young stable boy, Ivan, had retrieved for him from the fields and walked her out into the sunlight, where he mounted her and started riding to nowhere in particular. "I'm worried about Colin," he told her softly, knowing she would listen to his problems and offer no judgement or harsh words in response. "He's been with me for so long that I wouldn't even know what to do without him." He slid his hand over her mane as he talked.

"He gave himself up for Tessa...for me. Somehow he must have known that I would have this strange bond with the lass. He wanted me to be happy. He wanted me to fall in love again.

Love!" he said with a snort. "Then what? Watch her die? I doona think I can survive that again. And what if she gets pregnant? Must I also watch my own bairn die too...again? A man's heart can only take so much, and I fear mine has already had its fill."

Sadly he looked out over the land. The birds flew above him in a peaceful dance, trees grew around him and grass below him. Everything was so alive. For so long he couldn't understand how life could go on so normally after first Catherine, then Leah, had died. It just went on as if their deaths didn't even matter in the whole scheme of things. He had raged at God, at Finvarra and all the faeries. He had raged at everyone who got to die while he was forced to live on. The only one he hadn't been angry at was Colin because he knew that one day he might be dealt the same hand and have to watch those he loved die. As time passed he was proven correct.

He remembered sitting beside Colin, watching the pain of his wife's, then children's deaths tear him apart inside. He remembered the long nights filled with the rum and whisky his brother had used to dull his pain.

Although Isobel, Angus and Calum were Colin's children, he had also mourned heavily for them, feeling closer to them than any normal uncle could. He learned to keep a distance from Isobel's children and grandchildren so that he would not have to go through that pain again.

Colin on the other hand, loved each grand and great grandchild with all his heart, spending all his free time getting to know each one. Eventually there were so many of the greats that he wasn't able to know them as well as he would have wanted. Their descendents knew that their two ancestors were immortal because both he and Colin visited the oldest child of each generation to ensure that they understood the importance of keeping proper records of each marriage, birth and death in their generation for future generations to see, thus the MacLeods had a complete written lineage dating back for over many hundreds of years starting from Colin and Cailean's own great, great, great grandfather.

Though so many years had gone by since Katie's death, Colin still firmly believed in love and was happy that he had the opportunity to meet so many of his descendants and wouldn't have given that up for the world. His theory was that whether he lived to be seventy or one million and seventy, he still would no doubt have lived to see his two sons die, and possibly have outlived his wife as well. He said that living for so long was a gift in itself because of all of the people he was blessed enough to know and love.

Cailean had always had a great amount of love and respect for his younger brother, but never more than when he spoke those words while sitting at the edge of his great granddaughter's death bed after the disastrous birth of her third and last son, only three months after her husband had been killed in battle. He had seen the tears in his brother's eyes as he watched her draw her last breath. Colin had promised to take care of her children. And so his great granddaughter, Lisa, died in peace that day, knowing the children she left behind would be loved and cared for.

~9~

*C*ailean was brought back to reality when a particularly large
rain drop splashed against his hand. He'd been riding around for
almost an hour and hadn't noticed the black clouds rolling in above
the hills.

Resigning himself to the fact that he would be completely
soaked by the time he returned to the castle, he sighed heavily and
turned Destiny around, starting back at a fast trot.

About fifteen minutes later, the storm started in earnest and
rain pelted from the sky with the force of a hurricane. Needles of
rain felt as if they were piercing his neck and face and he picked up
the pace, eager to get home.

Sheltering his eyes, he looked out over the land and his jaw
dropped in surprise at the sight before him. He pulled Destiny up
short and sat with the tempest howling around him, looking at the
shimmering rainbow of colour that seemed to stand vertically
about fifty feet in front of him, reaching up to the heavens.

The opening, or so his brain seemed to want to interpret the line as, was pointed at both the top and bottom and widened visibly toward the center.

Shock suddenly crashed over him as he realized what the image before him meant, realized that he had seen it once before, hundreds of years ago, only that time it had been much, much smaller.

Kicking Destiny to a full blown run, he raced back toward the castle as if all the demons of hell were after him. He prayed he would reach Tessa in time.

* * *

By two o'clock, after an hour of sitting at her laptop, Tessa had managed to write a whole sixty two words. She sighed heavily and leaned forward on the desk with her chin in her hands, frowning at the cursor that seemed to be taunting her with its stubborn refusal to do anything other than try to blink her to death.

Sex was proving to be detrimental to her brain in more ways than she had realized, and try as she might, she just couldn't seem to come up with a good enough reason for her heroine to turn away the tall, dark stranger who had showed up at her doorstep the night before, helping her vanquish two vampires who had been intent on making her their next meal. The fact that he himself was also a vampire wasn't really an argument since he had killed his own kind to protect her.

She groaned and flopped her head onto her arms. She either had writers block or the distractions of this morning and last night were taking its toll on her. How could one man mess with her head so easily? It's not even like there was any possibility of a future with him. For one thing, the guy lives in Scotland. And not only that, but he's *immortal,* meaning he will NEVER die. What was she supposed to do, grow into an old haggard witch while her husband stayed a young, gorgeous, Scottish piece of....gorgeousness? As soon as she sprouted her first grey hair he would be off like the wind to trade her in for a younger model.

Oh Lord look at me...I already have myself married to the man!

A crash of thunder made her jump and she looked out the window in surprise. The weather had been sunny and fine just a little while ago. *Boy do storms move in fast here. Or maybe it's God agreeing that I'm an idiot,* she thought rather sheepishly.

She pushed back from her computer and went to the closed window, putting her hand against the cold glass as she looked out.

An almost creepy feeling overcame her as she stared out, open mouthed, at the fury of the storm. Uneasily she wondered if it was possible to get hurricanes in Scotland.

Backing quickly away from the window, lest she get stabbed by some kind of pointy flying debris, she turned and left the room in search of Cailean.

She immediately felt better in the hallway and went to his room, hesitating only briefly before knocking on his door. Sure he might think she was just a chicken, but she would just plead an interest in the storm for the sake of her book which was, after all, based in Scotland, so she should at least know about the kind of weather here.

That actually made more sense than she thought it would and she knocked again, a little more firmly this time, armed with a decent reason for wanting to know why the hell there was a hurricane going on outside her window.

There was no answer to that knock either, and frowning, she opened the door and glanced inside. He had obviously left his own window open, because the wind and rain was making a mess of everything. She bit her lip wondering what to do.

Reasoning that it might be too dangerous to go near the window, she closed his door and stood in the hallway, frowning. Now what?

Deciding to go downstairs in search of him, she again walked past her room, and jumped violently when she heard the sound of her own window breaking. Her laptop!

She opened her door and raced toward her computer, grabbing it from her desk and spinning around just in time to see Cailean standing at the door, panting, with a look of fury on his face.

"Did you seriously just risk your life to save your blasted computer you daft woman?" he yelled angrily over the storm.

She opened her mouth to yell back something about her computer being her life when she heard another missile crash through the window. Everything after that seemed to happen in slow motion as she turned toward the noise and felt something slam into her chest. The last thing she heard before everything went black was Cailean yell, "Tessa!"

* * *

Cailean was pretty damn sure that if he hadn't been immortal, he would have had a heart attack the moment he saw the metal pole shoot through the window and hit Tessa in the chest like a javelin. He had seen her eyes widen in comprehension and fear half a second before she flew backward from the force of the blow.

Right after she landed in a bloody heap on the floor some ten feet from where her feet had left the ground, one of king Teluth's warriors burst through the shattered window, landing on Cailean with a grunt and almost succeeded in stabbing him with a small dirk that he was damn sure was made of Senk.

He cursed and shoved the tall faery off him with such strength that his jaw actually dropped in surprise. What the hell? He shouldn't have that kind of strength. He was strong, but it was almost ridiculously easy the way he pushed the surprised faery off.

He saw a moment of hesitation in the things eyes before it lunged at him with a vicious growl.

In that one second, the creature had unknowingly sealed its fate by showing fear. Cailean's hand darted out and knocked the dirk away before grabbing it by the head and crushing it against the floor like it was no heavier than a chair. This gave him enough time to retrieve the small knife and jab it at the creature's neck, causing a fountain of blood to spill to the floor and splatter the walls. The once iridescent faery clutched its neck while looking in astonishment at the blood that covered the floor around it. It slowly changed to a drab grey colour before falling forward, dead.

Cailean dropped to his knees where he stood.

He closed his eyes as overwhelming grief poured over him. There was no way she could have hoped to survive that metal rod. It all happened so quickly that he hadn't even had time to move before it pierced her. He sank back on his heels and dropped his head into his hands.

"Cai...," gasped Tessa from across the room.

His eyes shot open and he slowly raised his head, not daring to believe.

"Cailean."

He turned his head slowly in her direction. His breathing ragged. "Tessa?"

"It hurts," she whispered.

When his eyes were finally able to focus on her, he saw that she was still lying on the floor. What he had thought was blood from the rod going through her chest was actually from the glass that sprayed over her when it shot through the window. He looked at her chest in disbelief. Where was the hole? There should have been a hole right through her.

"Please," she gasped again.

He suddenly came to his senses and shot to his feet, reaching her in seconds and gathering her into his arms. Still confused he looked around for the rod. Her laptop sat at an odd angle next to her, and when he reached out and pulled it over he saw the rod sticking partially out of it. She must have had it pressed against her chest when the rod hit. The damned machine had saved her life.

Relief coursed through him and he dropped his face to hers, holding on to her as if for dear life. "God Tessa, you're alive."

"Alive hurts," she said softly, rubbing at her sore chest.

He laughed, "Yeah," he said nodding. "It does."

"What happed?"

"Your damned computer stopped the rod from going clean through you. 'Tis dead I'm afraid."

She started to laugh, but stopped and rubbed at her chest. "Ow. Laughing hurts too," she grumbled.

Cailean took a deep breath and smiled down at her, shaking his head. "I'm glad it hurts lass. It means you're alive."

"Yeah," she agreed with a smile. "I guess it does huh?"

He hugged her close to him while the rain and wind howled around them. He decided at that moment that he was a complete idiot for letting his fears get in the way of his life. From now on he would love her with everything he had. He wanted to squeeze her but was scared of hurting her, so just settled for having his arms wrapped around her, wishing they could stay that way forever.

"Cailean," came a voice from the doorway.

He stiffened. He had known that voice from childhood. Could it be true?

Whipping around he saw his brother grinning at him. "Colin!" he yelled with joy. "How the bloody hell did you get back here?"

"No Tinkerbell is going to keep *me* locked up," he answered, grinning, then paused and looked more serious. "I hate to break up your little...," he gestured with his hand, "whatever you're doing, but you might want to get away from the windows."

Cailean's head jerked back to the windows, suddenly realizing that things were still flying through them. He picked Tessa up and followed his brother through the door into the hallway.

Tessa looked from one brother to the next in fascination after Cailean gently put her down to stand beside him, keeping his arm firmly around her. They were both so gorgeous that it was amazing to take them both in at once.

"Do you think he made an immortal?" asked Cailean, frowning. "'Tis how it opened last time. Only that time twasn't nearly this huge."

"Aye he did," confirmed Colin with a growl. "Ten!"

Cailean looked at Colin for a moment, as if he were searching him for answers. "What exactly happened when you were on the other side?"

Colin took a deep breath and sighed. "'Tis all a little fuzzy still," he replied before going on to explain that when he was taken captive, the Unseelie had locked him into a place very much like an oubliette. It was a narrow place, shaped like a wine bottle in the dungeon of their castle where he was lowered by rope. There was no way for him to get out and he had feared that he would be left there for eternity.

During his stay, he had overheard the fae above talking about king Teluth's plans to make some of his human warriors immortal. The plan was to see what that would do to the thin fabric separating the fae world from the human world in addition to making his army even more invincible. They'd said the king was planning to send a warrior through to attempt to kill Cailean to get him out of the way. Apparently the king's plan was to eventually send all his warriors through at once after making more immortals, so that the fabric between the worlds ripped open to allow his army through.

Sometime later, Colin had heard another voice, this time a woman. She promised to pull him out if he went back and told Finvarra of Teluth's plans. He was confused, but agreed, and she pulled him out, explaining that she refused to see her own Unseelie world destroyed by Teluth in his deranged desire to rule the Seelie. The ripping of the fabric by the amount of immortals he intended to make was sure to destroy both their worlds by killing the humans and angering the Seelie into destroying their enemy. She refused to allow that to happen.

It was at that point that Colin was sent back to the human side through the hole created by Teluth when he made those first few immortals.

"I had just assumed he would wait until the monthly opening of the faery mound to march them through. I had no idea he would consider this," said Cailean, feeling almost panicked. "How the hell can we stop something this big?"

Colin shook his head and started pacing the hallway. He ran his hand through his hair in frustration. "We need to talk to Finvarra," he said, looking into his brothers eyes. "He must know some way to stop it from happening."

"Onagh!" yelled Colin at the top of his voice, making Tessa jump violently.

Cailean ran a hand up and down her arm soothingly.

"Onagh where the bloody hell are you, you damned faery? Show yourself!"

"Who is Ooh nag?" she asked quietly, looking up at Cailean.

He glanced at her quickly and started to look back at his brother when he suddenly hit with how beautiful she looked, despite the fact that there were scratches and blood over her face. He turned back to her and held her face in both his hands, looking into her eyes. "I love you lass".

Her eyes widened and she opened her mouth to say something, but couldn't seem to get a word out.

*   *   *

Oh my God did he just say that? What on earth had gotten into him all of a sudden? Since the connection between her brain and mouth seemed to have gotten temporarily disconnected somehow, she concentrated on trying to figure out what was going on with Cailean. He loved her? Uh uh! No way! Not a man as sinfully delicious as him. Her toes curled at the thought and her heart felt as light as a feather.

Apparently he had continued talking after that but she hadn't heard a word. What on earth was he even going on about anyway?

"...and I know you're in love with someone else and...well...are planning to marry him when you return to Canada, which is why this is so bloody stupid of me...".

"Hold it!" she cut him off, realizing she had never told him what happened between her and Aiden.

He stopped abruptly and stared down at her. The look on his face was so vulnerable and hopeless that she wanted to just pull him to her and hug him.

"Cailean," she began, looking for the right words. "I know what you think, and..."

"Um Cailean," started Colin as he rounded the corner. "The storm has stopped completely." She'd been so stunned by Cailean's admission that she hadn't realized that he'd left.

"Stopped? Just like that?" she asked incredulously.

"Aye."

Cailean all but dragged her along with him as he opened her door.

Sure enough everything was quiet. If not for the utter disaster her room was in and her murdered laptop lying forlornly amid the debris, you would never have known that hurricane like winds had been raging only moments before.

She looked from Cailean to Colin in confusion and rubbed her hand along the back of her neck not quite sure what to make of the situation.

Somewhere a piece of broken glass tinkled to the ground.

"Well I'm at a loss," admitted Colin, throwing his hands in the air in defeat and turning around to leave. He tread carefully over the glass and branches with his long, jean clad legs, then stopped in amazement when he spied the dead fae in the corner of the room.

"Ummm Cailean, is that your doing?" he questioned with one raised eyebrow.

Cailean turned around to where Colin pointed and heaved a big sigh before speaking. "He came through the window at me," he said as he started walking forward, stooping once he reached the fae, to pick something up.

He handed Colin the dagger. "He tried to give me a present. I'm sure 'tis made of Senk."

Colin frowned and turned the dagger in his hands slowly. "'Tis definitely that! This would be the warrior Teluth sent over to kill you."

"Who are you talking about?" asked Tessa, confused.

"There's a fae in the corner of your room lass. He's dead. You canna see him because he chose to be invisible to you when he broke through the window."

"There's a dead man lying in the corner of my room?" she asked shocked, eyes wide.

"Faery actually," said Colin casually.

Tessa shivered and felt Cailean's strong arms wrap around her and pull her against his solid chest. Somehow, despite the fact that she was faced with impossible, and apparently invisible, fairy tale creatures trying to kill them, when Cailean wrapped his warm arms around her, she felt completely safe. She sighed into his chest and inhaled his amazing scent. Just his smell alone was enough to make her wish they were in his bed.

"'Tis ok Tessa, Colin and I will make sure you stay safe."

He turned to Colin again, "What was the name of the female that rescued you?"

"Kynleigh."

"Hm...I've never heard of her."

Suddenly, magically, a beautiful man appeared in front of them, startling Tessa. She let out a scream and tensed to run.

"Shhh, 'tis ok lass, 'tis only Onagh. He's one of the good fae," said Cailean in a soothing voice as he pulled her against him again.

"I'm so sorry Tessa, I did not mean to scare you," said the most beautiful man she had ever seen with a voice that instantly calmed her and brought to mind a peaceful ocean. He stood as tall as Cailean and was wearing white and red robes that sort of sparkled when they moved. He had the most amazing silver eyes and flowing blonde hair. He was also very broad under his robes which suggested a muscular body like Cailean's.

Her mouth opened in shock when she recognized him. "Crazy taxi man!"

Cailean looked at Onagh through narrowed eyes. "Oh Really? You drive taxi's now? I knew Finvarra had something to do with this! Damn it!"

Onagh looked at Cailean and Tessa and shrugged helplessly. "I do what I'm told Cailean. I am just as much a pawn in this as you and Colin."

Cailean growled to himself, still glaring at Onagh.

Tessa smiled shyly but said nothing, continuing to lean against Cailean's solid body, seeking whatever comfort he could give.

Unsure what they were talking about, she continued to look at Onagh, marvelling at his perfect beauty. It was almost as if she couldn't physically look away. She watched his hands as he gestured and was amazed at how perfectly masculine, yet gentle, they looked. His voice continued to calm her, and she felt almost like she was in a trance. Well even though he was so gorgeous, at least he didn't appear to be Scottish. In fact she couldn't place his accent at all.

It was really getting to the point of being ridiculous how many good looking men she was surrounded by all the time. She was starting to get a complex. There was nothing better to make a girl feel plain than standing next to three examples of perfection. She looked across at Colin. He stood talking to Onagh, looking like he'd just stepped out of a magazine. His long hair draped across his shoulders, and his thick dark eyebrows perfectly accented his almond shaped eyes. He had a straight nose that fit very nicely with the shape of his face, and his jaw, though not quite as square as Cailean's, was strong and wide. For some reason she couldn't seem to make out the words he was saying, but she could hear the deep resonance of his voice as he talked. She gazed at his hands as he too gestured, and noticed a small black shape on the inside of his left wrist. It looked like a sideways figure eight had been tattooed there in black ink. She would have to remember to ask him later what it meant.

She glanced down at Cailean's wrist and noticed the same tattoo. Must be some sort of brotherly bond thing, she thought sleepily. Wait a minute, why was she so sleepy? Could it be all the confusion of the day catching up with her? She blinked her eyes and shook her head slightly, causing Cailean to look down at her. She looked at him with a frown, too tired to talk, and saw a hint of a smile at the corners of his mouth.

He turned back to Onagh and said something she didn't catch and suddenly the sleepiness left her and she was alert again. Even their voices were clear. It was as if someone had given her a huge dose of caffeine that worked instantly.

"My apologies Tessa," said Onagh, looking at her with a heart wrenching smile. "I forgot to remove the enchantment."

"The what?" she asked, thoroughly confused.

Cailean smiled and explained it. "In order to keep you calm, Onagh put an enchantment on you, but we were so busy discussing the issue of Teluth that he forgot to remove it."

"Oh," was all she could say. It was a pity the all powerful Onagh couldn't make himself less beautiful, she thought in irritation, frowning at the man.

She suddenly realized she had to pee quite urgently and excused herself from group, heading toward the bathroom.

After finishing up in record time, she reached the door in time to hear Onagh talking to Cailean about soul mates. She stopped out of sight and listened.

"She is your soul mate Cailean. It is said that when a child is born, God splits that child's soul in half and puts it into another person. This means that each person has a soul mate wondering around. If those people are lucky enough to find each other, the bond between them in incredible. For an immortal, it means that when you have sex with her, your strength multiplies tenfold and you are capable of amazing feats, this is on top of the inhuman strength passed down through the MacLeod line. This is why you were able to defeat the Unseelie in the corner with so much ease."

"So you're telling me that in order to stay this way, I have to keep tupping the lass?"

Oh good God, thought Tessa horrified. *Why not just tell the world that I had sex with him,* she grimaced, blushing profusely.

"Yes Cailean. If you wish to have any hope of helping us to defeat the Unseelie, you must stay strong. It's why we guided her to Scotland."

"You knew?" bellowed Cailean angrily. "You put her in danger on purpose?"

"I'm truly sorry that Tessa has to be put in danger to make this possible, but yes, we subconsciously suggested to her that a trip to Scotland would be perfect. It was lucky for us that she was born when she was. The Fates had a lot to do with it. It would have been even better if Colin's soul mate had been born in this century as well, but we have no knowledge of her as yet."

"Nay!" said Cailean harshly. "I refuse to put the lass in anymore danger. I'm sending her back to Canada immediately."

Tessa gasped and opened the door. All three of the men turned to look at her. Colin at least had the decency to look a bit embarrassed.

"I'm not going anywhere Cailean," she bit out. "If doing...if having..." *God this was embarrassing.* "If I can do something to help save the world from this delusional Teluth person, then I'm not going to turn and run with my tail between my legs."

"Lass I'll no' be using you that way!" he replied firmly.

"It's not a big deal Cailean," she said, trying her best to sound casual and hoping he hadn't heard the slight hitch in her voice.

"Nay lass, we'll find another way. You're leaving."

With that said, he turned and left the room, leaving her blushing furiously in front of Colin and Onagh. Colin focused his gaze on Onagh and cleared his throat, clearly uncomfortable.

"What'll happen if he doesn't keep tupping the lass?"

"Oh Lord," mumbled Tessa, pretty sure she was going to die of embarrassment.

Onagh looked over at Tessa calmly before returning his gaze to Colin. "Then the fight will be in their favour, especially if Teluth makes more immortals. They already outnumber the Seelie with their human army and weapons. Teluth has succeeded in finding a surprising amount of senk for his knives."

Tessa shivered again, but this time it was in horror of what could happen. She suddenly laughed, causing the two men to look at her curiously.

"Do you realize what a story line this would be in one of my books?"

The men didn't answer.

"No seriously. The hero has to have sex in order to save the world?" she laughed almost hysterically.

She heard Colin stifle a laugh and saw Onagh smile.

"Actually I think it sounds like every man's dream," laughed Colin.

"I'm happy you find humour in the situation," said Onagh mildly. "But if you want to keep living, you had better find a way to convince Cailean that it's the only option he has."

That abruptly ended any humour Tessa may have felt and she sighed unhappily.

Onagh said his goodbyes and disappeared as quickly as he had come, leaving her looking at Colin helplessly.

He sighed and walked over, putting his arm around her and guiding her out of the room. "Well lass, I'll do what I can on my end, but Cailean's a very stubborn lad. He doesna want you to get hurt, and neither do I; but unlike him, I understand that there's no way around this."

It felt strange having this conversation with Colin. She wasn't accustomed to talking so casually about the fact that her job was now to seduce Cailean. Lord she had only just had sex for the first time, what did she know about seducing a man?

"I'll figure something out," she said. If she was going to do her part, she was going to have to get herself together and figure out a way to have sex with the gorgeous highlander. She could think of worse things. She shook her head in amusement and went downstairs with Colin to get some supper.

~10~

*A*fter Colin and Tessa finished supper, they joined Cailean in the drawing room where he was frowning at the television.

Tessa sat on the couch next to him while Colin took a seat to their right.

The news was on and Cailean's heart dropped when he heard the reporter announcing that a number of strange things had just been reported. There was a tsunami that had hit the coast of Florida and an earthquake in Africa measuring six point eight on the Richter scale. There was also a large atmospheric disturbance in the vicinity of Scotland, but so far nothing else has been reported. The number of casualties was still unknown but the reporter remarked that there were already over two hundred.

"Oh my God," whispered Tessa in horror with her hand over her mouth.

"Shit," growled Colin.

Cailean stared at the screen for a few moments, then closed his eyes and leaned his head back on the couch. What was he supposed to do? His first choice was to send Tessa back to Canada, but how could he be guaranteed her safety if crap like this kept happening. His only consolation was that she would at least be away from the fae who were trying to kill her. His second choice was to keep her here, in danger, and use her sexually. Either way the outcome wasn't guaranteed.

There had to be another way, he thought desperately. He refused to use her so crudely. She would be safer in Canada, away from him.

"You're leaving tomorrow morning," he spat out.

Tessa looked at him, horrified. "No!"

He raised his head angrily off the couch and looked at her, "Aye Tessa. 'Tisn't up for debate. You'll be safer in Canada than here where the fae are trying to kill you every damn second."

Colin sighed heavily and left them to their fight, wandering toward the kitchen.

"And then what Cailean? What happens when you're not strong enough to fight them and Teluth's army gets through? Do you think I'll be safe then?"

Cailean growled and looked at her angrily. "I'll find a way Tessa, but I canna fight them when I'm worried about your safety."

"You can't fight them if I'm not here helping you," she shouted angrily.

"I'll no' use you that way!" he said firmly, rising from the couch to leave.

"You're not using me if it's something I want to do," she said quietly as she watched him storm off, slamming the large castle door on his way out.

Cailean stomped around the castle making sure the wards were all where they were supposed to be. A small line was visible near the mound. The rip between their worlds hadn't been able to close completely. No doubt that was how Onagh had managed to get through. They would have to be extra cautious now. Thank God Tessa would be gone the next day, he thought with relief.

He sat for a time in the darkness, staring at the long glowing line that started from the ground and went straight up for about ten feet. It was just a sliver really, but enough that a fae or two would be able to force themselves through if they really tried. He was at a loss to figure out what other options they had against the Unseelie. There was no way to stop Teluth from making more immortals, and so far, none of the Seelie had managed to get close enough to him to kill him. Maybe there was some way to get in contact with the Kynleigh woman. It was possible she knew a weakness they didn't. He wasn't about to leave any stone unturned and decided to talk to Colin to see if he thought the woman might be willing to help.

He brushed his hand along the ground, gently over the grass. Soulmate. He just couldn't get over the idea that he and Tessa were supposed to be together. He had learned not to scoff at legends and folklore after meeting the fae and becoming immortal. That would be like holding a piece of grass in his hand and saying it didn't exist. He plucked at the grass and held a piece in front of him. No, if the fae said he had a soul mate, he would be stupid not to believe them.

He crushed the piece of grass between his fingers and pushed himself off the ground with a sigh. Tessa should be asleep by now. He would climb into bed, not think of how much he wanted her, and try to get some sleep. He was prepared for a fight in the morning and wasn't looking forward to it.

About an hour after he had finally managed to fall into a fitful sleep, Cailean's door opened soundlessly. As tired as he was he didn't wake up until the person was hovering over his bed, arm creeping slowly toward his neck.

Suddenly awake, he moved quickly, throwing the person over him and jumping on whoever it was. He pulled his arm back and was just about to beat him into submission when he heard Tessa's voice, full of fear.

"Cailean!" she shouted. "It's me."

Cailean stopped in shock, his fist inches away from her fragile face.

He sat back stunned, straddling her. He was completely horrified at what he had almost done and couldn't seem to remember how to breathe.

Finally coming to his senses, he rolled off of her suddenly and lay beside her panting, adrenaline still rushing through his system.

She sat up to face him. "I'm sorry I scared you."

He rested his arm across his forehead and willed his heart to slow down.

"Cailean, are you ok?" she asked as she rested a small hand lightly on his bare chest.

"I could've killed you Tessa," he said in a husky voice.

He felt her hand slide up and cup his jaw softly. "I would have forgiven you," she replied simply.

He let out a short soft laugh and shook his head, eyes still closed, trying to come to grips with what he'd almost done.

He felt her lean over and press her lips gently against his. He gasped softly at the contact as a line of fire shot from his lips straight to his groin.

He moved his arm from his forehead to restrain her. "What are you doing lass?"

"Kissing you," she replied simply, as if it were the most normal thing in the world.

He fought with his conscience for a moment as her lips pressed once again against his, with a little more pressure. He felt her breath against his mouth and his breathing sped up again as she kissed him gently.

Her hand lay against his chest and slowly started moving downward while she deepened the kiss.

Heat spread to his groin and he groaned softly when he felt her tongue slide tentatively between his lips. He wanted her so badly that his thoughts felt muddled. He tried to will himself to push her away.

In a few seconds, he thought. Just a few more seconds. Her hand had reached his stomach now and he suddenly realized that if he let her go any further there would be no stopping on his part. He ached for her. He was already rock hard and naked under the sheets. All it would take was for her hand to touch him there and any semblance of restraint he had would completely disappear. He would push her back on the bed, rip her clothes off and slide into her.

Her fingers slid perilously closer and his breath caught a second before he grabbed her hand, pulling it away from the part of him that wanted her so badly.

"Leave Tessa!" he growled.

"But..." she began before he climbed out of bed, pulling her along with him.

"Cailean."

He could hear the hurt in her voice as he walked her to the door. The sheet fell from his waist, revealing how much he wanted her, but he didn't pay any attention as he closed the door firmly behind her. He leaned his forehead against the door, struggling to control his breathing. His hands formed fists on either side of his head as he forced himself not to give in and yank the door open.

The woman could tempt a saint, he thought in frustration. He just had to stay strong until the morning. Once she was on the plane heading for home, she would be safe from the fae...and him.

* * *

Tessa huffed out a breath as she stood in front of his closed door with her arms crossed. Almost. Another minute and she was sure he would have given in. Goodness, another minute and she might have combusted from the heat that was racing through her body while she touched him. The man was definitely enough to make a vegetarian feast delightedly on a piece of steak. He had been naked, she remembered as a flush of desire rushed through her. She hadn't realized that he slept completely naked. She'd definitely file that away for later use.

She stood there for a while, wondering what he was doing on the other side of the door. She hadn't heard the bed creak so she knew he was still standing there...naked...hard. Good God this was more difficult than she thought. It was one thing to try to seduce a man, but it was another to be able to concentrate enough so that she could seduce him properly.

Convinced that he wasn't going to lie down again until he heard her go back to bed, she sighed and turned back to her room.

Sitting in her own cold, lonely bed, she tried to think up new ways to seduce him. Maybe she could catch him in the shower, or first thing when he woke up. Those were definite possibilities. She decided to try to get some sleep so that she could wake up bright and early and get a good start on her next seduction effort.

She snuggled down in the bed, under the huge down blanket and fell asleep quickly. She dreamt of lying beneath Cailean on a bed of soft grass. There were birds singing around her as Cailean thrust into her over and over. She could feel her orgasm building and was about to come when a knock on her door made her dream world shatter completely. She woke up in a bad mood and stared at her door in anger. Who on earth could that be and didn't they realize that if they had waited just two more minutes she would have had the orgasm of a lifetime?

"What?" she asked angrily.

She heard a chuckle from the other side of the door and then Cailean's voice, "Time to wake up lass, your plane leaves in four hours and 'twill take at least three to get to the airport."

She sighed heavily and flopped back into bed grumbling to herself. Well he can damn well come in if he wanted her to wake up, she thought as she turned over and snuggled under the warm covers.

"I have breakfast," he said temptingly.

She said nothing.

"Come on lass, you know 'tis the best way," he reasoned as he pushed the door open.

"I know nothing of the sort," she grumbled, beneath the covers.

She heard him put the tray on the table beside her bed and felt the bed sink as he sat on the edge.

"Please doona make this harder than it has to be Tessa. I doona want to have to carry you kicking and screaming to the airport."

She felt the blanket raise a little and a bagel being pressed to her lips. "Come on lass, eat something then get dressed," he encouraged.

She took a bite, more out of hunger than anything. He chuckled and grinned when she finally sat up and took the bagel from him. Glaring dangerously.

Still saying nothing, she ate the bagel and orange and drank her coffee while he watched in amusement.

Full now, she flopped back down and pulled the blankets over her again.

Cailean sighed heavily and she waited tensely to see what he would do. He was going to have a fight on his hands to get her out of bed because she wasn't going to give in.

She felt him lean over her, and gasped when he breathed softly into her ear. "Please Tessa."

So he was going to fight dirty was he? Two could play at that game, she thought as she shifted slightly so that she lay flat on her back.

"You're only making this harder than it has to be," he said, next to her ear again.

"Am I?" she asked with a wicked smile as she snaked her hand out from under the blanket and into his kilt in record speed, wrapping her hand around him firmly.

He sucked in his breath and grunted. Clenching his jaws together and shutting his eyes, he mentally fought for control.

"Let go lass," he commanded between clenched teeth as he stiffened in her hand. She began to stroke him, holding on firmly so he couldn't pull away.

He tensed and leaned forward with a groan, his hands gripping the edges of the bed as she continued her assault on him.

After a few seconds, he looked over at her with his mouth slightly open, trying to control his breathing and his reaction to her hand gliding up and down his cock.

When he continued to stare at her, obviously at the edge of self control, she felt a ball of heat spreading from her stomach to her crotch and her own breathing started to go haywire. She stared into his smouldering blue eyes. The way he was looking at her made her mouth go dry with desire. She could see the effort it was taking for him to control himself and felt warmth spread through her as she came to terms with the fact that she had this much of an effect on him.

Dragging in an unsteady breath he reached for her hand in an attempt to stop her, but as he did she quickly rose and pressed her mouth against his, sliding her tongue into the warmth of his mouth.

He let out a groan and turned, pushing her down on the bed, settling himself over her and somehow managing to move the sheets from between them. She let him go and felt him pressed against her, straining against her underwear. Oh God he felt amazing, she thought as she moved her hips against his. He pushed against her but made no move to remove her underwear.

She wrapped her legs around his hips and moved against him again, listening to him gasp as he again shoved against her at the same time that his tongue slid into her mouth. For a moment she was completely lost in the sensation of his tongue exploring her mouth and gliding along her lips.

Before she knew what was happening, he suddenly pulled away and got off the bed, walking out of the room without looking back. He slammed the door as he left.

She lay where he left her, gasping, wondering what had just happened. She was aching for him and shocked that he could leave so easily. Holding her hand over her mouth she struggled not to cry. How could he just walk out like that...like she meant nothing?

*   *   *

Cailean walked into his room and shut his door with as much restraint as he could manage. He was dying inside. He ached so badly that he had to squeeze his eyes shut as he leaned one hand against the wall for support. A groan escaped him as he stood there, in pain, shaking with desire.

God what was the lass trying to do to him? He had come so close to losing it that time. It was only the barrier of her underwear that stopped him the two times he was about to give in. Why the hell couldn't he control himself around her? She tortured his dreams and now his waking hours as well. He had felt so in control when he brought her breakfast. He was going to make her eat, force her to get packed and drag her, if necessary, to the airport where he planned to pack her into the plane and leave as soon as it took off. She had thwarted his plan so smoothly it was almost as if she had stayed up all night planning her moves exactly. Why the hell did he decide to wear his kilt today? Hadn't he learned by now that being in a kilt around her was a very bad idea!

He focused on his breathing and willed himself to calm down. He was just going to have to get Colin to help him, he decided angrily. Obviously there was no way he could trust himself around the lass anymore. "Soul mate my ass," he snorted. "She's the devil sent here to torture me."

Turning around, he leaned his back against the cool wall, finally gaining some kind of control over his traitorous body part. He was going to march over to Colin's room and demand he pack Tessa up and drag her to the airport.

As soon as got rid of the damn kilt.

Heaving himself away from the wall, he stalked over to his closet and quickly replaced his kilt with a pair of pale brown pants that tied up the crotch, and put his sporran on for good measure. She'd have to work much harder with this on to surprise him, he thought as he left the room in search of his brother.

He found Colin in the dining room working on his breakfast and sat with a grunt.

Colin looked up with an amused smile.

"I'm guessing it dinna go well."

"The lass is a devil in disguise," complained Cailean as he snagged a piece of toast off Colin's plate.

"Uh…did you change?"

Cailean glared at his brother.

Colin chuckled around a mouthful of eggs and managed to swallow before choking himself to death. "So what are you going to do now?" he asked with a grin.

"*You*," he said, looking pointedly at his brother, "are going to get that lass packed and to the airport while I hide."

Colin roared with laughter, almost upsetting his orange juice. His brother looked at him with a frown.

"I'm serious Colin, I canna do it. The woman's doing her best to get me into bed with her and damn near succeeding each time."

Colin tsk'd at Cailean, shaking his head. "What a very difficult life you lead brother, fighting off a beautiful wench who just wants to bed you."

Cailean frowned at him.

"You could give in you know."

"I canna do that Colin. I refuse to use the lass like that. We'll find a way to contact Kynleigh and see if she'll agree to help us."

"And if she says nay?"

"Then we'll find another way," growled Cailean, getting annoyed with his brother.

Colin started laughing. "Well brother, I suggest you think of something else because the lass just took off on Beauty."

"What?" He jumped up causing his chair to fall over backwards, and raced to the window, watching Tessa racing away from the castle on his horse. Her hair flew behind her as she rode like a bat out of hell. No doubt she had charmed the poor stable boy into helping her saddle the huge horse.

"Damn it!" he yelled as he raced for the door. "The lass is going to get herself killed just to avoid leaving."

Colin sat in front of his breakfast laughing at his brother's predicament. He wiped the tears from his eyes and quietly congratulated the lass on her quick thinking.

~11~

*T*essa, Cailean and Colin sat around the table at lunch in front
of a delicious smelling soup, and grilled cheese sandwiches. Colin
had Lara make the sandwiches especially for Tessa when he found
out it was one of her favorite meals in Canada. The room smelled
heavenly but that didn't ease the air of tension flowing off of
Cailean as he sat across from Tessa with a scowl.

It had taken him an hour and a half to catch her and get her
back to the castle. At that point, knowing that there was no way to
make the flight, she came willingly enough, trotting happily in
front of the fuming Scotsman while he ran through scenarios to
make sure she made the flight the next day. He would tie her to the
bed tonight if necessary.

The stable boy was told he would lose his job if he ever put
her on a horse again, and after Cailean escorted her back to her
room to pack, he went in search of Colin.

He found him lazily reclined on a chair in the living room with
one hand behind his head taking in the news. He looked so calm

and relaxed that Cailean was tempted to tip him head over heels for laughing at Tessa earlier escape. If it weren't for what Colin said next, he would have.

"The death count has reached three hundred and twenty seven."

Completely forgetting about getting revenge on his brother, Cailean sighed and sat on the sofa across from him.

"We need to do something fast Cailean," he warned as he sat forward and rested his elbows on his knees.

Cailean leaned forward as well and rubbed his hands across his face tiredly. "I know."

Tessa suddenly appeared in front of them and turned to Colin, ignoring Cailean completely. "Colin," she started, "can you take me to a nightclub tonight?"

"Nay!" roared Cailean, jumping up from his chair.

She looked over at him as if suddenly realizing he was in the room. "I'm asking Colin, not you," she stated abruptly. "If I'm being forced to end my vacation early then I would like to go out tonight to see what the night life is like in Scotland."

Colin tried to hide his grin. "Sure lass, how about we leave at five thirty and stop in at the Scottish Pheasant for supper first."

"*Colin,*" warned Cailean in a threatening voice.

"I'm sorry Cailean, the lass is right. If she's to miss out on the rest of her holiday, then she should at least get one night out on the town. I think we owe her that much."

Cailean glared at his brother, grinding his teeth before he opened his mouth to speak again. "I'm starting to think I'm outnumbered," he stated before turning to stomp off.

When he left the room, Tessa and Colin grinned at each other. "Well...I suppose I should act like I'm packing and make sure I pick out my sexiest outfit," she said, turning to do just that.

Colin grinned at her back and shook his head in wonder.

*   *   *

Tessa bounded up the stairs in a good mood and set to work on getting her outfit ready for that night. Normally she didn't wear revealing clothes, but this time she thought it might be a good idea to make the effort since jealousy was what she was going for. The only problem was that she didn't bring anything even remotely sexy.

She rifled through the clothes still left in her bag and was pleasantly surprised when she came across a low cut blue dress that went to her mid thigh. It was tight and silky. Laney had obviously snuck it in when she wasn't looking. She grinned happily. Yes it would definitely do. She'd have to remember to thank her later.

She spent the rest of the afternoon absorbed in her writing. Colin had gone out and bought her a new laptop to replace her murdered one, and luckily she had remembered to back up everything on her flash drive except for part of the last chapter.

Her vampire had now officially fallen in love with the human main character and was battling himself as he tried to focus on kissing her rather than killing her. The storyline was really good and she felt confident that this book would be another hit.

She had unintentionally gathered a huge cult following because of her romantic vampire series. It continuously surprised her how many people dreamed of being in love with a vampire. Personally she wasn't convinced that it was a good idea to be with someone when you had to worry that his every kiss might be your last. Intriguing maybe, but definitely not comforting.

"Oh well," she sighed happily. She would just continue to write what her fans wanted to read. Luckily for her she enjoyed these kinds of books so the words came easily. She constantly had to force herself to finish writing one book before starting another because she had so many ideas. She was always making notes on her next book while trying to finish whichever one she was working on.

She had decided long ago to look the next book as a reward. She refused to allow herself to start writing another book until her current one was completely finished and edited. Sort of like not being allowed to have ice cream until her supper was done. It forced her to write quickly which got her books to her editor on time and made her publisher very happy. All in all it worked out very well for her and her fans ended up with a new book three or four times a year which delighted them immensely.

It had taken her a long time to get to the point she was at now with her writing. She had started no less than eighteen books before finally completing one. It wasn't that the books were no good, it was just that she had no real idea of how to write a book and it had taken that many false starts and many, many years of research and reading up on writing to finally get the rules straight and to teach herself to be patient when she came up with a new idea half way through writing a book. Everything she did taught her something new, and she had managed to get a little further which each new book she started.

One day, years after her first attempt, she managed to write a synopsis from start to finish and sat staring at it in awe. She had finally planned a book out completely. It had just flowed so easily that she was in shock for a few days after. She realized only at that point that she probably should have written a synopsis for each book she had tried to write. Thinking of all the wasted years upset her until she realized that those first writing attempts wouldn't have ended very successfully anyway because she knew nothing about writing back then and had only learned what she knew now through trial and error.

When she was finally able to sit and start writing her first real novel, everything seemed to come together so naturally that it felt as if she had been writing forever, which she supposed she really had.

The day she finished that very first manuscript, she sat staring at the last page for nearly an hour, unable to believe it was finally done. The emotions she felt at that moment were very mixed, ranging from relief to sadness.

When she had completed the editing part, she sent some queries, along with the first few chapters, to a few editors and spent an incredibly tense few months waiting for a reply. The first few replies were simply to tell her that there weren't accepting any more new writers at that time, one said she had potential but wasn't what they were looking for, and one said they liked her work and asked for the rest of the manuscript to be sent in.

She sat staring at that letter in disbelief for days until her mother finally asked why she didn't seem very excited.

Shaking her head in wonder she replied that she was actually *so* excited that she didn't know what to do. They eventually decided that actually packing up the manuscript and sending it in would probably be the best idea. And so began her writing career.

The publisher loved her story and she was an instant hit with the paranormal romance readers, causing her book to become a bestseller with weeks of publication. Since then, she had written twelve more just as successful books, and was constantly asked to appear on talk shows and at book readings. Many of those requests had to be turned down, unfortunately, or she simply wouldn't have had the time to write. She considered herself incredibly lucky that she had a job she loved and actually made money at.

She sat back for a moment, biting the end of her pen; a habit she had picked up as a child. Her gaze dropped absently to the time at the bottom right of the screen and she suddenly jumped up when she realized that it was already four thirty. She only had an hour to get ready for her night out.

She hit the save button and raced to the bathroom.

When she got there, she immediately turned around and went back to the room to save her manuscript on to her flash drive, mumbling about freak storms and faeries. Satisfied that her book was now protected from all manner of accidents, she finally made it back to the bathroom.

Fifteen minutes later, she was walking back to her room when she saw Cailean leaning against the wall with his hands crossed over his chest. A shadow passed over his face as he looked at her. "So you're really going out tonight?" he asked quietly.

Tessa gripped her towel, digging her fingers into its softness. She considered dropping it to see what he would do, but decided against it incase Colin or one of the maids suddenly appeared.

"Yup. You can come if you want."

He gave a short humourless laugh and shook his head.

She continued her charade even though it hurt her that he didn't want to spend her last night with her. "Your loss then," she threw over her shoulder as she shut the door behind her and leaned against it with her eyes closed.

Her heart raced like a rabbit. Christ it took a lot of effort to appear nonchalant. She grinned and shook her head. Well she could always hope he changed his mind and showed up.

With a sigh she pushed away from the door and laid her towel over the chair at her desk to dry before spending the next forty five minutes dressing and touching up her makeup and hair.

At five thirty there was a knock at the door that turned out to be Colin. The man was definitely prompt.

She gathered her small purse and opened the door to find him lounging against the wall dressed in black jeans and a grey shirt that fit him like a glove. The girls were definitely in trouble tonight she thought with a smile.

They left for their night out in Colin's silver Corvette Stingray. She instantly fell in love with it when the door opened upwards instead of outwards like a normal car. Inside was just as amazing. It had bucket seats and the dashboard on her side wrapped around her, making her feel as if she were in a spaceship of some kind.

"Colin," she said breathlessly. "This is amazing."

He grinned like a kid at Christmas as he closed her door and walked over to his side. "She's my new toy. I think this is my favorite century so far," he laughed as he got in and closed his door.

She reached up and slid her hand along the chrome dashboard in awe. Maybe she should buy herself one of these beauties.

As soon as her seatbelt was on Colin hit the gas, making her gasp at the speed of his takeoff. They glided effortlessly through the winding roads, countryside whizzing by. She wasn't sure how fast he ended up going, but she wasn't about to complain. It was exhilarating racing along so low to the ground. Her only cause for concern was when he narrowly avoided missing some sheep, but after that the roads were relatively animal free and she relaxed, enjoying the ride.

About thirty minutes later they pulled up at the Scottish Pheasant, which was more of a bar than a restaurant. Every single eye was on Colin's 'toy'. One man almost walked his date into the path of an oncoming vehicle as he stared in awe at the car.

Tessa giggled and felt entirely like a teenager on a date at that point. It was a nice feeling to be so relaxed and happy.

Colin caught her hand, spinning her around in a mock dance as they walked toward their table. She laughed and went along with him, twirling unselfconsciously.

He tried his best to convince her to try the Scottish favorite, Haggis, but she almost threw up when he explained what it was. He finally decided to get something other than Haggis, telling her he didn't want to listen to her gag during the entire meal. She stuck her tongue out at him and grinned.

She had a surprisingly good time with him during supper and got to know him much better than she thought she would, but when the topic turned to Cailean and what they were doing, an uneasy flicker passed across Tessa's face. "Are you sure we are doing the right thing Colin?" She tugged nervously at her dress.

He looked at her over his wine glass and sighed. "I'm no' sure what the best thing is in this situation lass," he admitted, running his hand through his long, soft hair. "But I do know that without the strength you give him, we are at a great disadvantage."

She bent the corner of her napkin into a triangle as she considered his words.

"Well I have to admit I'm having fun trying," she grinned, blushing.

Colin laughed and caught her hand in his. "'Tis a good thing lass, because I would no' encourage this if it were against your will."

They smiled at each other for a moment and he let her hand go as the waitress walked up and handed him his bill. "Here you go gorgeous, and what are the two of you planning for the rest of the night?"

Colin laughed and pulled the waitress onto his lap, causing Tessa to giggle. "We'll naught be getting into too much trouble lass," he teased. "Maybe you could join us later; we'll be at the Cradle's Edge."

The waitress giggled and pulled herself away from Colin. "Maybe I will then if 'tis ok with the lass," she replied, looking questioningly at Tessa.

"Umm, yeah, that would be great!"

Still grinning at Colin, the waitress hurried off to take another customers order. Colin left some bills on the table and reached for her hand, pulling her along behind him.

"Do you know her Colin?" she asked curiously.

He laughed and reached out to open her door, tucking her into the car quickly. "Nay lass, but maybe tonight I can remedy that situation."

Tessa shook her head, laughing. The man was a chick magnet. And why not? He was tall, muscular, sexy, had long hair and beautiful eyes. Oh and he was immortal, let's not forget that.

She sat back once again, cocooned in the softness of the bucket seat as Colin drove expertly though the narrow streets.

Suddenly nervous, Tessa looked over at Colin. "Did you tell Cailean which nightclub we were going to?"

"Aye."

He reached over and engulfed her small hand in his comfortingly. "'Twill be ok Tessa. If I know my brother, he *will* show up at some point." He let her hand go and put it back on the steering wheel.

They pulled into a spot across the street from a brightly coloured building. Music was pounding through its slightly open door and there were people lined up, impatiently waiting their turn to enter the club.

She couldn't say she was entirely surprised when Colin took her hand and guided her to the side of the building, embracing the bouncer in a friendly hug and clapping him on the back before they went through the door.

Once inside, the music was about twenty times louder and she could barely hear Colin as he started telling her some nonsense about proper club etiquette with the lasses. He marched Tessa into the bowels of the club, pausing occasionally to greet friends he found along the way. By the time they made it to the dance floor, she had met at least fifteen of them, both male and female, but definitely more female. The ladies looked after him longingly, and at her enviously.

As they reached the middle of the dance floor, the music suddenly changed to the Lambada. She was shocked that she would hear a song like that in Scotland of all places. She actually didn't even know they still played it, as old as it was.

Colin's eyes had a mischievous glint in it as he pulled her to him, wrapped an arm around her waist while holding the other in the air and started moving his hips in a way that caused her eyes to go wide.

Apparently he knew how to Lambada.

This made her laugh because it seemed so absurd that a Scottish immortal would be familiar with a dance like this. What were the odds? She decided that maybe the smug looking immortal could use a shock as well, and she started moving her hips in time with the familiar rhythm of the dance. She had practised this dance with her girlfriends in high school just incase that particular song played at their annual school dance. It had been very popular back then and although there were many complaints about how sexual the dance was, she had been lucky enough to go to a non-catholic school that didn't care much.

The song was indeed played at their dance one year and she remembered having the time of her life dancing it almost expertly with Dylan Senter, causing some other boys in her grade to suddenly take notice of her. The next year of school was a very busy one for her.

She giggled at Colin's shocked look when she moved along with him, never breaking rhythm. He tried to spin her and even leaned her back at one point with her straddling his thigh but she matched him step for step, hips swaying against his, making him laugh in delight. Although it was supposed to be a sexual dance, with Colin it was more fun than anything. He had a way of making her feel completely comfortable in his presence.

When the dance ended, he grabbed her hand and pulled her along to the bar where a seat was waiting for her. He lifted her effortlessly onto it and leaned across the counter to ask the bartender for a couple beers. "So where did you learn to dance like that lass?" he asked, as she worked on catching her breath.

"High school."

He put his head back and laughed. "Well you do that very well." He expertly grabbed the beers that slid along the bar top toward him.

He rested his arm casually on the counter behind her in a protective gesture as he leaned against the bar and took a swig of his beer. The music had switched to something slow and the couples made their way on to the floor, holding each other gently as they swayed to the music. She glanced sideways at Colin leaning next to her and was surprised to see a look of sadness flicker briefly on his face as he watched the couples dance.

She supposed after almost three hundred years the poor guy had every right to be lonely, but other than right now she had never seen any indication of his life being anything other than fun and games, except for maybe a fae fight or two, but even those he seemed to enjoy. She wondered sadly how long it would be before his soul mate would be born.

After a couple hours, the waitress from the Scottish Pheasant showed up and Colin decided that he should dance with her to give the other guys a chance to talk to Tessa without him hovering over her.

About three minutes after he left for the dance floor, a tall, handsome man with brown hair and green eyes moved in to take his place at the bar.

"Are you two together?" he asked in a friendly way, glancing at her from very attractive, deep set eyes.

She laughed as the scene brought to mind a speed dating service she had once attended at Laney's urging.

"No," she yelled over the music. "Just a friend." She took a drink of her beer and smiled to herself.

He scratched the side of his neck nervously as the music changed to a slow song. "Would you like to dance then?"

This was the opportunity she had been waiting for. She only hoped that Cailean would show up soon so that she didn't have to keep dancing with strangers.

Hopping off the stool, she took the man's hand and led him on to the floor, making sure to stay beside Colin incase the man tried to be a little too friendly.

Even though she had assured him that Colin was a friend, he was fairly tense as he pulled her closer to him to dance. Colin chose that moment to grin at the man which did a lot to relax him.

It was about an hour later, during another slow dance with yet another man when she suddenly heard a gruff voice behind her. "May I?" he asked, his polite request nowhere matching the tone of his voice. The man she was currently dancing with opened his mouth to complain, but as soon as he took in Cailean's towering, muscular form and angry face he backed up, almost tripping over another couple in his hurry to leave.

Tessa grinned with her head turned away from Cailean and quickly composed herself, giving off an air of annoyance.

"Couldn't you wait your turn?" She gasped as he grabbed her hand and spun her toward him.

"Nay!"

She could feel anger radiating off of him as he held her against the solid wall of his chest. He was wearing a black long sleeved shirt that looked amazing on him. One hand held hers in the air while the other was on the small of her back, holding her securely against his jean clad hips. She could feel his erection and almost forgot to breathe at the contact.

"I thought you didn't want to join us."

He pressed her against him a little more firmly, causing her to momentarily forget her game.

His head dipped and she felt a rush of desire go through her as he whispered into her ear. "I got lonely."

Her breathing got a little ragged at those simple words.

"Obviously *you* weren't," he growled into her ear.

She shrugged nonchalantly, "It's a bar, people dance."

She felt him grind against her as he glided along the floor. "You seemed to be enjoying yourself."

Struggling to control her breathing, she pushed against his chest just enough so that she didn't have to talk into his shirt. "I *was*," she said, knowing that answer would annoy him.

She heard a growl in his chest and gasped as he suddenly turned and walked off the dance floor, towing her behind like a petulant child. She glanced back at Colin and he gave her a tiny little wave then turned quickly to hide his smile.

~12~

*C*ailean didn't speak as he drove them home in his

Lamborghini.

Although not quite as impressive as Colin's Corvette, it still made the hairs on her arm raise as she was pressed flat against her seat from the speed. She eventually started to relax as they drove, and tipped her head back to look up at the stars that flew by. Her hair whipped out behind her, and when she closed her eyes, she felt like she was flying.

After a while she opened them again and caught Cailean looking at her. This alarmed her since he was going fairly fast, but she refused to say anything.

After a few seconds, he turned back to the road and she could see his fingers turn almost white as he gripped the wheel with a scowl on his face. She slid her own hands under her thighs to stop herself from reaching out to him.

The material under her hands felt soft and fuzzy and she leaned her head back, closing her eyes once again, enjoying the moment.

A short time later they turned on to the bridge that led to the castle. He slowed down and parked a bit away from the front door.

The purr of the motor stopped, leaving them sitting silently for a moment.

He took a deep breath and got out, coming around to open her door for her. In all her years she had never seen a man look quite as deliciously sexy as he did right at that moment. His black shirt was tucked into blue jeans that were secured with a black belt. She could almost see the muscles of his thighs under the jeans and ached to run her hands along them. Could a man look any sexier? The sleeves of his shirt wrapped around arms the size of her thighs. He had pulled the sleeves up during the drive and each cord of muscle stood out in relief as he held his hand out toward her.

She lifted her hand and placed it into his larger one, amazed at how small she felt as his strong fingers closed over hers. He helped her out and shut the door, saying nothing.

It took Tessa a moment to realize that he had pressed her back against the car.

She looked up at him questioningly and he slowly lowered his head toward her, pressing a kiss gently against her lips.

She shook as she parted her lips, willing him to continue.

*   *   *

Cailean wasn't quite sure why he was torturing himself like this. He had gone to the bar telling himself that it was just to make sure she was ok. The argument that Colin was watching over her was quickly discarded.

He had been home, looking out the window, wondering when they would return, when he started feeling something he had never felt before. It took him a while to realize that the bitter feeling in his chest was jealousy.

He knew she was safe with Colin and that his brother would never touch Tessa in any way other than friendship, but he knew the other men at the nightclub would have no such restraint.

At first he had managed to convince himself that Colin would keep the other men away from her, but then he realized that it wasn't Colin's job to babysit Tessa and that he would probably be too busy dancing with every woman in the bar to keep a good eye on her.

He'd sat by the window for a good five minutes more before giving in and heading to the club. He refused to admit to himself that his abrupt decision was because he couldn't stand the thought of another man touching her.

He had gotten to the club in record time and stood at one end of the bar for a long time looking at Tessa dance with man after man, and enjoy it. A furious rage built in him as he watched the men sliding their hands along her back, pressing her against their bodies as they swayed to the music. He had closed his eyes, fighting for control as he tried to convince himself that he had no right to her.

The last piece of his control left completely when one of those men leaned down and whispered something in her ear, causing her to laugh. He forced himself to walk slowly and calmly over to them and gritted his teeth together as he basically glared a hole in the man's head. Lucky for the man, he knew when to pick his battles and all but threw Tessa at him.

Almost shaking with fury, he made himself hold her and dance with her, attempting to calm himself down. His plan backfired when he pulled her against him and felt her mould herself to his body willingly. He had shut his eyes as desire ripped through him and tried his best to focus on dancing. He heard Colin chuckle softly beside him and knew he was laughing at the torture he saw on his brother's face. There was definitely going to be another battle between the two as soon as he could get Colin alone. The whelp deserved to be put in his place after laughing repeatedly at his misery.

When he leaned to whisper in Tessa's ear and felt her shiver he almost lost it. She wanted him as much as he wanted her and knowing that made it even harder for him to resist her. She was sexy, enticing and inviting, and it had taken all of his strength not to kiss her on the dance floor, knowing he would have one hell of a time stopping if he did.

In all his years he had never imagined he would find a woman who affected him so strongly. He had loved Leah with all of his heart, but she had been so different from Tessa. She had been unhappy for so long that it put a great toll on their marriage.

Years after Cailean had been made into an immortal he asked Onagh if it were possible to make her immortal too. Leah had looked at him in horror when he told her. At first he thought she was upset that Onagh said no, but quickly realized that the thought of having to live forever and never making it to heaven to be with her baby had terrified her.

"How can I go on knowing I will never be able to hold Catherine? At least in death I know I shall see her again. I will finally have the chance I never had to hold my child in my arms."

174

He suddenly realized that she had been counting down the days until that moment. Because she was Catholic, ending her own life meant she would never be allowed into heaven with her child, so she was forced to live through each day, praying that it was her last. Praying for the day she would finally be able to hold the daughter she had loved for so long. His love had never been enough to take away her pain and longing.

Tessa moaned softly against his mouth as he slid his tongue along her lips, teasing her. He was drowning in sensation, the feel of her mouth against his, her softness against his stiff erection, her breasts pressing against his chest.

"Tessa," he whispered hoarsely. "Why do you make me so crazy?"

He kissed the corners of her mouth and felt her lips relax against his, mould to his, open for him.

"Amazing," he whispered, unaware that he had spoken aloud.

She slid her tongue into his mouth and desire slammed through him so completely that he shuddered. His hands found their way down her back and he tugged her harder against him, drawing a groan of pleasure from her.

"I won't leave," she whispered against his neck, sending shivers through him.

"You must," he countered, nipping softly at the soft silk of her neck.

He lifted her and sat her on the edge of the door and she wrapped her legs around his waist, pulling him toward her, coaxing a moan from him.

He felt her hands move across his back and down to his waist before sliding back up to his neck. She dragged her fingers through his short hair and forced his mouth more firmly against hers.

He shifted slightly so that his rigid flesh pressed rock hard between her legs. He rotated his hips, rubbing against her in erotic circles, causing her to gasp in pleasure.

Tessa arched against him, almost destroying his control. His tongue explored the soft heat of her mouth with an urgency he had never known, probing her silky depths. He revelled in the sensation of her soft tongue against his.

He pushed them off the car and walked toward a crop of trees with her still wrapped around him. When he got there, he tumbled her gently to the ground and lay on top of her.

*   *   *

Tessa gasped in pleasure when he pressed his entire body against her as smoothly as a lion. She felt him nudge her legs apart with his knee and settled himself between her legs, pressing firmly against her.

This was heaven, she decided as she wrapped her legs around him, pulling him hard against her in one smooth motion. She felt a shudder rip through him and captured his face in her hands, looking into his eyes.

He looked at her through smouldering blue eyes, his lips parted as he breathed heavily. She tried to memorize every inch of his handsome face as she watched him struggle to control himself. She took in his wide jaw and square chin, lightly covered in stubble. She remembered the feel of that stubble against her breast and shivered.

Tessa saw complete surrender in his smoky eyes as he lowered his mouth to hers, demanding wordlessly that she surrender as well, and he kissed her so deeply that she no longer knew where she ended and he began.

Her hips thrust against his with a mind of their own and he thrust back, a deep growl rumbling in his chest.

"Tell me I can stay," she whispered against his mouth, forcing her hips to stay still.

A wordless moment passed as their breaths mingled with one another's, lips barely touching.

Don't make me agree to that...don't ask that of me, pleaded his eyes as he looked down at her.

Her hips thrust against his again, seducing him, begging him to say yes.

He sucked in a breath, fighting for control as she pressed against his swollen ridge.

She tilted her head so that her lips grazed his mouth. Forcing herself to stop moving was taking all the willpower she possessed. Her tongue darted out, tasting him, and he closed his eyes in torment.

She pushed him off of her onto his back. His skin was soft, yet firm beneath her fingers as she trailed a feathery soft line down his neck, over his chest and then down over his taunt stomach. She could feel his muscles contract at the touch and knew she was close to pushing him over the edge.

Her tongue flickered against the sensitive skin at the side of his neck. As she marked a trail across to the other side, he tilted his head back, allowing her access, jaw clenched.

Not sure who was more aroused by her actions, she lay on top of him and lightly scraped her finger nails along the nape of his neck. He thrust against her with a grunt, almost against his will.

Don't make a sound, she reminded herself. Don't let him know how close you are to your own undoing. She forced herself to stay quiet as she continued her assault on him, her body screaming at her.

"Enough," he whispered hoarsely into her ear, sending delightful shivers down her spine.

"Tell me I can stay," she demanded.

"Nay," he whispered huskily as a tremor ran through him.

The word was so simple yet so devastatingly harsh that her whole world came crashing down around her. She had failed...again!

"Go inside lass," he pleaded quietly as he rolled her off of him and lay on his back in the grass for a few seconds.

When he finally stood up, he held his hand out to her.

She let him pull her up and then walked away, waiting for her heart to break. How could he turn her away so easily? She had been so sure that he would give in this time.

The wind whispered through the trees as she made her way to the castle. The soft spongy grass cushioned her steps as if it were trying to comfort her. She felt tears well up, threatening to spill over, and suddenly realized that she was in love with him.

Awestruck, she turned to watch him as he leaned against his car, muscles bunched and rigid, head down. She looked at his wide back and followed the line down to his trim waist and hips. A soft breeze played with his hair and she understood in that one moment that leaving him right now wasn't an option. Tonight was all they had and there were no guarantees for tomorrow.

Knowing that he would probably turn her away again didn't stop her. She walked toward him with a purpose in her step and only stopped when she was standing right behind him.

She lifted one hand hesitantly. Would he push her away?

She decided that she didn't care because if she didn't try, if she didn't push aside her fears and touch him one last time, she would spend the rest of her life wondering if there could have been more for them. The 'never knowing' would be so much worse than if he just turned and yelled at her. Looked at her with hate in his eyes and told her that it was all a mistake. As much as she wanted to take the less painful route of just walking away, she couldn't force herself to turn around, to leave this complex bear of a man without finding out what could have been.

*   *   *

Cailean knew she was standing just behind him. She had started to walk away, but for a reason he couldn't fathom, had turned around. He gripped the top of the door, careful not to dent it, and waited to see what she would do next. He felt as if he were coiled so tightly that he would explode.

Turning her away had been the hardest thing he had ever done. It wasn't only sexual for him. Somehow the lass had managed to get through his defences despite his best efforts, causing his heart to almost tear in two when he told her to leave. He had no strength left to deny her and didn't know what he would do if she touched him again. His muscles trembled slightly as he stood still, waiting for her next move. *Please doona touch me lass,* he begged silently, *I doona have the strength to turn you away again.*

179

A strangled sound escaped him as she slid her arms around his waist from behind. Lightening shot straight to his groin and he held on to the car like a drowning man would grab a life preserver. This time his fingers dug into the metal of the door, denting it in his effort to keep from turning around. "Tessa," he choked out, not sure if he was asking her to stay or go anymore.

Her arms tightened around him and dipped lower as she leaned her cheek against his back, causing another round of electricity to shoot through him. His whole body was shaking at this point and he dragged in a shaky breath and blew it out through his clenched teeth.

All around them a light wind blew through the trees, whispering an ancient melody. The air smelled of summer and flowers and a lone bird sang in the distance, adding a feel of magic to the night.

"If you give me tonight," she whispered softly against his back, "I'll leave in the morning."

Cailean turned and dragged her against him with a groan, kissing her with so much passion that he could almost feel her melting in his arms. The soft sounds of surrender coming from her were too much for him and he moved them quickly to the grass.

They were almost rough in their rush to rid him of his pants, and only managed to get it unbuckled and pulled down slightly before she pushed him back onto the grass and raised herself over him, her legs on either side of his hips. He was throbbing hotly, and the moment he felt her heat touch his cock, he wrapped his hands around her waist and slid inside her hard, grunting at the insane amount of pleasure that move shot through his aching body. She gasped and started moving her hips along with his, so turned

180

on that she came immediately, making him grind his teeth in his effort to hold back his own release.

He couldn't remember ever having to purposely control himself this much with a woman and it amazed him how much willpower it was taking not to let himself come. He was determined to make this unforgettable for her, but each time she pulsed around him brought him dangerously close to the edge.

Her head was tilted backward as she sat on his hips, gripping handfuls of his shirt and groaning in pleasure as she throbbed hotly around his shaft. He held on to her tightly, eyes shut, willing himself to wait. His breathing was ragged and his whole body was tense when her orgasm finally subsided. Pulling her down, he kissed her and moaned when she started moving her hips against him again. He could only last so long and she was definitely testing his limits.

Rolling her over, he lay on top of her and started sliding slowly in and out. Tessa moaned and met him stroke for stroke. He couldn't remember sex ever feeling so amazing. Each time he slid into her hot, wet sheath, a part of his mind tried to make him give in. Just a little longer, he promised himself as he moved faster. She was writhing under him now, head twisting from side to side, gasping.

"Oh God Cailean, you feel...mmm."

He could feel the pressure build inside him and knew this was it. He felt her orgasm coming and knew that he would not be able to ride it out this time, the urge was too strong, the pull too intense. As she started to pulse around him again, something inside let go and he came with blinding force, burying his head in her neck, trying to force himself to remember not to hurt her, not to squeeze her arms or shoulders or he would surely break her. His fingers dug into the grass and dirt as he came, making deep furrows in the soil and he groaned as pleasure wrapped like a cloak around him. He felt his seed spill into her and marvelled at the way her orgasm seemed to milk him, drawing even more out. God but he had never felt anything so insanely pleasurable in his entire life.

At last she had taken everything from him that he was able to give, and he managed to shift to the side slightly before collapsing into the sweet smelling grass beside her. Their breathing sounded loud and ragged in the quiet of the night.

They said nothing for a time and just lay on their backs looking up at the stars, drifting pleasantly in an ocean of soft grass and aromatic flowers. His whole body seemed to be vibrating and he chalked it up to the incredible orgasm he'd just had. She had made all of his nerve endings sing.

Tessa turned slightly and lay her hand on his chest, sliding one leg over his thigh while her head lay nestled against his shoulder. She still had her dress on and he could feel the silk of it slide against his body when she moved. She slid her hand under his shirt, gliding her fingers along the ridge of his sternum.

"I love this part," she mumbled sleepily against him, brushing her fingers gently along it.

"My chest?" he asked, trying to make sense of what she was saying.

"The dip in the middle." He felt her smile against his chest.

What a curious woman. Forget his chest, she liked the dip?

She played with his chest for a while longer, her fingers soothing him and almost making him fall asleep.

After about ten minutes she moved up slightly in his arms and started nibbling on his neck, making his breath catch.

"Tessa," he warned. "What are you doing?"

"I can't seem to get enough of you."

He moaned softly as her teeth scraped along the sensitive skin of his neck, followed by her tongue. She made her way slowly along his jaw, causing him to harden instantly under the thigh she had draped across him.

She shifted slightly as he turned his head, dragging her thigh exquisitely across his rock hard shaft. Electricity shot through him just as if it were the first time. Would it never be normal with this lass? He constantly felt like a horny teenager around her.

Forcing himself to pull away, he shifted and pulled his pants up, leaving his belt undone. Tessa let out a soft sound of disappointment and he stood and dragged her up against him, kissing her.

"How about we try it on my bed this time?"

She melted against him at his suggestion.

"Mmmm hmmmm."

He laughed softly and took her hand, pulling her along behind him. They made their way into the castle and went straight to his room.

As soon as he shut the door behind them, he pulled his shirt and pants off and whipped her dress over her head. He looked at her for a few moments as she stood self consciously in front of him. She was so beautiful. Her soft round breasts seemed to be begging him to touch them and he didn't make them wait long as he lifted her against him. She automatically wrapped her legs around his waist and he walked toward the bed, laying her down on the soft thick blanket before crawling on after her and finding her nipple with his hot mouth.

She arched with a gasp and he swirled his tongue around the pointed bud, making her cry out. She tasted so perfect, so wonderfully Tessa, he thought as he nibbled his way along to the other one. Soft sounds of pleasure escaped her as she squirmed under his mouth, making it hard for him to concentrate.

After a few minutes, she grabbed his head and pulled him up so that she could kiss him. He gave in because of the drugging effect her kisses seemed to have on him. They spent the entire night making up for the time they had missed. Somehow his stamina never waned. One move or touch and he was ready for her again and again. He didn't think he would ever understand the effect the lass had on him, but for now, for this one night, he was content to lie with her cuddled protectively in his arms, doing whatever she wanted him to do.

~13~

*T*he next morning Tessa woke with a start and looked around

for Cailean. The night had been long and filled with tender loving, with a bit of roughness here and there. Thinking of that got her going again but she figured it was a good thing he was up already because she was so sore she could barely move without wincing.

Instead of getting up right away, she just lay in his bed, snuggled into a nest of pillows and blankets, thinking about the night before. She relived each touch, each soft caress, and knew without a doubt that sex would never be like this with any man other than Cailean.

There seemed to be some kind of a bond between them that made each touch spark with electricity. She knew she had given her word the night before that she would leave without complaint in the morning, but God she didn't realize it would be this hard to even get out of his bed, to willingly separate herself from his tantalizing, masculine scent. Maybe she *was* addicted to him after all. She smiled sadly at the thought of having to go without her addiction.

She lay a pillow over her head with a plop and wondered how he was feeling about what happened. Would it be easy for him to let her go? Probably. Men don't form these stupid attachments the way women do. Laney had told her that a few times while crying on her shoulder over one lost love or another.

She shook her head in defeat. She was going to have to leave him today. She was going to have to get on a plane, fly back to Canada, and all she would be left with was memories. There was no telling when this conflict would be over, when she would be free to come back to see him. Years maybe. Not in her lifetime possibly. That sudden thought had her heart plummeting to her toes. God she hadn't even thought of that. She felt a rush of icy hopelessness pour though her veins. She might never see Cailean again. Suddenly her whole world seemed dreary and black. A tear slid helplessly down her cheek and she fought to control the overwhelming darkness that threatened to wrap its sharp claws around her heart.

Life without Cailean.

Ok deep breath. Calm down. You can't let him see you falling apart like this. She felt so close to losing her mind at that moment that she almost didn't hear the door to the bedroom opening.

When she realized someone had entered the room, she froze, forcing herself to breathe normally.

"Tessa, are you awake lass?"

His voice was soft and husky. She wanted so badly to hear that voice every morning for the rest of her life, and every night before she fell asleep.

186

"I brought you breakfast."

How could she even think of eating when her happiness was about to be ripped out from under her. *Oh God get a hold of yourself. Breathe.*

She took a slow, hesitant breath in, willing herself not to start crying.

"I'm up," she mumbled from beneath the pillow. "Not hungry."

She heard him sigh and then the sound of the tray being placed on the table. The bed dipped when he sat on the edge. Was he trying to figure out what to say to make this easier? Didn't he know nothing would?

His hand touched her hair, softly stroking.

"If there were any other way to keep you safe, I'd choose that instead."

He sounded so honestly regretful that she wanted to hold him, reassure him. But that would do no good, she couldn't even reassure herself. The decision was made and it was up to her to make it go as painlessly as possible...for his sake. In those few words he'd spoken, she had known that he felt the same as she did. Felt the same loneliness and emptiness, the same hopelessness.

She felt the bed move again as he moved the blankets and lay down beside her, pulling her to him. He held her as if he would never let her go, and for a moment she wished with all her heart that was true. They lay facing each other and she buried her face in his neck, wrapping her arms around him. Silent tears slid down her cheek as imagined the life they could have had.

He let out a shaky breath. "Ah lass, 'tis so much harder than I thought it would be."

They lay that way for a long time, just breathing each other in.

Eventually he spoke. "We have to leave for the airport soon my love."

Tessa nodded into his neck, then turned and rolled off the other side of the bed. After she pulled on her clothes, she left his room without a backward glance, not wanting him to see the tears in her eyes. He hadn't moved from the bed and she knew he was watching every move she made. She could almost picture the sadness on his face.

She walked into her own room and closed the door, leaning against it as if she could keep it shut against the pain. Her heart was breaking into a million pieces and she didn't know what to do about it. Her hand went to her mouth as she stifled a sob and slid down the door to the cold floor.

*   *   *

When Tessa had gotten out of his bed, Cailean had to force himself to stay put so that he wouldn't give in to the insane urge to grab her and tell her he changed his mind. His hands held the sheets in a death grip and he forced himself to breathe deeply and evenly while she got dressed and walked out without looking even once at him. He knew she was hurt, he saw it in her eyes, felt it in the fierce way she had clung to him in bed a few moments before.

She would get over him in time. She would marry Aiden and forget all about him. She would live her life with a normal man who would grow old with her. She would have children with him, and her time in Scotland would become a distant memory.

Only those thoughts kept him from grabbing her. He couldn't take that away from her, he had done enough damage already.

Inch by inch he released his death grip on the crumpled sheets. They fluttered back to the bed, lying still and limp. He had no choice, he told himself firmly. Making her leave him to keep her safe from the fae was the only possible option. Still, he wished it weren't the only option. What he would give to have her stay with him in his castle for as long as she lived. He would watch her grow old and love her still. He couldn't understand the emotions that were going through him. She was his soulmate. Maybe that was why it was so incredibly difficult to make her leave him, because they were meant to be together.

He swiftly erased that thought from his head. Those kinds of thoughts weren't going to make it any easier on either of them.

There was a knock on the door and for a moment his heart froze.

"Cailean?"

He released the breath he had been holding when he heard Colin's voice through the door, and got out of bed quickly, opening the door.

"Aye?"

"We only have a short time to make it to the airport. Tessa has just come downstairs, are you ready?"

He took a deep breath and let it out in a rush. It would all be over soon. The quicker he could get her safely on that plane, the quicker he could start trying to forget her. His heart immediately crashed at the thought and he knew without a doubt that forgetting Tessa Anderson would be an impossible feat.

"I'll be right down," he said, pinching the bridge of his nose in frustration.

"Are you doing ok?" came the tentative question.

"Aye, just...I'll be there in a minute."

Colin spared him one last concerned look before heading back downstairs.

After pacing back and forth a dozen times, he finally decided he was calm enough to finish the job, and walked out, slamming the door behind him.

Colin and Tessa were already settled into his car when he got there and he climbed into the driver's seat and put the car in gear, skidding the tires on the gravel as he slammed on the gas.

Tessa gasped but didn't say anything as they took off over the bridge and headed for the airport.

He could feel her looking at him as he navigated his way through the winding country roads and waited for her to say something.

She stayed stubbornly quiet.

Even Colin, who was known for his easy way of calming tense situations, was eerily quiet, no doubt very uncomfortable. He had only come along because they were to stop at the McGowans' castle after dropping Tessa off.

The McGowans had a vast library dating back to the turn of the century. The MacLeods were always welcomed since it had been documented in one of the McGowans' books that Cailean's ancestors had once saved the McGowan line hundreds of years before when John McCreary had tried to poison Gabe McGowan, who at that time was the only living McGowan. Cailean and Colin had caught the fiend red-handed as he poured a vile concoction into Gabe's whisky.

In repayment of his deceit, Gabe forced John to drink the whisky himself, resulting in a terribly painful death for the man.

The silence stretched on as they made their way to the Inverness Airport.

For some reason, instead of the three hour drive taking forever, it seemed to fly by with each mile. By the time they had reached the Skye Bridge, the tension in the car was thick enough to cut with a knife.

Tessa had turned to look out over the water, a look of surprise on her face. He had forgotten that when she had made this drive previously it had been night time. She probably didn't even realize she had driven over this bridge. He glanced at her as she tried to take everything in at once, and hoped the beauty of it would improve her mood a little.

Colin fidgeted in the back seat and Cailean looked into the rear view mirror in time to see him put headphones on and lean his head against the seat with his eyes closed. He couldn't blame him, it was almost as if the silence was deafening. Tessa glanced at Colin as well and then turned back toward the view, saying nothing.

"Aren't you going to say anything lass?"

She looked down as if suddenly finding her hands in her lap simply amazing, and he sighed in frustration.

"'Tis no' safe for you to stay Tessa. The fae would see how important you are to me and keep trying to kidnap you. They would kill you in a heartbeat just to hurt me."

"So you'd rather not have me at all?"

The question was whispered so quietly he almost didn't hear it.

"I'd rather you were safe...alive, rather than dead, aye!"

"Either way you will never see me again."

His heart contracted painfully at her words. "We doona know that for sure lass. It could happen."

"Yeah, maybe you'll come looking for me in fifty years! Maybe I'll get to see you once more while I'm lying on my deathbed? I'd rather you remembered me as I am now, not a wrinkled old woman about to die," she added sadly.

Her words brought back sharp memories of Leah as he'd last seen her, lying still in bed, almost happy knowing she would soon be seeing her Catherine. Happy to be leaving him.

He remembered holding on to her weak, wrinkled hand as she drew her last breath. "Tell Catherine I love her too," was all he said before she closed her eyes for the last time. A small frown appeared on her peaceful face at that last second, almost as if she had suddenly realized, in the moment of her death, that he too had suffered from the loss of their only child. That he too had been in pain all these years and missing the daughter they almost had.

Her next breath never came, and he gently laid his head down on her still hand. Anger and sorrow mixed together, forming a worldwind of emotions that he had no idea how to deal with. He sat holding her hand for an entire day, even as it grew cold and stiff in his. He told himself it was to make sure her soul was truly gone before leaving her body all alone, but in truth it was because by releasing her, he was acknowledging to himself that the life he knew was over.

The moment he let her hand go for the last time, he promised himself that he would never love another woman. Never have to lose someone he cared about so much.

A lot of good that promise did him.

He looked over at Tessa with sadness in his heart. No, he would not find her as an old woman. He would let her die with pride, not be embarrassed by what she felt she had become. It would be better that way anyway because seeing her again after so long, just to let her go again so soon, would tear his heart out.

He reached over and held her hand in his while he drove. They didn't talk again after that and the rest of the drive went by faster than he would have liked.

They arrived at the Inverness airport at quarter to one, and after a quick hug from each of the brothers, and a lingering kiss goodbye from Cailean, she was ushered onto the waiting plane, minutes before it took off.

* * *

Tessa was lucky enough to have three seats to herself, and she sat slouched against the window, looking down at Scotland as the plane rose into the clouds. The tears had started as she walked along the corridor toward the door of the plane, much to one of the stewardess's concern.

Muttering something about being tired, she found her way to her seat and leaned her head back while the tears streamed quietly down her face. She had been doing ok until Cailean had hugged her, kissed her softly and said, "I will love you for as long as I live." She realized then how much worse his pain would be when she died, knowing he would have to go on forever without any hope left of ever seeing her again.

The stewardess had made a couple rounds to check on her, still worried, but Tessa assured her that she would be ok.

When the stewardess found out she was leaving behind the only person she had ever really loved, she looked truly sorry and even sat to talk with her a while.

The flight from Inverness to Winnipeg took forever, but after two stops she finally found herself coming down the escalator in the Winnipeg International Airport.

She looked out over a sea of expectant, happy faces. Most of the crowd were waiting to see their loved ones. There were young kids being held by their parents, looking out for someone they knew, smiles lighting up their innocent faces, never guessing how their lives could drastically be changed one day just by having to board a plane.

Some of the people had signs held up; waiting to pick up people they had never met before. Others looked bored as they sat behind the crowd, maybe waiting for someone they couldn't care less about.

One woman in particular captured her eye. She was standing, looking longingly at the line of people filing down the escalator like ants. She wiped away tears as she held her hands together, almost praying. Tessa new the minute she had found who she was looking for because her face erupted in a smile so wonderful and bright that everyone around her seemed to fade into the background. She envied the woman so much it hurt.

When she got to the bottom of the escalator, Tessa looked behind her, searching for the face that made the woman smile. A tall, dark man walked past her, straight into the woman's arms. The couple stood there, holding each other tightly. The woman buried her face in the man's neck and he whispered something in her ear. After a second the woman looked up, smiling that bright, all consuming smile, and they kissed passionately, completely oblivious to anyone around them.

Tessa looked at the couple for a minute, her heart breaking into a million pieces, before turning and heading for the baggage wheel. Would that be her one day? Could she ever be lucky enough that Cailean would defeat the Unseelie and come to get her? The sadness in her was so deep, so strong, that she almost let her bag roll right by her on the conveyer belt. She snagged it at the last second, dropping it to the ground at her feet with a thump. She ended up wrestling with it for a good two minutes before finally convincing the collapsible handle to come out of hiding.

She hadn't told anyone that she was returning to Winnipeg so soon because she couldn't bear the thought of talking to anyone and answering their questions. The pain was just too much to deal with.

Walking out of the airport, she looked across the pickup lanes to the hotel that was attached to the airport and decided that she would just stay there for the night and call Laney to get her in the morning. It had been a ridiculously long flight and she just couldn't face the long drive home, so she hitched her laptop bag over her shoulder and pulled her other bag along behind her, its small wheels rumbling loudly across the road.

After checking in, she lay on her bed and stared at the ceiling of her hotel room, overwhelmed by a feeling of intense loss.

Not knowing what else to do, she decided to have a quick nap before supper. She lay fully clothed on the bed without even bothering to pull the covers down, and cried herself to sleep.

She was surprised when she woke up and saw that it was eleven at night; apparently she had been more tired than she thought.

Deciding on room service, she ended up picking at a stack of pancakes before falling into a fitful dream where she was surrounded by the most beautiful looking killers she had ever seen.

In her nightmare, Laney was standing in front of a tree screaming for her. She tried to tell Laney that she was right there in front of her but she didn't seem to hear her. Tessa woke with a jump, gasping and sweating.

God what a way to start the day, she though miserably as she sleepily grappled for her cell. She dialled Laney's number and sighed with relief when her friend answered on the second ring.

* * *

After seeing the state she was in when she arrived at the airport, Laney insisted that Tessa stay at her house until she was sure she was going to be ok.

It took an hour for Tessa to relay the events of the past couple weeks to her friend, who sat wide eyed and enthralled throughout the telling.

"Honey, if I didn't know you so well I would have believed that you had just gotten too caught up in one of your novels and started thinking you were one of your own characters."

"I know," groaned Tessa, rubbing her face. "I wish that *is* what happened."

"Oh honey." Laney looked at the pure misery on her best friends face and was convinced that her decision to make Tessa stay with her was the right one.

She had never seen her friend look so broken in her entire life, or so depressed. It really worried her. First her stupid fiancé, Aiden, cheating on her just before they were supposed to get hitched, then she went and fell in love with a man who was so completely unavailable that there was absolutely no way around it. Immortal? She didn't believe the part about him being immortal, but the rest of it seemed realistic enough. A man in trouble with some people who wanted to hurt the people he was close to. He sent her away to protect her. Makes sense. She was just glad whoever this guy was, that he had the sense to keep Tessa out of his screwed up life. Feeding her the line about being immortal seemed a little crazy to her though. But maybe he *was* crazy. If so, it was a good thing that Tessa came back before he went all Ted Bundy on her. The thought made her shiver.

She watched Tessa pick at her taco salad and looked at her with sympathy.

"Hon, you realize you only knew this guy for a very short time right? I've never known you to get so involved so fast." She hesitated a second before continuing. "Do you think maybe, it might have to do with the shock of finding Aiden with that little slut?"

"No."

Well at least she sounded pretty sure of herself, but Tessa's strong feelings toward the Scottish guy was really making her worry.

"Onagh said we were soulmates," she began. "Maybe that's why I feel so connected to him...why it feels like I'm dying without him."

Those words had the hairs on Laney's arms standing up. *Dying?* Oh God, Tessa was worse off than she thought. Definitely depressed! *I'm going to kill Aiden! Stupid asshole!*

Tessa must have seen the look of horror in Laney's eyes because she added blandly, "Oh geez, not *really* dying Laney, I'm not that stupid."

Laney relaxed almost immediately, relief flushing through her, and let out a sigh before realizing what she was doing.

Tessa looked at her and shook her head with a smile. "You read way too many books hun."

"Well," she said defensively. "My friend comes home with no notice from a holiday and starts talking about faeries, immortal men and dying. What would *you* think?"

Tessa let out a small laugh. "I suppose it does kind of strange."

"Ya think?" replied Laney sarcastically with a smile.

"Alright, I knew you would have a hard time with the immortal and faery part, but what about the soulmate part? Is that so hard to believe?"

Laney thought about it for a while. That wasn't something people just made up right? When you find that one person who makes you feel as if all your problems just melt away and that life was nothing before you met them...that's what people call their soulmate. So if she were thinking along those lines, yeah sure this Cailean guy could be Tessa's soulmate. It was definitely possible.

"Ok Tess, I'll give you the soulmate part, and the part about him making you leave to protect you from whatever mafia he has chasing after him."

Tessa grinned at her long time friend, knowing that was as much as she should expect any sane person to believe. "Thank you."

"No problem. There's just one thing I was wondering about though."

"What's that?"

"If these so called faeries can just appear out of some kind of porthole, what's to stop them from appearing in your closet or something?"

Tessa laughed at her friend's question.

"They can't just *make* a porthole Laney. There is only one at Dunvegan as far as I know. Any others would be made if they made another immortal. And it would be preceded by a serious hurricane-like storm."

"Ah of course...silly me, what was I thinking."

"Alright smart ass," said Tessa as she threw one of Laney's hand embroidered pillows at her. She caught it with a laugh and they ended up talking for another hour before Tessa started yawning.

"Jet lag huh?"

"Yeah, I guess it will take a couple days to get back to Canadian time."

"Well you go to sleep then, and I'll keep an eye out for Fairy Mark or whoever."

Tessa shook her head with a smile and Laney grinned, feeling better now that she had gotten her friend to smile. She would definitely have to take her out tomorrow to get her mind off of that crazy Cailean dude.

~14~

The next day Tessa woke to a racket outside the bedroom window. She jumped out of bed and raced over, looking down into the immaculate yard below. There were flowers everywhere of every colour you could imagine, and in the middle of it all was Laney, racing around like a mad woman with a rake above her head.

"Stupid animal," she yelled as she chased some as yet unseen offender around her garden.

Tessa leaned her arms on the window sill and laughed as she watched her friend peak around flowers, trying to locate the mysterious beast.

"You can't hide from me forever. One of these days I'm going to get you and your furry little friends too," she threatened loudly.

Tessa put her hand over her mouth and giggled quietly, shaking her head at the insanity.

"Sweetie, let the poor thing live another day," she called through the open window.

Laney looked up in surprise, rake poised over her head.

At that same moment, a grey bunny hopped out of the flowers and raced away.

"Aww damn it!" she yelled when she realized she had lost her opportunity.

Tessa laughed out loud at her accusing expression. "Yeah Laney, like you have it in you to kill a cute, innocent little bunny."

"Innocent?" she sputtered, rake hanging dejectedly at her side, looking at Tessa as if she had just turned on her. "Those furry little rats keep eating my flowers! No matter what I do they won't go away."

"You could really kill one?" Tessa asked, knowing perfectly well that Laney didn't have it in her.

"Well...no," she admitted with a pout. "But I figured if I gave it a bop on the head it wouldn't come back again."

Tessa giggled again.

Suddenly Laney looked up and smiled, "Wanna go to a movie?"

"Oh I don't know sweetie," Tessa sighed. She wasn't ready to go out yet and face the crowds, watching the happy couples kiss and hold each other the way she couldn't with Cailean.

"Please? I really want to see that Twilight movie," she begged, looking all doe eyed.

"God you're such a baby," Tessa laughed, shaking her head. "Fine I'll go, but don't expect me to enjoy it."

She squealed in excitement, "Awesome. We'll get some breakfast and then head out. There's a matinee at Cinema City."

After a delicious breakfast of homemade hash browns, eggs, toast, and jam, they got dressed and headed to the movies.

They navigated their way through construction and pulled into the large parking lot, managing to find a spot close by the doors.

"So what's this movie about anyway?" asked Tessa cautiously. Laney was known to pick the strangest movies.

"Vampires!" she replied happily, slamming the door shut on her red Intrepid. The car was the first thing she ever owned outright and even after ten years she refused to get rid of it.

She claimed it was a matter of not leaving behind your old friends when you made it big. She was an administrative assistant at the University of Manitoba and did pretty well for herself. Years ago she swore that she would drive her 'old friend' until she got to the point that she felt ok about letting it retire in peace.

It was so hard not to smile around Laney. She had such a contagiously happy and crazy personality, and for some reason being around her made you forget exactly how bad your problems really were for a while. Maybe the movie would be just what she needed to stop thinking about Cailean for a couple hours.

They walked through the doors and past posters of all the movies that were currently playing and paid for their tickets. They had made a deal when they were still in high school that no matter how rich or famous either of them got, they would still make the time to spend together doing the simple things like movies, dinner and shopping. Even after all these years they still managed to get together at least once a month to keep their promise to each other, and always had a great time. The rest of the time they kept in touch through phone calls or emails.

They made it to the concession stand, happy to note that it wasn't too busy. Going to a week day matinee helped ensure that Tessa wasn't accosted by her fans too much. She bought herself popcorn and coke, and Laney got her usual coke and Twizzlers before they headed in to the movie, snagging a seat in the middle of the back row.

Tessa wasn't too optimistic about the movie, judging from its slow beginning, but by the time the vampire, Edward, came into the picture she had decided that it wasn't so bad after all.

Laney sighed beside her.

"The actor playing Edward is Rob Pattinson. If he wasn't ten years younger than me I'd be so into him."

Tessa giggled at her friend, "You already are into him you fruitcake."

She just giggled at that and continued to munch on her Twizzlers, eyes wide, not wanting to miss a moment of the sexy vampire.

Tessa shook her head and rolled her eyes in amusement. Laney was known to drool over at least one actor in every movie she had seen.

Focusing on the movie again, she took a better look at Edward the vampire as he sat smiling and talking to the human girl, Bella, during biology. She grudgingly decided that he was actually kind of drool worthy as far as twenty something year old guys went. Square jaw, strong chin, gorgeous smile, sexy bedroom eyes.

If Laney had her way she would want to be permanently twenty with a thirty year olds wisdom. She complained that they were making the younger men so much hotter now days, and decided that since she couldn't stay twenty, she would just have to be content drooling over the hot young actors at the movies.

Tessa on the other hand, preferred the more mature men. She had her fill of immature partners, including Aiden, and was ready for someone like Cailean. *Oh Lord, how did her thoughts keep getting back to him? Ok focus!* she commanded, forcing herself to pay attention to the movie. Edward had just told Bella that he didn't have the strength to stay away from her anymore, and Laney 'awwd' beside her. *Great! A sappy love story...just what I need.* Tessa sighed in frustration.

She was determined to make it through the movie for Laney's sake, not wanting to ruin their movie date.

By the end of the movie, Tessa was even more bummed out because she thought it very unfair that Bella got her vampire but she couldn't have her immortal man. At least the person *she* was in love with had a heartbeat and didn't want to kill her every second!

Laney looked at her quietly as they walked back to her car. "You ok hon?"

Tessa smiled sadly at her.

"I'm fine," she sighed. "I just think it's incredibly unfair that Bella got her man and I didn't. He's dead, or undead or whatever, and she *still* got him."

Laney laughed so hard that she had to stop and hang on to the railing to prevent herself from collapsing.

"Oh God Tess," she managed between laughs, "You're really pathetic, you know that?" she said, wiping the tears from her eyes.

Tessa grinned sheepishly at herself. "Yeah I know!"

Laney shook her head in amusement. "But you have to admit, Edward is hot!"

"Yeah, yeah...he's hot!"

Satisfied with Tessa's answer, Laney led the way to the car, almost skipping.

They decided to head to the mall after that to kill time with some shopping before supper. Laney decided that she simply had to have a new outfit for work on Monday and possibly new shoes as well if she found any that screamed at her.

Tessa laughed. To say Laney was fashion impaired was understating things, which was why she always dragged Tessa along on her little clothes shopping expeditions.

In the mall, they grabbed a coffee from Tim Horton's and had only managed five steps before Laney promptly bumped into an incredibly tall, good-looking man, spilling her coffee down his shirt, causing him to grunt in pain.

"Oh Jeezus...holy shi....damn that's hot!!!!" he gritted out, plucking his soaking shirt between two fingers and flapping it to cool it down.

His eyes were squeezed shut as he took deep calming breaths and Laney immediately started to panic. "Oh my God, are you ok...oh God Tessa I burned him...oh Lord...here let me..." she scrambled out, unbuttoning his shirt.

He grabbed at her busy hands, stopping them. "It's ok...no...uh...really don't want to get naked in the middle of the mall lady."

Laney stopped at once. "Oh God you're right. I'm so sorry! Oh please forgive me...I'm seriously the most sorry person you've ever met. Well not sorry as in pathetic...well maybe that too...oh God."

The handsome man looked down at her with a small laugh. "Really, it's ok."

"Do you need to go to the hospital or something? That coffee was really hot."

"No...I'm fine," he assured her, looking right into her eyes, obviously hoping she would finally believe him and stop making a scene. There were about twenty people crowding around the three of them wanting to know if he was ok.

"Oh God...well at least let me buy you a new shirt then."

He looked over at Tessa, silently begging for help.

"You might as well agree or she'll follow you around like a lost puppy to make sure you don't pass out anywhere."

The man sighed in surrender and held his hands up. "Ok you win, you can buy me a shirt...if," he stopped and looked her in the eyes again, "you promise to stop freaking out...I'm really ok. And by the way, my name is Alex." He held his hand out to her, dimples appearing in his cheeks as he smiled.

Laney smiled back, a little embarrassed. "Ok, I promise Alex." she agreed as she took his hand and pulled him off toward the men's clothing store they had passed on their way to get coffee. He followed along, not really being given an option, and was a remarkably good sport about it all.

Laney wasn't just happy to buy him a new shirt. She made him try on at least five before deciding that the navy one looked best on him. Tessa had to give him credit; he put up with her crazy friend and even pretended to model on a catwalk, obviously sensing that she needed some help getting the guilt off her chest.

When he was sufficiently decent, Laney invited him to join them at Moxie's for supper. By that time he seemed to have become somewhat entranced with Laney's crazy ways and agreed as long as he would be allowed to pay for it.

After much bickering between the two about who was paying for supper, Laney finally gave in when he promised to let her pay the next time. In truth, Tessa was sure Laney only gave in because she was shocked that there might be a next time. She was definitely taken with guy.

"He's just as gorgeous as Edward," she whispered to Tessa on their way to Moxie's, causing her to almost choke with laughter into her cold coffee.

Supper was an amusing experience as Tessa sat back and watch the two of them laugh and talk. She was happy that Laney had met him, even if she had to scald him to death for an introduction. Maybe he would be just nuts enough to put up with her funny friend.

Laney's parents had died in a car accident six years before. They had been very close and it took her about five years to get back to her normal, happy, loving self. Those five years were the longest in Tessa's life as she watched her friend slowly get worse and worse, sinking into a deep depression that was so unlike her.

Two weeks before last Christmas, Laney suddenly came out of her depression with a vengeance. She had called Tessa up sounding happy and told her things were going to be much better from then on. Tessa was so shocked at her friend's sudden change that she practically flew over to her house to make sure she was ok.

It turned out that she had woken up that morning and suddenly decided that if her parents really were watching over her, they would be extremely upset seeing her that way. She swore from that point on to live life to its fullest and save the depression and sadness for situations that really warranted it...and even then, only in short bursts.

To this day she kept true to her promise and was always a joy to be around.

"Aren't you hungry Tessa?"

She jolted out of her thoughts to see Laney and Alex looking at her. The question had come from Alex.

"No ah...," she shook her head, trying to find words. "Not really," she smiled apologetically.

Laney looked at her with concern. "You wanna go?"

"No, no I'm fine. It's nice actually, to be out doing stuff."

Alex looked questioningly at Laney and she shrugged. "Ok then, just let me know when you're ready to go."

Tessa nodded and forced herself to join in their conversation, not wanting to ruin the moment for her friend. It wasn't everyday she found a cute, decent guy who wasn't an unavailable movie actor.

*   *   *

"Focus Colin," said Cailean in an annoyed voice from the corner of the large stone room. They had been looking through tome after tome for three days now and had yet to find anything they could use against the Unseelie.

The room was at least one thousand square feet and filled from floor to ceiling with books of every kind. There were multiple ladders on tracks so that a person could climb up to the higher books and slide themselves along to the next column of shelves if necessary. The brothers had been up and down these ladders so often in the last few days that it got to the point where they were flipping coins to see who would go next. Book after book was taken down and replaced after finding nothing pertinent to their situation.

At one point in their search, Colin chuckled and Cailean look up expectantly.

He read aloud from the book in his hand. "'Twas known that the brothers McLeod, strong in their love for their dear friend Gabe, intervened in his sure demise, allowing the McGowan line to continue..."

That got a smile out of Cailean and he shook his head at his brothers obvious amusement and continued flipping through the large tome laid out on the table in front of him. The pages were brittle in his hands and he was very careful to turn them gently to avoid tearing them.

Gliding his fingers down the page, he could feel fine dust on his fingertips as he skimmed passage after passage. Some of the books in the McGowan library were so old that they had been re-written a few times to avoid losing that piece of history when they finally fell to dust.

Ryan McGowan, a short, friendly man with a balding head and a limp, came into the room just as Cailean closed the book.

"Find anything useful?"

Although he didn't know what the brothers were looking for, he had a general idea that it was about faery folklore. He was more amused than anything that the brothers were taking their search so seriously.

"Nothing yet my friend," replied Colin dejectedly from his corner.

"Why is it so important to you...this folklore?"

Colin answered that one.

"Well, Cailean here is thinking of writing a book and wants any information he can find on the beliefs about faeries in the past. Naturally I got drafted to help with the search."

Cailean's eyes narrowed on his brother.

"I see," replied Ryan.

"Got it!" yelled Colin suddenly, before clearing his throat to cover his excitement.

Ryan raised his eyebrows and looked at Cailean who just rolled his eyes.

"He's a little too into the story. I promised I'd use his name," he said by way of explanation.

Ryan chuckled. "Alright then, I'll leave you two to it. Let me know when you get hungry."

"Thanks Ryan," said Cailean.

As soon as Ryan closed the heavy door behind him, Cailean rushed over to Colin who was mumbling and skimming through the page he'd found.

"Ok, so it says that the Unseelie were once members of the Seelie court who fell from grace....blah blah blah...no method of reproduction...enslave mortals...Tuatha de Danann...live in the sidhe which are faery mounds...like at the castle I suppose," he added, glancing at Cailean who was growing impatient. He looked back at the page and continued on. "Fairy flag of Dunvegan when unfurled was said to save the lives of certain clanfolk...multiply clan's military forces. Eldest male is the only one allowed to unfurl the flag...wave it three times...given to McLeod by queen Titania. Can only be unfurled three times, last time would either mean victory over enemies or the total extinction of the McLeod clan. Well crap that's no' good!" ended Colin with a groan. "Do you think there's any truth to this?" he asked with a frown.

Cailean just stared at the book.

"Cailean?"

"Well Colin, do you think there's any truth to faeries or immortal men?" Cailean asked sarcastically.

Colin slumped into his chair with a look or horror on his face.

"Well at least we know where the flag is if it comes to that."

"That miserable looking scrap of cloth willna help us. If we took it out of the case 'twould fall to pieces," said Colin with a sigh.

Cailean dragged in a deep breath and blew it out in frustration. "I know."

* * *

Tessa was finally allowed to go home two days later, but before she left she overheard Laney on the phone with Alex. He had called the day after their supper, asking Laney if she would like to go for coffee with him the next day. After much prodding and poking, Tessa finally managed to assure her that she was doing much better and was in fact planning to home anyway. Laney eventually gave in, and walked around alternating between happiness and total terror.

"I can't believe I'm going on a date with this guy," she began for the fifth time.

"Sweetie, it will be fine. He already past my rigorous approval standards, so what else are you waiting for?"

"It's just been so long since I've been on a date, and then to jump right in with Mr. Model Man?"

Tessa giggled at her. "He's just a man Laney! Just like every other man you dated. After a couple weeks he'll start pissing you off and you'll just dump him as usual. Until then, why not?"

Laney sighed. "Am I that bad?"

"Yes!"

"Well maybe this time will be different."

"That's the spirit! Come on, get dressed, he'll be here in twenty minutes. The first test will be to see if the man is punctual or not."

Laney sighed, obviously very nervous, and Tessa smothered a smile as she pushed her toward her bedroom to change.

She truly hoped that this guy would work out. Laney was a wonderful person, but the fact that she was a feminist occasionally turned men off. Mostly they were more scared of offending her than anything, but it also seemed to bother their sense of manliness. At least Alex looked manly enough to be able to deal with that. After all, he did agree to let her pay for coffee on their date today, which was a good first step.

The doorbell rang at exactly three thirty which got Alex some immediate points in Tessa's opinion. Laney just stood staring at the door, biting her lip until Tessa spun her around.

"Listen to me. You're amazing. You're a wonderful, sexy woman. He's lucky you agreed to honour him with a date. And I love you!"

Laney couldn't help grin at the last part and grabbed Tessa in a back crushing hug. "I can do this!" she told herself firmly.

"Yup," grunted Tessa, still being squashed in a bear hug. "Must breathe!"

Laney laughed nervously and let her go.

When she opened the door, both their jaws dropped in amazement.

Standing in front of them was a huge bouquet of flowers. They were pretty sure there was a man behind them, but couldn't be positive since the bouquet took up the entire doorway.

"Oh!" was all Laney could manage.

"My God!" finished Tessa.

The bouquet moved aside and Alex peeked out from behind with a huge grin on his face. "I couldn't find a bigger one...I hope this will do."

Laney blushed furiously as she stammered that it would definitely do, and Tessa reached out to take them from him.

"I'll just go put these in water while you guys go for coffee," she said as she stuck her face completely in the bunch and inhaled. "Oh that's wonderful."

"Maybe I should have brought some for Tessa too," he laughed as they walked to his car.

Tessa peeked around the flowers in time to see him open the car door for Laney. Oh this should be interesting. She expected her to inform him immediately that she wasn't ok with that kind of thing, but Laney just thanked him and got in, throwing a sheepish look Tessa's way which caused her to grin. Maybe she decided to save the feminist talk for the third date.

Sighing happily for her friend, she closed the door and went into the kitchen to find a couple vases for the garden he had left behind.

After making sure they were all tucked away safely, she went upstairs to finish her packing. She would have to remember to stop at the grocery store on her way home since she had emptied nearly everything from her fridge the day before leaving for Scotland.

While she packed, she couldn't shake the ominous feeling that something bad was going to happen. She hadn't had feelings like that since she was a teenager, and just like then, it was very unpleasant.

Turning a hairclip over in her hands, she wondered briefly if it had anything to do with Laney going out, but decided that she was just overreacting. Sure her friend was a little accident prone, but she was pretty sure Alex would be able to keep her safe from herself. She hoped so anyway.

~15~

"*N*o!"

Tessa awoke in a panic and sat straight up in bed, sweating and gasping for air. It was the second night in a row that she had dreamed about the fae. It had come out of nowhere and grabbed her, taking her through a faery mound and into their world. It was a dark and scary place, filled with desolation and hopelessness.

Holy crap! She wasn't even in Scotland anymore and the damn fae were haunting her dreams. She wiped the sweat from her forehead and slumped back against her pillows. She wished she could talk to Cailean, but he told her that it would be safer if they cut all contact completely. He refused to risk one of the Unseelie overhearing them and seeking her out.

"Ok, I'm just going to have to accept the fact that it's over. I will never go to Scotland again and I will never see Cailean again."

Somehow saying the words only made everything seem worse. Her heart ached for Cailean. She itched to touch him again, to feel his lips against hers.

The phone on her bedside table rang, making her jump violently.

"Calm down you idiot," she grumbled to herself, reaching for the annoying, screaming thing.

"Hello?"

"Tess, Alex invited you to join us for a barbeque tonight at his place. Say you'll come." The words tumbled out of Laney's mouth and it took Tessa a few moments for her sleepy brain to make sense of them.

Laney!

Yesterday it was drinks at the bar. She turned her down, pleading a headache.

"Pleeeeze?"

Tessa shook her head and sighed loudly, making sure Laney knew how she felt about this. "Ok Laney, I'll go!"

There was a pause on the other end. "Really?" She sounded surprised.

"Yes fine," she said in an exasperated voice. "I'm just having nightmares here anyway."

She heard the phone moving around on the other end as if Laney had switched ears. "What kind of nightmares?" she asked.

"The ones about evil faeries sucking me into their evil world and having their evil way with me," she answered with a soft laugh.

"Well are they cute?"

"Laney!"

"Ok, ok, you had just mentioned how good looking that Onagh one was, so I was just curious."

"You're insane, you know that?"

"Yup! Guilty! Soooo?"

Tessa shook her head in surrender. "Yes they were cute ok. What time?"

"I'll come get you at five."

"Alright, see you then."

Laney giggled and hung up.

Maybe she just needed a distraction so that she could stop thinking constantly about Cailean. She hadn't even been able to write a word since she'd been back, she just sat and stared at the screen as it stared rudely back, refusing to say anything at all. Stupid computer!

She looked at the clock beside the bed and figured it was probably a miracle that Laney had been able to wait until eight thirty before calling her.

Well she was up anyway, so she might as well try to write a little.

She eyed the computer in the corner of the room accusingly. "You better do your job this time," she threatened.

It stayed stubbornly quiet as it sat there, mocking her.

She climbed out of bed, going through her usual morning rituals, glad for once to have her bathroom attached to her bedroom instead of down the hall like in the castle.

"What are you doing Tessa?" she sighed in exasperation.

"No thinking about Scotland! No thinking about castles! And definitely...no thinking about Cailean!"

She sniffed, satisfied that she had set herself straight, and continued brushing her hair.

The omlet she made for breakfast satisfied her hunger and when she could find no more excuses, she turned and stomped unwillingly toward her bedroom computer. As she reached the chair, she was suddenly overcome by sadness and almost detoured right back to her bed. The only thing that stopped her was the fact that her agent had left ten messages on her machine when she had been gone, begging and pleading for the completed manuscript that she had promised to deliver the following week.

Grace knew Tessa had never been late, but she also knew that her wedding had just been cancelled and why. On top of that, she had fled the country. She wasn't surprised that Grace was having a heart attack about the latest manuscript being ready on time.

Giving her computer a wide berth, she picked up the phone and called Grace who sounded like she was on the verge of a nervous breakdown. It took about five minutes to calm her down and reassure her that the manuscript was going well and that she would indeed have it by the next week. Grace thanked her over and over and finally hung up after promising to take a Valium.

"Wow! That's why I'm the writer and not the agent," she thought in relief.

Standing about five feet from the computer, she stared at it menacingly with her arms crossed.

"I've had just about enough out of you," she threatened. "You're going to behave yourself now and do what I tell you. I'm the boss, understand?"

The computer just stared back.

Glaring, she walked toward it cautiously and sat down, took a deep breath and turned it on.

After a couple minutes it was finished loading and a sky blue screen looked back at her. She had put a picture of an eagle soaring through the skies on it because normally that's what she felt like when she wrote. Free. She was definitely considering changing it to a pair of handcuffs at the moment. She had never had this much trouble getting focused before and it was really starting to annoy her.

Half an hour later, after checking her emails and messing around a bit, she finally decided that opening her manuscript would probably be a good start. She double clicked on it and the word document opened up instantly. The cursor blinked slowly at her, waiting.

Hesitantly, she hit the enter key to start a new paragraph and almost cringed as the cursor jumped to the next line, waiting expectantly for her next order. She quickly re-read the last paragraph she had written in Scotland and then looked at the blinking cursor again, willing it to move.

Nope.

She decided to re-read the last two paragraphs this time. When she was done, she looked at the cursor again...waiting.

Nothing!

Alright, enough of this crap. She paged up to the beginning of her chapter and started reading it in earnest. She had already written just over three thousand words for this particular chapter, and by the time she had gotten back to the cursor, she was finally starting to get back into the story. She took a deep breath, closed her eyes and imagined what her vampire was going to do to get himself and his human partner out of their current predicament. Suddenly the words came to her and she opened her eyes and yelled in triumph.

"Ha!" she yelled at her computer. "I told you I'd win!"

The computer knew when it was beaten and had the decency to accept it.

Her fingers started flying over the keyboard, racing in their effort to keep up with her thoughts. The story poured out of her just the way it used to before her life had gotten complicated. She felt exhilarated and managed to write another one and a half chapters before she heard a honking through her open window.

Looking up in astonishment, she realized it was already five o'clock.

"Damn...crap!" she said as she clicked the save button and raced to get changed out of her pyjamas.

Laney opened the front door with her own key and started banging her way up the stairs. "Woman, if you're sitting in front of your computer in your p.j.'s I'm not going to be happy!"

"I'm sorry! I lost track of time," yelled Tessa from the bathroom where she was hurriedly applying makeup. "No p.j.'s!"

She heard a suffering sigh from the bedroom. "I'm not even sure you remember how to tell time anymore. Doesn't your computer have a built-in clock?"

"Yeah but it's so small that I never notice it!"

"Humph. Well I can fix that!"

Alarmed, Tessa almost poked her eye as she quickly finished with the mascara and peaked around the door to see what Laney was up to.

On her desktop where her eagle used to be, now pictured a huge digital clock.

Laney stood beside it, arms crossed with one eyebrow cocked, looking smug.

"Oh you're hilarious," said Tessa sarcastically as she unwillingly laughed at her friends pretend put upon attitude.

Laney started laughing as well and walked into the bathroom behind her to peak into the mirror, holding up Tessa's recently discarded pyjamas. "No p.j.'s huh?"

Tessa grinned guiltily.

"Come on Tess, I'm the one who has to look good here. You're going to steal my spotlight if you do anything else."

Tessa turned to face her friend with a smile. "Laney, there's not a woman for miles who could be remotely capable of stealing your spotlight." It was true. Laney was a truly beautiful woman by any standard; tall, slim, smooth oval face and long blond hair. For some reason she could never see that about herself. It was probably why she made friends so easily, because she never saw herself as better than anyone.

"Alright, enough with the ego boost and let's get going," she commanded impatiently.

They managed to make it to Alex's house exactly on time. He lived in a dark grey stone house in Charleswood. The place was huge and beautiful and the driveway curved gently to the right toward a double garage. They parked in front of one of the garage doors and sat in the car for a minute.

"Ummm, so apparently he's rich," Laney squeaked.

Tessa laughed. "So am I Laney, you don't seem to have a problem barging into my house."

"Yeah but I knew you when you were just normal, it's different."

"Are you saying I'm not normal?" Tessa asked in mock horror.

Laney glanced at her with a grin.

"You are a cruel, cruel woman Laney Ferrel," she sighed, shaking her head as she opened her door and got out.

They walked to the front door and Tessa reached out to push the doorbell. It took only a minute for the door to swing open. Because of the light shining behind Alex, he looked like he was standing in a halo of light.

He grinned at them. "Welcome ladies."

"Hi," said Laney, almost shyly.

"Hi Alex."

He waved them in and shut the door before leading them toward the back of the house. "The potatoes are almost done."

"Wow you are efficient," remarked Tessa in surprise.

"I aim to please."

They walked out onto a large wooden deck, complete with a beautiful glass patio table and a hot tub. There were lights strung up over the deck that Tessa was sure would look amazing when it got dark.

Alex walked ahead and pulled out a chair for each of them.

Tessa glanced at Laney to see what she thought of his gallant behaviour and noticed that she hadn't even raised an eyebrow. She decided that it was entirely possible Laney had given up her feminist ways because of Alex. Well then. Maybe he was the one after all if he could make her change so drastically without even trying.

"Quit looking at me like that," she whispered hotly. "I've decided a little pampering isn't so bad."

Tessa smothered a giggle and looked over at Alex who had gone to check the potatoes.

"So how do you ladies like your steaks?"

"Medium," replied Laney.

"Dead!" answered Tessa.

Alex looked up from the potatoes in surprise and laughed. "Dead?"

"Let's just say I will be very offended if it moo's at me," she clarified. "Or bleeds on me," she added for safety.

Alex roared with laughter. "Dead it is then," he promised.

Laney grinned at Tessa, silently thanking her for breaking the ice.

Tessa winked at her and turned back to Alex.

"So what do you do Alex?"

"I own Greystone Financial Corp on Broadway," he said simply, as if it were just another job.

Tessa choked on the wine he had set in front of them. "Own?"

He smiled at her and nodded. "I bought the company eight years ago and it's been doing pretty well."

"I'd say," remarked Tessa, amazed. "They are the number one financial group in all of Canada. Good Lord, could you just be a little more humble please?" she added with a laugh.

He laughed at her teasing and looked at Laney. "Would you ladies like an appetizer?"

Laney nodded, keeping a close eye on his butt as he walked inside to get some nibblies.

"God that man has a gorgeous butt."

"Laney!" Tessa gasped, pretending to be shocked at her friend's observation.

"Come on, I know you noticed too," she teased.

"Yeah ok, his butt ranks up there with his looks."

The both jumped when his voice came from nearby. "Here you go ladies, shrimp ring and wiener wraps. I hope my choice of appetizers doesn't offend you."

"It's perfect," remarked Laney, grabbing a wrap while Tessa skewered a shrimp and dipped it into the sauce.

"Oh and thanks, by the way," he added mysteriously to Laney.

Tessa and Laney looked at each other in confusion as if each could tell the other what they'd missed.

"For the butt compliment," he grinned as he turned to walk back the barbeque.

"Oh God," whispered Laney as she put her head down on the table in embarrassment. Tessa just giggled at her.

Laney peaked over at him and went even redder when she saw he was still grinning at her with a mischievous glint in his eyes.

When the steaks were ready, they ate and chatted about trivial things.

Along with steak and potatoes with all the fixings, he had also served a side of roasted vegetables, and crusty bread smothered in butter. The desert that followed was caramel apple cheesecake and biscotti served with a gourmet coffee that tasted heavenly. When he told them that everything was homemade, Tessa promptly proposed, making them all laugh.

As the evening continued, Alex piped some classical music through hidden speakers and they relaxed and talked about everything from their first dates to Tessa's writing career. He was such an easy man to talk to that they both felt extremely comfortable with him.

The night drew on and the lights strung over the deck did indeed turn out to be amazing. It was almost as if the three of them were in a world of their own. Tessa had to give the man credit; she didn't once feel as if she was a third wheel that night. He included her in every conversation he and Laney had and made her feel just as welcomed as Laney did. She really did hope everything went the way Laney had hoped. He seemed like such a wonderful man. The only thing nagging at her was why he was still single if he was so amazingly wonderful and incredibly sexy.

After a while, the nagging voice in her head insisted it have its way and she found herself blurting out, "Why aren't you married?"

"Tess!" Laney gaped, astounded.

Alex just smiled and looked down at the table. "No, it's ok. I don't mind answering that."

Laney glared at Tessa who shrugged apologetically.

"I actually *was* married to an amazing woman for just over ten years. She died of ovarian cancer four years ago. We never had any children."

Tessa closed her eyes, mortified. Laney started apologizing in a rush. "I'm so sorry Alex. For your loss and for Tessa's mouth..." she glared at Tessa again.

"No it's really ok. You have a right to know things like that if we are going to be seeing more of each other."

Laney stopped with her mouth open. "We are?"

He looked suddenly unsure and glanced at her. "If that's ok with you," he said quietly.

"Uhh...yeah. Of course. I'd love you...Oh God I mean *to*...I'd love to! Not that I'm ruling out the idea of love possibly in the future but..."

"Hon." Tessa interrupted her friend's speech, patting her on the knee. "I think he gets it."

Laney suddenly stood up. "May I use your washroom? I think I need to plaster some powder on before I blind you with my blushing."

Alex laughed aloud at that and gave her directions to the bathroom.

After she had gone, he looked at Tessa with a grin, shaking his head. "That friend of yours is quite amusing."

Tessa laughed. "Yes she's definitely one of a kind. I don't know what I'd do without her...or with her," she added with a grin.

"Would you like to go for a walk around the garden while we wait?"

Tessa frowned slightly. "But it's dark," she said hesitantly.

He smiled and walked over to the door, flicking a switch when he got there. The whole garden was bathed in soft light. She hadn't noticed before, but the rest of the garden had also been strung with lights, forming a path between the flowers.

Tessa threw aside the slight feeling of apprehension she had felt when he'd first asked, realizing how silly she was being. "Well that changes things," she joked. "I'd love to go for a walk. With any luck, by the time we make it around your whole yard I would have burned off some of the million calories I gained tonight."

He walked back and held his hand out to her, pulling her to her feet before letting go again. They headed off the deck and angled to the right toward a huge Weeping Willow that looked forlorn and beautiful at the same time. There was a small hill on the ground in front of it, lying peacefully below its long, droopy branches.

"What's this?" she asked as they got to it, feeling an unnervingly strange sense of déjà vu.

226

"You have no idea?" he asked quietly.

She looked at it again, images fluttering, but nothing sticking. "No."

He moved behind her. She tensed instantly at his next words. "It's a faery mound Tessa."

Her eyes went round in horror as she felt his hands grip her arms cruelly. "No," she gasped. It didn't make sense. The idea of a faery mound here – so far from Scotland – was so out of place that she couldn't get a grip on her thoughts. Nothing was making sense. Alex wasn't a faery...he couldn't be.

"Yes my beauty. King Teluth is quite anxious to see you. He plans to use you as bait for your precious MacLeod." His voice, though still velvety, had a mean twist to it now. God was this really the same man who had cooked them that fantastic supper and talked of his wife dying? She was hyperventilating now as he forced her forward toward the mound where she could now see a faint silvery line standing vertically from its base.

"Please," she pleaded, barely loud enough for her own ears to hear. Terror rocked through her, almost paralyzing her. "Laney."

"Don't worry about your friend, I'll be here to get her through her grief."

"No! Laney!" But again her voice was just barely above a whisper. Her throat felt like it had closed shut and she was struggling for air. Panic set in rapidly. He was incredibly strong and lifted her the rest of the way as if she weighed no more than a child, shoving her through the slit that hovered in the air. She disappeared without so much as a sound and he grinned as he stepped through behind her.

Tessa stumbled to her knees as soon as she was through. The darkness of night was suddenly replaced by a blood red sky, and the peaceful night was alive with screams of some kind of creature that didn't sound like anything she ever wanted to meet.

Before she could even make sense of what had happened, Alex appeared behind her and yanked her upright. "Come on Tessa, I don't have time to waste," he said harshly, dragging her along behind him.

"Please Alex," she begged as she tried to stay on her feet. "This isn't you. Please stop."

He stopped suddenly and pulled her around in front of him almost hard enough to give her whiplash and laughed harshly. "Oh my dear, I'm afraid you're mistaken. This is very much who I am. I'm an Unseelie faery Tessa. We are not known for our kindness where humans are concerned. I am, however, a very convincing actor which is why king Teluth assigned me the task of luring you out of your world. I've lived in the human realm for a long time now. It will be very simple for me to suddenly appear out of the woods, bleeding and sliced up, looking like I was tortured. Naturally I will have to comfort your darling friend, Laney, after she finds out what horrible things were done to you by that madman that attacked us and killed her dear friend." He tsk'd at this point. "Such a waste."

Tessa looked up at him in horror. Her mind refused to grasp what was going on. He was so completely different from the Alex she had known just five minutes before. How could someone so evil lie so absolutely convincingly?

"It's called glamour Tessa," he said. He had obviously read her mind which scared her immensely. "I simply made you and

Laney see what you wanted to see. You both wanted so badly to believe that I was a good, honest, and caring man. I used glamour so that you wouldn't see when I was getting annoyed at your stupid human thoughts and reactions." He looked at her curiously. "Why is it that you humans act so stupid around good looking people? Is that all your race cares about?"

It was obvious that he didn't want an answer to his question when he abruptly turned and started pulling her along behind him again.

She was trying so hard to keep her feet under her so that she wouldn't be dragged along the sand, that she didn't notice the other man until he was right beside her.

"Good job Alex," the man said in a commanding voice. "I knew I was right choosing you for the job."

Alex bowed low to the other fae. "Thank you my king, I am glad I have pleased you."

"And what of the other woman?"

"I will go back and say this one was killed by a madman."

The fae tossed a dagger to Alex who caught it deftly. The blade was a strange colour. "Make it realistic, I want no mistakes."

"Of course my king," he said softly with a look of resignation on his face as he bowed low once again.

"Go now! MacLeod will find out soon enough. I must deal her before they try to rescue her."

Bowing again, Alex turned and walked back the way he had come, leaving Tessa staring behind him in terror. She turned to look up at the king. He was just as good looking as Alex, but more imposing. Her brain had finally taken in all it could, and as she blacked out, Cailean's name whispered softly past her lips.

~16~

"*S*he has been taken, my king," said Onagh as he appeared beside king Finvarra with a worried look on his face.

Finvarra sighed heavily and shook his head. "This is going too far, even for Teluth." He had been dreading this news. Dreading what it meant would now happen.

Onagh stood silently beside him, robes flowing softly around him as if being caressed by a slight breeze. The sound and smells of the ocean floated around them, calm and peaceful; such a contrast to his heart which was now filled with chaos and misery.

"Where is she?"

"Past the Dark Hills, somewhere in the caverns," Onagh answered softly.

Finvarra sighed and shook his head.

"I will go, my king."

He looked up at Onagh with sadness in his eyes. "I know you will Onagh, that's what I fear."

"It must be done. I am the only one who is able to feel the human's spirit. I'm the only one who can find her."

He looked at Onagh, seeing a fae unlike any other, and beckoned him closer.

Onagh walked to him and knelt at his feet, head bowed.

After a moment, Finvarra placed his hand on his head and felt him trembled slightly. It was not often he touched anyone because of the power that coursed through him. It was often too much for one to bear, like a prolonged electric shock.

"I do not want to lose you Onagh," he Finvarra softly. "You are a son to me. Please be careful."

With that said, Finvarra removed his hand and Onagh stood. He had already shown more emotion than Onagh was accustomed to and didn't want to alarm him.

"I will return to you, my king," he promised softly before disappearing to find Oberon, who would accompany him to the Dark Hills.

Finvarra looked down at his clasped hands when Onagh left.

His heart ached at the thought of losing his long time companion. He had gone to dissuade Teluth the previous night but it had done no good. The Unseelie king was determined to rule their world and did not care much what happened to its current occupants or the humans. He warned Finvarra that any Seelie who tried to stop him would be killed on the spot, no matter who he was. He had also warned him that his men had gathered enough senk to make enough daggers to seriously deplete the Seelie's numbers, if not kill them off completely.

With a heavy heart, Finvarra looked out the window across from him. The sky was a pale blue with no clouds in sight. It never rained in his world, much to his disappointment. After spending time in the human realm he had grown to love the fresh smell of grass after a rainfall.

*   *   *

"Cailean!"

Colin's voice echoed up the stairs to Cailean's bedroom, waking him from a sound sleep. He groaned and turned over, pulling a pillow over his head to drown his brother out. A few minutes more. Was it that much to ask to get a full night's sleep for once? He and Colin had been at the McGowans' library for almost a week trying to find as much information on the Unseelie as they could. They had only just gotten home the previous night and Cailean had crashed immediately.

"Cailean?" the voice came from his doorway this time. Obviously Colin wasn't going to let him sleep any longer.

"What?" he grumbled.

"There's a woman on the phone who's babbling like a crazy person about a cute guy and a barbeque and I think I heard Tessa's name in there somewhere."

Instantly alert, Cailean pushed the pillow away from his head and looked at Colin with a confused frown. "Tessa?"

"Says she's her friend and she needs to talk to you immediately. Sounds really upset."

Cailean's heart dropped like a stone and he reached for the phone on his bedside table with a trembling hand. It wasn't possible! They couldn't have hurt her there!

"Hello?" he said into the phone as he held the cold plastic to his ear.

"Are you Cailean?" asked a panicked voice.

232

"Aye, and who would you be?"

"I'm Laney, Tessa's best friend. She's gone!"

It took Cailean a second to process what she said. "What do you mean gone?"

"I'm at my new boyfriends house...well I'm not sure if we are really going out yet or not, but his name's Alex and he lives in this huge house in Charleswood and he invited us over for supper which went great and all but then I went to the bathroom and when I came back she was gone...like completely gone, I couldn't find her anywhere."

Cailean forced his breathing to remain calm. "Is your boyfriend gone too?"

"Yes, that's what I'm saying...they both just disappeared. I checked his garage and his car is still here, I know because I parked in front of one garage door and when I checked inside the garage, there was one car in it and it was parked behind the second door, so he didn't go anywhere with it and my car is still here too."

Her voice hitched at this last part and she started sobbing into the phone. "Oh God what if something horrible happened to her. Tessa told me some stupid story about faeries or something, which I totally didn't believe at the time, but then I searched the house looking for them, thinking that maybe they came inside or something and I found some kind of weird looking robe of some sort that's kind of shimmery and obviously not normal, and notes on Tessa. He should not have any notes on Tessa because he had only met her once and that was only like a few days before when I first met him because I bumped into him in the mall and spilled coffee all over him."

She finally took a breath and Cailean heard her crying softly over the line.

"You said they were outside the house when you went to the bathroom?" he asked carefully.

She sniffed loudly. "Yes, I was only gone for like five minutes."

"What does the back of his house look like Laney?"

"Well," she began, confused. "It's pretty big, there's a deck and a hot tub and...oh and the lights were on in the garden, they weren't on when I went inside, so they must have gone for a walk around the yard or something...it's a pretty big yard."

"Laney, is there any kind of a hill or large mound of hard packed earth forming a large lump in the landscape?"

"Ummm I don't know...what does that have to do with anything?"

"'Tis very important Laney, please go check."

He could hear Laney walking and a door opening.

"There's a small hill like thing by the Weeping Willow."

Cailean's heart hammered in his chest. Colin was looking at him with a worried expression on his face. "What is this Alex person's last name?"

"Ummm, Fay?"

"Shit!"

"What? That's bad isn't it?" she yelled loudly enough for Colin to hear.

"Thank you for calling Laney, I have to go now but I'll call you as soon as I know anything." He took her number and hung up before Laney had a chance to ask him anything else.

"They have her?" said Colin softly, his hand gripping Cailean's bedpost so hard that his knuckles had turned white. It was more of a statement than a question.

He nodded, staring at the phone. "He told Laney his last name was Fae. He wanted us to know."

"Damn it!" yelled Colin, smacking the bedpost.

"I have to find her Colin."

"I'm coming with you. There's no way you are doing this alone."

"I canna ask you to do that..."

"You dinna ask, I told you I'm going!"

The discussion was over and Cailean dressed as fast as he could and they both ran out of the castle toward the faery mound.

Just before reaching it, they noticed a body lying on the ground near it. There was blood all over it and it was turned face down.

Cailean would have had a heart attack right there if the body hadn't been way too large to be Tessa's. They moved slowly, inching up on the unmoving form, torn between wanting to get to Tessa as fast as possible and needing to make sure it wasn't an ambush.

When they got close enough to recognize the clothes, they both let out an expletive and reached out to gently turn the body over.

"Onagh, can you hear me?" asked Colin, holding gingerly onto the fae's torn and bloody arm. They rested him gently on his back and Cailean leaned in to listen for a heartbeat.

"He's alive," he breathed in relief, "but barely. His pulse is very weak."

"Onagh, wake up. We need to know what happened to you."
Colin shook him gently.

Onagh's eyes opened partway and he gasped in a horrible wet
sounding breath. "I couldn't save her."

Cailean let Onagh go and dropped to the ground in shock, not
daring to believe that Tessa was dead. "No!" he whispered.

Colin looked at Cailean in disbelief, then back at Onagh
whose eyes had shut once again. "Onagh, is Tessa...dead?"

After what seemed like an eternity, Onagh shook his head
from side to side. Cailean released the breath he didn't realize he
had been holding and gasped for air. Oh God she was alive! He
shut his eyes in relief and hung his head between his legs, shaking
in relief.

"Dark Hills...Oberon dead. She's..." he paused and drew a
wet, rattling breath as blood dribbled out of his mouth. "...in a
cave...under the...Seven Sisters...ten guards."

He drew another wet breath before passing out again in
Colin's arms. "We need to get him inside and call Doctor
Bentley!"

Cailean jumped up and grabbed Onagh's legs while Colin got
him under the armpits and they carried him as gently as they could
manage into the house. They lay him on Tessa's bed, and Colin
called Dr. Bentley while Cailean gathered hot water and rags, as
well as a couple of the maids to help.

"Doc will be here within fifteen minutes. He said to keep him
calm and lying on his side to prevent the blood from choking him
too much. He said it sounds like his lung was punctured. We also
have to put pressure on as many of the deep wounds as possible to
keep him from bleeding out. The doc will bring some blood incase

he needs a transfusion, though I'm no' sure if his body will take human blood."

They wrapped pressure bandages on as many of the wounds as they could and the maids wiped as much blood off his face and body as possible so that the doctor could see his wounds better.

Because of the need to get Tessa as soon as possible, they left Onagh in the maids' capable hands and raced back to the mound, jumping though as soon as they got there.

It was daylight when they broke through to the faery realm, and the ocean was crashing softly against the shore. The sky was a pale blue and shared space with two suns and two moons that were all visible at the same time. No birds flew in the sky and there were no animals to be seen. It was complete silence except for the soft waves.

The peacefulness of the fae world calmed them somewhat and the atmosphere surrounding them made their worries start to fade. It was only Cailean's nails biting into the palms of this hands that kept his mind focused on their task. He grabbed Colin roughly by the shirt and tugged him along, snapping him out of his semi trance. "We need to go Colin," he said gruffly.

Colin shook his head and blinked a few times. "Wow, this feels weird."

Cailean looked at him, confused. "Haven't you been here before? When you were taken?"

"Nay," said Colin, shaking his head as if he was in a daze. "It dinna look anything like this."

"The only other time I've been here, I was zoned out for five days. It has a sedative-like effect on humans, makes them forget what they came here to do. A defence mechanism of sorts," he explained quickly. "The trick is to make sure you are feeling pain somehow. It helps you to keep your focus." He lifted his hands and opened his fists, showing Colin the deep nail marks in the palms of his hands. "Do it!"

Colin nodded and made fists too, forcing his nails to dig into his palms. The effect was immediate and his eyes cleared as his focus returned. "Ok, where to now?"

From what I remember, the Dark Hills are at the end of the beach. 'Tis better to no' try and think too logically in this place. What I understood from Finvarra the last time I was here, was that either end of this beach ends up being the Dark Hills which is the entranceway to the Unseelie world. If we turn and go in the opposite direction from the water, we get to the Seelie world. Walking into the water itself will take us back to our world.

"Well that's just weird," grumbled Colin.

Cailean shrugged. "Like I said, 'tis best to no' try to be logical here, and for God's sake make sure you stay in pain or you'll never make it to the water."

They both took a deep breath and started walking to one end of the beach. After about ten minutes, Cailean stopped. "This isn't working," he said worriedly. "We've no' moved an inch. That tree is still right beside us," he said as he glanced to the left.

Colin turned to look at the tree with a frown. "What are we missing?"

Cailean kicked the sand in frustration. "Damn it this is stupid!" he yelled. "I doona have the time to play games with this bloody place!"

Colin frowned and looked around him. "Cailean? You said it was better to no' think logically. Maybe we are supposed to play a game of sorts. Why no' try imagining where we are going while we walk? Like picturing the Unseelie world in our heads."

Cailean looked at Colin with a frown, thinking. "I guess it wouldn't hurt to try, except that I have no idea what it looks like."

"The sky is red, the ground dark, and there are big black looking hills all around."

A soft breeze blew through their hair, feeling more like a caress than wind. Colin yawned. "We'd better try now, I'm getting sleepy."

"Ok let's try it your way."

Colin yawned again and they started forward while imagining shadowy hills in the distance. As if by magic, mountains started taking shape in the distance, shimmery and vague at first, then more solid as they drew nearer.

Suddenly they were standing in a valley with dark, shadowy hills on either side. The sky above had turned a blood-red colour and the suns lost their shine in favour of the moonlight. It was like walking from daylight into night.

The sleepy feeling immediately left Colin and they both started feeling extremely anxious instead. "It feels like something is going to jump out at us at any second," whispered Colin.

Cailean nodded and looked around warily. "We need to find the Seven Sisters...whatever that is."

"Should we imagine it again?"

"Aye."

They started walking forward while imagining seven women standing side by side. Nothing.

Colin shook his head. "You think the Seven Sisters are mountains perhaps?"

"Let's try." They started forward again imagining seven mountain ranges in front of them. Nothing.

Cailean growled in frustration.

They decided to walk a little bit further to see if that took them anywhere, but they didn't seem to move, it was almost like being stuck in quicksand but without the drowning.

Cailean's eyes suddenly lit up. "Wait a minute, dinna Onagh say there was a cave?"

"Aye," agreed Colin, obviously not seeing where Cailean was heading with that question.

"So what if we imagine a cave with Tessa inside it?"

Colin raised his eyebrows, considering. "Sure. I doona have anything better."

This time when they started walking, a cave appeared in the distance. Above the cave was a huge metal ring that had what looked like seven metal crosses attached in equal spaces all around it.

"Of course!" exclaimed Colin in excitement. "The Seven Sisters are seven female symbols joined together."

They didn't rejoice for long though because almost immediately they noticed that the cave was indeed being guarded by ten powerful fae warriors. Each had a dagger in his hand, ready for combat.

The brothers heard a piercing scream come from the cave and Cailean gritted his teeth in anger.

Colin put a restraining hand on him. "Patience Cailean. We'll do no good if we race off without a plan to fight ten inhumanly strong fae."

He knew Colin was right, but he could barely concentrate when he thought about what they could be doing to her. What could cause her to scream like that? He shoved the thought out of his head and focused on making a plan. He was easily strong enough to take on at least five of the warriors with his new strength. It had only been a week since he'd had sex with Tessa and he found his strength hadn't diminished noticeably since then. Colin on the other hand would only be able to deal with one or two at once. They were outnumbered.

There was also the unknown...the warriors were holding daggers made with senk. He knew it slowed the fae's healing powers down to human speed. What would that do to a human? Immortal or not, it had to be bad.

Another scream pierced the air, causing Cailean to rise slightly. Colin stopped him again. "Think Cailean!" he ordered him.

Although he felt like punching something, he forced himself back into a crouch behind the large boulder and looked at Colin with pain in his eyes.

"We canna help her if we're dead Cailean. And there's no one else to come after her if we doona make it."

Cailean sighed heavily, glad for the sharp bite of his nails. He could feel wetness on his palms and knew that he had drawn blood. "The only thing I can think of is for us to either find our way to the Seelie and beg for help, or rush the guards and hope for the best."

"No!" The scream was laced with pain this time and Cailean pressed his fists to his eyes as his heart pounded in agony. "She might no' have time to wait," he said tensely. "We have no choice but to rush them."

Colin nodded in agreement.

After thinking it over for a minute, Cailean decided that he would attack first from one side to get their attention. Once they started attacking him, Colin would come from behind and start his own attack. With any luck they might live to save Tessa.

They looked at each other with sorrow in their eyes, and Colin took a deep breath. "If I doona make it..."

"Shut up you idiot, you know as well as I do that you'll make it." Cailean couldn't bear to hear the rest of what Colin had been trying to say.

"Let's go," he said. "I'll leave you one or two to fight so you doona feel too left out."

Colin grinned at him. "See that you do."

They each crept off in different directions and made their way slowly to the sides of the cave, hiding behind the rocks. After a few minutes Cailean suddenly walked out toward the guards and yelled, "Hey!"

The guards looked at each other in amusement, obviously thinking the human had a serious death wish. They all started to walk toward him when the leader yelled for two of the men to stay back and guard the cave. "The eight of us are more than a match for this stupid human," he said tauntingly.

Cailean narrowed his eyes at the leader. "Come get me then if you think I'm so pathetic."

The eight guards converged on Cailean and started lashing out with their daggers. One caught Cailean in the arm and a severe burning sensation spread down his forearm. The pain was worse than anything Cailean had ever felt in his life and his breath hissed between his teeth. The guard to his left laughed. "The human doesn't like that Orin. Looks like it hurt a little."

"Poor human," spat the one called Orin.

Cailean yelled as he lunged at them with a dagger of his own. He stabbed Orin straight in the heart. The warrior stopped and his jaw dropped as he looked down at his chest in surprise, watching the blood spurt out in sickening red streams. The others seemed fascinated with Orin's gushing wound as well and stared at him agape until the leader yelled in anger, snapping them out of it. "Stupid human! How dare you turn our own weapon on us?" He lunged at Cailean, who dodged him effortlessly, coming up beside him in time to slide the dagger into his ribs. The leader screamed in pain and frustration and spun round to attack again.

By this time Cailean had already spun round and whipped the blade of his dagger across another warrior's neck. The fae dropped to his knees in pain, grabbing his neck, gurgling. Within seconds he fell to the ground, dead.

The leader attacked again, along with two other warriors. Cailean was trying to figure out what to do when one of the warrior's eyes suddenly opened wide. He stopped in his tracks for a second before his eyes rolled back and he collapsed into a heap where he stood. Colin moved out from behind him grinning.

Cailean heaved a sigh of relief, and together the two of them finished off the remaining warriors, only getting minor cuts in the process.

When they were all dead at their feet, Cailean looked at Colin in confusion. "How did you deal with the two at the cave?"

"Wasn't so hard since they were staring at the fight instead of guarding the cave," he laughed. "You should have seen the insulted look they threw my way before they died."

Cailean grinned at his brother's obvious satisfaction and clapped him on the back. "Well the good news is that the bloody knife wounds hurt so much that I doona have to keep my fists clenched anymore."

A deep, threatening voice jolted them out of their celebratory mood and stopped them in their tracks.

"I have to admit MacLeod, I didn't think you had it in you to make it past so many guards, of course I didn't plan on your brother coming with you."

The brothers looked over in shock to see king Teluth standing at the entrance with his hand around Tessa's neck. She was white with pain and struggling to breathe as he squeezed.

"Let her go," yelled Cailean, starting forward.

Tessa's eyes bulged and she whimpered in pain, scraping ineffectually at the kings hand. Cailean stopped immediately.

"Oh don't stop on my account MacLeod," he grinned, as Tessa started to turn slightly purple.

Cailean looked into Tessa's eyes and in that one moment saw his life flash before him. Tessa was in every scene. He stood helplessly and watched her eyes roll to the back of her head as she tried desperately to take in a breath. Her knees gave out but she didn't drop. King Teluth's arm remained in position, as if she was as light as a feather.

"Drop her Teluth!" commanded a loud voice to their left.

They all turned in time to see king Finvarra appear out of nowhere. Teluth growled menacingly, dropping Tessa as he turned to face his enemy.

~17~

"*A*hhh, brother!" growled Teluth menacingly as he pulled a dagger from his belt.

Cailean and Colin looked at each other in shock. Brother?

Cailean called to Finvarra, and tossed his own dagger to him. He caught it gracefully as if it had been thrown in slow motion.

"So you have your little minions here for help. Seems a little unfair to me."

"You were never one to fight fair Teluth, why start now?"

"Oh I'm not concerned Finvarra, I just wondered what you would do if I killed one to make the playing field more even."

As he said that, he reared back and threw his dagger with deadly precision into Colin's chest.

Colin flew backward from the impact with a surprised grunt and landed with a jarring thud on the ground, a grimace of pain contorting his face.

Cailean look at the dagger sticking out of his brother's chest in shock. "Colin!"

246

"Pull it out Cailean, it burns like Hades," begged Colin as he lay prone on the dusty ground. His fingers dug into the dirt at either side of him.

Cailean ran to his brother, dropping to his knees by his side. He grimaced as he wrapped his hand around the dagger, sliding it out in one smooth motion. Blood pooled and soaked Colin's shirt in a matter of seconds.

He pressed his hand firmly to the hole in his brother's chest and his heart contracted at the thought of losing him.

Colin's breath hissed through clenched teeth. His eyes were shut and he swallowed convulsively, then grunted and opened his eyes again. "I'll be ok, just kill that bastard for me."

Cailean looked down at his brother in sympathy. He knew Colin had to be in an extraordinary amount of pain.

"Aww isn't that sweet," said Teluth, his words dripping with sarcasm.

Cailean gently replaced his hand with Colin's and stood up. Blood pounded through his veins and his vision narrowed so that all he could see was Teluth. He looked at the smiling fae with pure hatred and stepped forward. A haze of red spun around him as he took another step with deadly intent.

Before he could take another step he felt a firm, unmoving hand on his shoulder and a sudden jarring shock fly through him. He jerked back reflexively from the pain and his mind cleared for a second. He looked questioningly at Finvarra.

"Don't throw yourself to your death Cailean; I can take care of my brother alone."

Despite the rage that encompassed him, he knew Finvarra spoke the truth. He knew it was something he had to do alone. He shut his eyes, fighting for control, and nodded almost imperceptibly.

"So you want to kill me yourself?" asked Teluth menacingly, teeth bared in a snarl.

"If I must," answered Finvarra.

"Well then make your choice brother, because I have," growled Teluth right before lunging at him.

Finvarra sidestepped Teluth smoothly and shoved the dagger into his back, ripping a howl of indignant frustration from him.

Cailean watched as the two kings battled each other. They seemed to be an even match.

Leaning down he put his hand over Colin's wound again, noticing that his brother's hand had slipped. He pressed, causing Colin to grunt in pain and tense. The fact that Colin was still alive meant that the knife must have missed his heart. For at least that small amount of luck, he was thankful.

His eyes moved to where Tessa lay. She was looking at Colin with tears in her eyes. She knew that he had only come to make sure Cailean was safe. He knew her well enough to know that she'd take the blame of Colin's injury onto herself instead of where it rightly lay, with him. He should have moved faster to protect his brother. He knew that Tessa might also have been killed because of him, because he didn't have the foresight to see that she would be in danger no matter where she tried to hide, and that if he had let her stay in Scotland with him, they might have avoided the whole situation of her kidnapping.

Colin wrapped his hand weakly around Cailean's. "'Tis no' your fault Cailean. I know what you're thinking and you're wrong. The blame lies completely with Teluth."

248

Cailean looked down at his bother with sorrow in his eyes. His gaze slid to his chest. His own hand was covered in Colin's blood as he pressed against the hole the dagger had made. A flicker of sorrow crossed his face.

The battle continued in the background for a few more minutes until suddenly there was silence. Cailean looked around sharply and immediately sagged with relief when he saw Finvarra kneeling alone on the sandy ground. Blood was all over him and some of it dripped into the sand below, turning it red. Teluth was nowhere to be seen.

Finvarra looked at Tessa with an expression of pain on his handsome face as he put one hand on the ground to keep his balance. She raced over to him and touched his arm, jumping back with a surprised yell as a bolt of electricity ran through her body at the contact.

"What on earth?" she asked bewildered.

"You can't touch me Tessa," he whispered weakly.

"But I have to stop the bleeding," she cried anxiously.

He shook his head and his arm trembled with the effort it was taking to stay upright.

"Tessa," called Cailean from his brother's side. "Come take over for me so that I can help him."

She scrambled up and ran over to switch off with him.

Leaving his brother, he ran over to Finvarra who was shaking his head, "No Cailean, too much will kill you," he warned.

"I'm stronger now," he said as he made him sit, gritting his teeth in pain from the contact. "Besides, 'tis only bad when I'm in full contact with your skin."

After he got Finvarra onto his back, he ripped his own shirt off and tore it into pieces that he folded to press against the worst of the wounds. With the material between them, the shock was reduced tenfold and he was able to stop the blood.

"I need to know how to get us back to our world Finvarra, we have doctor there who can help you and Colin. He's already working on Onagh."

"Onagh? He's alive?" gasped the king, his eyes searching Cailean's.

"Aye, but badly hurt."

Finvarra sighed heavily in relief, a small smile on his face. "I thought...when he didn't return..."

"He came to tell us about Tessa, but he lost a lot of blood so we had to keep him in our world. Our doctor is good. He'll no' ask questions."

Finvarra nodded. "Ok."

"How do we get you back?" he asked again, slightly alarmed at Finvarra's white face.

"Think of the beach...walking into the water." He passed out at that moment and Cailean swore and looked over at Tessa where she sat with her hand pressed to Colin's chest.

"Tessa you need to think about the beach."

"What beach?" she asked confused.

"The one you saw when you first got here."

"There was no beach," she said confused and slightly panicky.

Cailean looked at her as if she were crazy. "What do you mean no beach?"

"When we went through the porthole we ended up in this horrible place."

"Damn it!" he growled. "The Unseelie must have a way of getting straight here."

"What do you mean?"

He sighed and looked around. "Ok. This will no' make much sense to you but you have to do what I say or you'll no' be able to get back."

She looked at him, horrified.

"This place doesn't follow a normal line of thinking. You have to imagine you're somewhere or going somewhere to get there."

"Well can I imagine I'm back at the castle?"

"No, it will no' work that way. You have to get back to the beach and then imagine walking into the water."

She looked at him as if he was crazy. "But I've never seen the beach."

"It may work if she's touching me when I think of it," said Colin with a grimace of pain.

Cailean's face lit up suddenly. "It just might, 'tis what I'd have to do anyway to try to get Finvarra back," he said looking down at the unconscious king.

"Ok good," said Tessa. "Then let's try it."

Colin gripped Tessa's hand and closed his eyes.

When Cailean opened his own eyes, they were all on the beach. He immediately relaxed.

"It's like the complete opposite of the other place," said Tessa in amazement as she sat with a dazed look on her face, looking around with a smile.

"Tessa," called Colin weakly, trying to get her attention. "Tessa focus."

She kept looking around as if she couldn't hear him. "God it's so beautiful here."

"Cailean!" said Colin urgently.

"Shit!" he groaned as he came to Tessa side, not at all liking what he was about to do.

He reached over and dug his nails purposely into her soft skin and cringed.

"Ow!" she yelled, looking accusingly at him as if she couldn't believe what he had done. "What was that for?" She tried pulling her hand away from his but he held his grip.

"Cailean you're hurting me."

"I'm so sorry lass. You must be in constant pain or your mind will wonder and you'll no' be able to leave this place. So please just dig your nails into your palm so that I can stop hurting you."

She held up her hand and showed him that she had done what he asked and he immediately let go. "I'm really sorry I had to do that lass."

"No..., it's ok." She immediately put her other hand back on Colin's chest wound, causing him to wince and grind his teeth.

She looked down at him apologetically and used her clenched hand to move the hair out of his eyes.

She turned to Cailean. "How's your patient doing?"

He looked down at the still unconscious fae and shook his head. "He's no' good, we have to get going. You need to hold on to Colin and imagine walking into the water."

She took a deep breath and closed her eyes. "Ok."

Within a second she opened them again and they were all back at the faery mound outside the castle.

She looked from Colin to the castle and back again. "Ummm Cailean, how do we get them inside?"

He looked down at the two men with a frown then turned and started running toward the barn. "I'll be right back," he yelled.

After a couple minutes, he came back with three other men, and together they lifted Colin and Finvarra carefully and moved them into the castle. They put both of them side by side on Colin's king size bed so that the doctor would be able to treat one while keeping an eye on the other. He never once looked surprised about the state of his two patients, and the only time he looked concerned was when he touched Finvarra and got the shock of his life.

He jumped back and flapped his stinging hand, looking questioningly at Cailean.

Cailean just shook his head at the doctors questioning look and told him that he would have to tell him what to do because the shock wasn't as bad for him.

Colin was stitched and bandaged in no time while the doctor calmly explained to Cailean how to clean and stitch Finvarra's wounds.

Once it was done, Cailean dropped into a chair with his eyes shut. The multiple shocks had taken a huge toll on his body and he breathed heavily as sweat dripped from his forehead.

Almost straight away he felt Tessa's soft hand brush through his hair. "Are you ok?"

He kept his eyes closed for a minute, imagining that they were alone and that nothing bad had ever happened. Imagining what life could have been like with her. He longed for peace. Longed to live like a normal man.

Tessa spoke again, this time with a hint of panic in her voice.

"Cailean?"

Not wanting to worry her, he pushed the pain away and looked up with a smile. "I'm fine, just tired." He took her hand in his and kissed it gently before pressing it to his cheek. "Thank you for all your help Tessa. One of them would have died if it weren't for you."

She snorted. "They wouldn't have been in that situation in the first place if I hadn't been stupid enough to get caught."

He looked up at her in surprise and tugged her into his lap. "Tessa! There was absolutely no way you could have known about Alex. We dinna even know."

She sighed and looked down at her hands. "Yeah but seriously? Alex Fae? I should have had some idea."

"No lass. He was being purposely obvious about it. Hiding in plain sight. Twas what he was counting on. Oh, that reminds me," he said abruptly. "You should call Laney to make sure she's ok. She was a wee bit panicked when she called."

"She called you? That's how you knew?"

"Apparently she started to believe your story when she found Alex's robe and some research he had on you. It wasn't a far leap from there."

"Oh the poor thing," she said, jumping up from his lap and reaching for the phone.

After talking to Laney for twenty minutes, she hung up and looked at Cailean who was waiting impatiently to hear her side.

"Alex apparently showed up with cuts all over him, spouting a story of being kidnapped and attacked by some madman. He told her I was dead and that he had tried ever so hard to save me. She said she would have believed him too, if she hadn't already found evidence of his obsession with me. He had gone upstairs right after appearing, on the pretence of cleaning his wounds, and must have hidden those things she found because the police never mentioned them. She didn't say anything to him because she was scared he would kill her too. Fortunately when he couldn't lead the police to me or show proof of any signs of a struggle they arrested him. He's in jail now."

Cailean frowned at the news.

"What? That's good isn't it?"

"Lass, no human jail is enough to hold a fae. All he has to do is bend the bars and he'll be out in seconds...or simply disappear for that matter."

The blood drained from Tessa's face. "What about Laney?"

"Laney's in need of protection, but as long as she dinna let on that she knows who he is, she should be relatively safe until she can get away from him."

Tessa immediately dialled Laney's number and almost dropped to the floor in relief when she answered. "Laney, you have to get over to Scotland right now. He can get out of jail."

"Oh my God, are you serious?"

"Yes Laney. I'm deadly serious. You need to leave your house right now and call the airlines on your way to the airport. And Laney, if you do see him before you can get away, play stupid. You don't know who or what he is ok."

"Oh God, oh God. Ok I'm leaving now. Do I have time to pack?"

"LANEY! Get out!"

Laney almost screamed in fear. "Ok I'm gone! I'll call you when I get a flight."

She hung up before Tessa could say anything else and she and Cailean stared into each other's eyes, trying to figure out what to do.

*   *   *

"Shit! How the hell did I end up in this mess?" she asked herself as she ran downstairs, grabbed her keys and ran for the door.

She got as far as the hallway before she slammed into something big and hard. She bounced back with a scream and would have fallen to the ground if Alex hadn't grabbed her arms. "Laney, are you ok?"

She stared into his eyes in horror. *How did he get here that fast? Oh crap, her life was over.* He shook her gently. "Laney? What's wrong?"

Think! Oh God think of something. Say something damn it! "Uh..." *Crap what a time for her brain to take a vacation.* "How did you get here so fast?"

He looked confused for a second before his eyes narrowed suspiciously. "What are you talking about?"

"The ah...the police called and said they were releasing you," she rushed on. "I was just racing over to get you."

He continued to frown at her, obviously trying to figure out what was going on. "They did?"

She tried to force her breathing to calm down a little, she was practically panting from fear. "Yeah, just a minute ago. Did you take a taxi?"

He nodded hesitantly. "Yes, I'm surprised they only just called you."

"Well they said they didn't have enough to hold you on, which is pretty obvious. It was ridiculous for them to even accuse you in the first place. They are actually lucky you got here before I left or they would have had an earful from me." She changed her tone so that she sounded indignant enough about what he had been put through.

"I'm confused Laney, aren't you upset about Tessa?"

Her heart stopped. He was right! She should be a wreck, barely able to function. Her best friend had just been murdered.

She looked up at him, allowing tears to well up and her chin to tremble slightly.

"Don't!" she whispered as she turned away from him. "I can't..."

As if he suddenly realized his mistake, he quickly turned her back around and pulled her to his chest, whispering into her ear. "I'm sorry, that was stupid of me. I'm so sorry."

Almost giving herself away with a sigh of relief, she forced her arms around his waist and really imagined how it would feel to lose Tessa so that she could do a good job of the tears.

He held her and rubbed her back in what he must have assumed was a comforting gesture. She tried not to cringe in disgust and focused even more on her pretend loss, managing to get some good sobs in.

Alex led her to the couch and made her sit while he disappeared into the kitchen to make her some tea.

As soon as he was gone, Laney yanked her cell out of her pocket and sent a text to Tessa, praying that she would receive it. Typing two simple words in, she pressed the send button, erased the sent message and jammed her phone back into her pocket.

257

* * *

Tessa's cell buzzed in her pocket just as she leaned over Onagh to check his temperature. It had been so long since she had gotten a text message or even a phone call on her cell that she jumped in surprise when it vibrated, almost stabbing the thermometer into Onagh's nose. He looked at her warily.

"Sorry," she said with an apologetic grin as she calmly placed it under his tongue.

Wrestling her phone out of her pocket, she flipped it open to read her text and immediately froze in horror. The two words that comprised the message made the blood drain from her face.

alex here

"Oh God," she gasped as her knees gave out, causing Onagh to reach for her instinctively. He jerked forward, caught her and gasped in pain as the stitches on his abdomen ripped open.

Immediately realizing what she had done, she stood again and forced him to lie back, yelling for the doctor. He let out a strangled curse as his face drained of colour. A few seconds later the door burst open and Cailean appeared with the doctor on his heels.

"I'm sorry, I fell and he grabbed for me...his stitches ripped and Alex is with Laney."

Cailean jerked his head back to her while the doctor ran to his patient's side and pressed down on the wound to stop the bleeding that had started up again.

"What did you say?" he demanded, grabbing her arms.

"She sent me a text a second ago." She held up her cell so that he could see the two words that had instantly changed her world. Her hand was shaking violently. "Oh God Cailean, what are we going to do?"

"Doona text her back," he warned. "We doona want him to know she got a warning to us. Since she's obviously still alive it means that so far she has managed to fool him."

"Oh God." Tessa paled at the words 'still alive'.

Cailean pulled her to him and held her. "She'll be ok lass."

Tessa pressed her face to his warm, naked chest, tears sliding down her cheeks. What would she do if she lost Laney? That thought was just too unbearable. She and Laney had been friends since they were teenagers. They had gone to the same high school, been there for each other through breakups and deaths, and complained to each other about each wedding they were forced to attend as bridesmaids. She had no idea how to have a life without Laney in it. Her heart ached, and her head throbbed. She had to figure out a way to help her friend. She was a genius after all, there had to be something she could think of. How did those faery portholes work anyway? If Cailean was able to get to Canada through it, he could possibly get there as soon as five minutes from now. If the stupid murdering fae could do it, there had to be a way.

"Cailean," she said suddenly, looking up. "Can you use the faery mound to get to her?"

He frowned as he considered it. "Well I had no' thought of that, but I suppose it only makes sense that if Alex could deliver you to the faery realm through it that I should be able to get to the porthole at his house as well."

She looked up at him with hope in her eyes, praying that this was the answer.

Cailean looked over at Onagh and noticed the doctor looking at them with one eyebrow cocked and the needle he was currently using to re-stitch Onagh with, frozen in mid-air. They had forgotten he was in the room.

"Ah..." Cailean began, but the doctor held up his hand, shaking his head to stop him.

"I doona want to know Mr. MacLeod, because if for one minute I even thought to entertain the idea that what you are saying might actually exist, I'd never sleep again." With that, he finished with Onagh and left the room to tend to Finvarra and Colin. Onagh chuckled at his departure then grimaced in pain.

"So?" Cailean asked, looking at him expectantly.

"Yes you can do it," he assured them. The only problem is that I don't actually know what the thought is that would get you to Alex's porthole."

Tessa's heart fell. "Of course. Only an Unseelie would know something like that."

Onagh nodded sadly. "I'm sorry. I wish I could be of more help."

"Wait a minute!" Tessa said excitedly. "Didn't you tell me that Colin was rescued by an Unseelie woman?"

"Yes..." said Cailean.

"Do you know how to find her?"

"Colin can," said Onagh from the bed. "He's seen her. All he has to do is go through the porthole, remember what she looks like and he will automatically be taken to where she is."

Cailean frowned. "Right into the dragon's lair."

Onagh shifted uncomfortably. "Well...it's not without danger of course."

"Even if he could find her, there's no guarantee that she would help us."

"Well actually, I'd say that there's very little chance of that indeed," said Onagh honestly.

Cailean sighed. "I suppose any chance is better than none at all...if Colin is willing to do it."

"Of course I'll do it."

They all turned to see him grinning from the doorway. "After all, I had to miss most of the last fight. I'm still a wee bit pissed about that."

Tessa went over to him and hugged him gently, careful of his stitches. "Thank you Colin," she said softly.

He grinned even more and hugged her with one arm. "Anything for you luv."

~18~

"*A*ll set?"

Cailean handed his brother the senk dagger which he put in a holder on his forearm that was covered by a loose, long sleeved cotton shirt.

"As ready as I'll ever be," he answered in a confident voice.

"Stick to the plan Colin," Cailean warned. "Find her. Convince her to tell you. Get back here."

Colin laid a hand on his brother's shoulder. "I'll be fine Cailean."

He nodded and gave him a slight smile. "I know."

"All right then, be right back," he said as he turned and walked toward the porthole, disappearing instantly.

"Will he really be ok?" asked Tessa, her voice choked with fear.

"He's a strong warrior lass. He'll do fine."

He put his arm around her shoulders, pulling her closer and she nestled her head against his chest and sighed.

"You need to get some sleep Tessa, you've been up forever."

"So have you," she complained.

He sighed and shook his head at her in amusement. "Ok fine, we'll both lie down for a bit until Colin returns." This seemed to appease her and she went with him back to the castle.

They dragged themselves to his room and lay down under the soft sheets. He had to admit that they felt like heaven at that moment.

Tessa turned and snuggled into him, her leg sliding across his thigh, causing an immediate response that he tried to ignore.

He thought he had everything under control until she shifted and moved her leg again. He felt the heat of her knee glide against his throbbing erection and inhaled sharply.

"Cailean?" she asked, tilting her head to look at him.

Ok concentrate. "Aye?" He kept his eyes closed.

"I was wondering..." she trailed off.

He was just trying to decide if he should ask what she was wondering of if she had fallen asleep mid sentence when he felt her hand slide slowly down his chest and past his stomach. She pulled his kilt up and wrapped her hand firmly around him, wrenching a gasp from him that turned into a grunt from the intensity of the feeling.

He opened his eyes and looked down at her. Her teeth were pressed into her bottom lip and she was looking up at him with a wicked gleam in her eyes. It took only that one look for him to push her back against the bed. He found her mouth with his and thrust his tongue between her tantalizing lips. She was giving as good as she got and within seconds every thought in his head was replaced by the one telling him to get away from her hand so that he could slid into her and end his torment.

He moved his hand down to hers and tried to pull her away from him but she hung on tighter and started sliding her hand up and down. They rhythmic motion felt like heaven. He groaned as desire shot through him like a knife, making him jerk forward in her hand.

She turned onto her side and lifted her leg over his thigh so that with each stroke he slid into slightly, but because her hand stayed wrapped around him, he couldn't get any further.

God and this woman was a virgin up until two weeks ago? She was driving him crazy and she knew it. It was like it heightened her excitement to control him in this way.

When he finally decided she'd had her way long enough, he pushed her away and pulled off her clothes. She grinned and allowed him to pull her underwear off, lifting her hips in an effort to help.

When she was well and truly naked, he leaned back for a moment and drank in the sight of her body before dragging her into his arms and kissing her deeply, his tongue hot and hungry in her mouth. She moaned as his tongue caressed hers and groaned when he pressed himself firmly against the vee of her thighs, his own thighs on either side of her legs, making it impossible for her to open for him. She struggled against him, making him hotter and harder as he thrust against her, teasing.

"Please Cailean," she begged as she dragged her nails down his back, making him shiver and thrust against her involuntarily. He growled softly and pressed his lips against her neck, nipping softly one second and soothing with kisses the next.

He allowed one of her legs to escape, but kept the other firmly between his thighs. After a few seconds he realized that his decision had been a mistake. She wrapped her free leg around his hips and pulled him against her very effectively.

He pulled his head back and looked down at her, breathing heavily. Her eyes were clouded over with desire as she looked back at him, her lips parted.

Her soft panting became more frantic as she continued to push herself closer to the brink against his leg, and he thrust hard against her thigh with a groan when her nails dug into his back. Tessa kept up the pressure as she slowly dragged her nails further down his back. By the time she had reached his butt he suddenly found himself pushing against her soft, wet heat, completely oblivious to the fact that he had somehow let her other leg escape. It was only when he felt both legs wrapped tightly around his waist, forcing him to slide into her that he realized what had happened. Damn she was good.

She was bringing them both to the brink without any help from him whatsoever, using her legs to force him into her. He groaned in surrender and started pumping into her in earnest, dragging gasps of pleasure from her each time he thrust.

"Cailean," she whispered, seconds before she arched against him and screamed with the intensity of her release. He drank her scream into his mouth, kissing her savagely until he was almost mindless with need. Finally - unable to stop himself - he plunged into her once more and felt his orgasm tear through his entire body, his seed pumping into her with each shuddering contraction of her body.

When he finally stilled, she rubbed her hands soothingly along the burning lines on his back. They were already starting to heal.

He brushed his lips gently against hers, kissing her tenderly. "I love you lass."

Her hands stilled on his back and he felt her breathing stop for a second. He tensed, knowing he shouldn't have said that. He cursed himself for his foolishness.

"I love you too Cailean," she returned tentatively.

He raised up on his forearms and looked her in the eyes, confused. "What about Aiden?"

"Aiden?" she asked incredulously, looking even more confused than he felt. "It was over with Aiden before I first met you."

"What?" he asked in shock.

She grinned at him. "Yes. I left him because I caught him with another woman."

Cailean frowned immediately. "Stupid fool!"

"I'm glad he was," she laughed. "I would never have met you otherwise."

He smiled at her, his eyes glittering in the dim light. "I owe him dearly."

Tessa grinned and pulled him down for another kiss.

And what of my promise never to fall in love again? He shrugged mentally at the question. He would find a way to deal with anything that may come. For now, he would enjoy what time he had with the most fascinating woman he had ever met.

Feelings crashed through him that he had never imagined. Feelings of happiness and love. The relief of acceptance.

"What are you thinking?" she asked with a shaky laugh.

He looked at her with passion in his eyes and slid his thumb across her smooth cheek. "I'm thinking that I've done the one thing I promised myself I'd never do."

"Oh and what's that?"

"Fall deeply in love with a mortal."

He leaned down again and kissed her softly, running his tongue along her kiss-swollen lips. "Tessa Anderson. I will love you for as long as I live."

He kissed away the tear that crawled slowly down her cheek and started sliding himself into her again. She closed her eyes in pleasure and matched him in his exquisitely slow thrusts.

* * *

Once Colin arrived in the faery realm, he immediately dug his nails into his palms and imagined Kynleigh. Within seconds, he was standing in a dark bedroom looking at the woman herself as she lay sleeping soundly.

He wondered how much trouble he would be in when she woke up and saw a human staring at her. Thinking about that for a moment, he decided it would be a wise idea to move to the other end of the room before making his presence known.

This turned out to be a very good idea because once he called her name, she was out of bed and across the room with a dagger at his throat, all within seconds.

"Please..." was all he could manage before he felt a tiny drop of blood trickle down his neck.

She frowned, recognizing him, and released the knife's pressure on his throat fractionally.

'What do you want human? Was it not enough that I freed you...do you have a death wish now?"

"I need help."

"I gave you help!" she growled menacingly.

"I need to know how to get to Alex's porthole."

"Why should I help you again? Are you under the impression that I need another complication in my life?"

"I just need the image...please. Cailean will no' help defeat Teluth's army until the woman Alex has is safe."

She growled and let him go, turning away from him. "I knew helping you would turn around to bite me in the ass, as you humans say."

He reached out to touch her shoulder. "Kynleigh..."

She spun round and shoved at his chest. "Don't touch me human."

Colin grunted in pain and doubled over, grabbing the edge of the table with one hand in his attempt to stay upright, and his chest with the other. In his mind he saw the pain as a bright white light starting from his chest and arcing its way through his entire body. Sweat immediately beaded on his brow and he did his best to take a breath.

Kynleigh looked at him in shock, not sure what kind of game he was playing.

He went down on one knee, face contorted in a painful grimace, struggling for that elusive breath.

Little by little he managed to take in tiny gasps of air. He rested his forehead on the arm that was still gripping the table tightly and focused on his breathing.

"MacLeod?" whispered Kynleigh hesitantly, reaching out a hand but not quite touching him.

He couldn't answer her. He tried, but the pain took away his ability to speak.

She shifted from one foot to another anxiously, as if unsure what to do. "Are you really hurt?"

He nodded slowly. His face had gone completely white and his breathing was shallow, hissing between his clenched teeth.

"Is it your heart?"

He shook his head.

She knelt on the floor in front of him, putting her hand on top of the one he was gripping the table with.

Slowly, he started to feel his muscles relax. Inch by inch his tension eased slightly, and within a minute, although the pain was still there, it had eased to a tolerable level because it wasn't being made worse by the tensing of his muscles around the wound.

He raised his head slowly and looked into her eyes in astonishment. "Did you do that?"

She nodded and kept her hand on his. "Are you able to sit in the chair?"

"I think so."

She put her other hand out and he let go of his chest to grab hold of it. With her help he managed to stand up enough to slide into the chair behind him. When he let go she looked at her hand with a frown.

"You're bleeding," she said simply before turning and leaving the room.

He looked after her with a confused frown. Well that was weird. Was she offended by his blood? The pain was back now that she wasn't touching him, but it wasn't as bad now that he had gotten past the tensing up part. He pulled his bloody shirt away from his chest and looked at his stitches. None had ripped. The blood was probably the result of the hit and because his heart had started pounding like a drum from the pain. Good God that had hurt.

She re-appeared a couple minutes later with a soft white cloth and a bowl of water which she set on the table next to him.

"Use that to..." she motioned with her hands, "wash." He noticed her hand was clean once again. She didn't seem to want to touch him any more than was necessary.

"Thanks," he managed, before dipping the cloth in and squeezing it out. He sucked in a pained breath when the water touched the wound, but grit his teeth and continued until it was cleaned off.

She picked up the bowl and disappeared for another few minutes before returning with a gauze bandage and some tape.

"Put this on it," she commanded, thrusting the items at him.

He looked at her a little confused and took the items, careful not to touch her.

After he had gotten it secured, thanking God he didn't have much chest hair to contend with, he looked back at her and frowned. "You doona like being touched do you?"

"No," she said simply, not volunteering an explanation.

"Why?" he insisted.

She frowned at him and moved to sit on the edge of her bed.

He looked at her walking away and wondered what would make such a strong woman so skittish about touching humans.

"It's not just humans," she said.

"You read minds?" he asked, shocked.

"Yes, that too," she sighed. "I also feel pain that others are feeling and have the ability to take it into myself. If I'm touched by surprised, it's like a very unpleasant shock that goes through me. I don't like it, but I realized that since I was the one who hurt you, it was only right that I reduced your suffering."

He looked at her surprised. He had thought that all Unseelie were heartless and cruel.

"That's not true," she replied to his thought. "We were banished because of who we followed, but just because one agrees with another doesn't mean that they are completely without morals and ethics."

"Well then why did you follow Teluth?"

"He wanted a world where we could exist without hiding. He spoke of freedom, and for most of us, that was all we had ever wanted. We went willingly. It was only after that some of us realized what kind of an impact our supposed freedom would have on the lives of humans. By that time it was too late, we had been banished with Teluth and had no way of proving that we believed the humans should remain unhurt."

"Why don't you just tell king Finvarra that you've changed your mind?"

"Finvarra chooses not to believe the few of us who have tried. He thinks it's Teluth's version of a Trojan horse, and he would be right in some cases, but not all...not mine." She said this part softly as she looked at the ground, obviously upset.

"There has to be a way to find out who is sincere. You said you read minds, isn't there a Seelie equivalent of you? Can someone no' read your mind to know the truth?"

She shook her head sadly. "Only a fae with both the power to read minds and emotions as well can know for sure. They have to feel the truth behind the words that are thought because a mind reader can only read the thoughts that a person purposely puts in their head. If one wishes to deceive a mind reader and are strong enough, they only have to think the words that will do it. Confusing one who reads emotions is even easier because although they can feel what the person is feeling, that person may not be saying what they feel."

"And there are none other than you who can do both?"

"As far as I know, I'm the only one."

He saw what she was getting at. "And Finvarra can't take the word of an Unseelie."

"Exactly."

He thought about that for a moment before looking up with a smile. "Do you no' think 'tis possible that he might have no choice but to believe you if you are helping us to defeat Teluth?"

She frowned and looked away.

"What?" he asked, confused. By all rights she should be happy about this news.

"Teluth...well..."

"What Kynleigh?"

"He's my lover. My partner for all intents and purposes. Even if I helped you, Finvarra couldn't be certain whether or not I did it because of a plan Teluth had that just didn't work."

Colin was now thoroughly confused. "How could you be with someone you believe is doing something so wrong?" he asked quietly.

She looked at him with a sneer. "And is everything you do honourable, human?"

He was taken aback by that answer.

"Have you not taken lives for a reason you thought was right?"

"'Twas to protect humans," he argued, rising to his feet.

"From what? A perceived threat...something someone told you was going to happen?"

"Well...aye," he admitted, realizing how stupid that must sound.

"Did you even bother to get information from the other side before agreeing to mercilessly kill fae?"

He shook his head slowly, a small thread of doubt entering his mind. It was a most unpleasant feeling.

"Teluth believes that building an army is for the good of the fae. Finvarra is content to sit back and wait. He too thinks that what he does is for the good of the fae. But who is right? Should we or shouldn't we have an army to protect us incase the humans stumble upon a way to deceive us? Shouldn't we have an army to protect us from the Seelie who attack, believing their intentions noble?"

"Teluth wants to kill fae to rule Basteerus and eventually earth, Finvarra does no' want that...'tis pretty clear to me who's on our side," argued Colin.

"Who said Teluth wants to kill humans?" she asked softly.

"Finvarra," he said, frowning at that answer.

"How do you know you can trust Finvarra?"

He thought that over for a while. "'Twasn't Finvarra who tried to kill me," he said, pointing at his chest.

"Did you never wonder why he just didn't give the order for the human, Tessa, to be killed on the spot?"

Colin didn't like this. She was making him question everything he believed. Why didn't Teluth kill Tessa immediately? Cailean would have come searching regardless. Tessa was of no use to Teluth after her capture.

"That's correct," she said.

He didn't like the fact that she could read his thoughts, see him question himself.

"All you have to do is ask and I will stop," she said.

"Stop."

"As you wish."

"Right! And I'm supposed to believe you would just stop like that?"

"It takes effort to read minds, and is quite tiring and unpleasant...I prefer not to do it," she said simply.

Colin ran his fingers through his long hair and sighed in frustration. He sat down again and looked at Kynleigh. She was beautiful even by fae standards. Her bright silver eyes stood in stark contrast to her long raven coloured hair, and her smile was mesmerizing. He'd only seen her smile once, very briefly during their conversation.

"Are you denying that Teluth has killed humans on purpose?" he asked pointedly.

"No. I am saying that he does what he believes is right to achieve a goal that he thinks is best for all fae."

"He tried to kill me!"

"He was outnumbered."

274

Colin sighed. He was obviously getting nowhere with the woman.

"Weeping Willow," she said tiredly.

"What?" Now he was confused. What did a Weeping Willow have to do with anything?

"What you came for."

He looked at her for a moment, wondering why she suddenly chose to help him after all.

"I will not help you again, so do not ask."

He nodded, understand how hard it was for her to help at all, knowing the possible outcome. "Thank you Kynleigh."

She nodded and turned, climbing back into bed. When she was lying down again, she pulled the sheets up to her neck and closed her eyes. He could see the strain on her face and wondered what was going through her head at that moment.

After a few seconds, he closed his own eyes and pictured a Weeping Willow. When he opened them he was standing in the dark under a tall tree, facing the back of a huge house with a deck.

Satisfied that she had given him the correct image, he turned and walked back through the porthole. As soon as he found himself on the pale white sand, he walked into the water and out of the porthole at his castle. Cailean and Tessa were waiting for him impatiently.

*   *   *

"Good Lord 'tis about time Colin," yelled Cailean in relief. "Did you get lost?"

Tessa gasped. "Colin what happened to you? You're bleeding!"

"No, 'tis no' bleeding anymore, I just bumped it."

"Are you sure you're ok?" asked Cailean worriedly.

"Really I'm fine, but there's something we need to discuss before you leave."

Cailean and Tessa looked at each other in confusion and turned to follow Colin to the castle where they watched him grab some buttered bread, hungrily stuffing it into his mouth. He downed that with a full glass of milk before speaking.

"There's a small chance that Teluth may no' be as bad as we were led to believe."

"What?" yelled Cailean angrily. "Did you hit your head?"

Colin sighed. "I know 'tis hard to believe...I still doona, but the fact is that Teluth dinna kill Tessa when he had the chance, he dinna kill me when I was first captured, and as far as we know...Tessa's friend is still very much alive and well."

Tessa and Cailean both looked at each other in surprise.

"He's right," she whispered.

Cailean shook his head. "Nay! He dinna kill you that time, Colin, because he was using you as a lure to get me, but he did throw a knife at your chest first chance he got. He did try to kill Tessa but Finvarra distracted him, and if we doona get to Laney, she will probably be killed as soon as Alex realizes that she knows about him."

"Cailean...just think about this objectively for a minute. Kynleigh can read minds and emotions...she says that Teluth truly believes that what he's doing is best for the fae and that he has no plans to kill off humans. He just wants us all to live side by side. Finvarra is against this and is trying to stop Teluth from building his army so that it'll never happen. The army is supposed to protect them from any humans or Seelie who doona like the idea of fae living among humans."

Cailean shook his head. "Uh uh...nay. Colin I'm sorry but even if that were the case, the fabric between our worlds is there to protect humans from being taken advantage of by the fae. What human...besides us of course...can hold their own against a fae? In two weeks they'll rule our world completely."

Colin thought about this while chewing on the end of a carrot. It made sense that humans wouldn't stand a chance against the fae if they were planning to overrule them. Maybe the real question was why Teluth was so determined to live among humans in the first place. What was wrong with his own world? He wished he had some answers. It was all too confusing.

"Colin," said Cailean gently. "Did you ever think that maybe Kynleigh was saying these things to get us out of the way? That maybe 'tis all part of Teluth's plan?"

Colin nodded in agreement. "But what if she was telling the truth?"

"Then I guess we'll deal with that when we get there. For now the most important thing is getting Laney away from Alex just incase I am right."

"Aye," he said sadly.

Tessa heaved a sigh of relief.

~19~

*C*ailean gave Tessa a kiss, promising to return quickly, and turned to walk into the porthole. From the beach he found himself standing beneath a huge Weeping Willow, looking at Alex's back porch. He had gotten Laney's address from Tessa and was given instructions on how call for a taxi.

Breaking into Alex's home, he quickly found a phone and made his call.

While he was waiting, he decided to take a look around. He rooted through Alex's personal documents for about fifteen minutes before hearing a honk from below the window.

He got into the white taxi and gave the man Laney's address, asking to be dropped off a block away. The cab driver didn't question him, just drove off toward her home whistling some tuneless melody while Cailean sat in the dark wondering about Colin's words. Was it even possible that Teluth may not be as bad as they were led to believe? He knew without a doubt that it was impossible to expect the fae, especially the Unseelie, to live peacefully among humans, but was there even a slight possibility that Teluth could be persuaded to call off his plans without any bloodshed? He hadn't seemed too inclined toward peace when he threw his dagger at Colin. The terror of that moment still caused chills to run through him. Just the fact that he had come so close to losing his beloved brother made him shake in anger.

No! Teluth wasn't about to sit and peacefully discuss anything. He and Colin needed to talk to Finvarra to find out what exactly was going on and what all the options were, but first he had to try to get Laney away from Alex without him suspecting anything was up.

The cab driver pointed out Laney's house as he drove by, and as he was told, dropped Cailean a block away. He paid the man generously and started walking back toward her house, keeping carefully to the shadows.

At the edge of her property, he slipped quietly into the trees and made his way around the house, looking through the windows as he went. Somewhere nearby a dog barked.

As he approached the living room window, he saw shadows moving on the ceiling as the occupants moved around inside.

Peaking over the sill, he saw a woman who he presumed was Laney, sitting at a table with a tea cup in her hands. She was frowning as she looked down at it. The woman had long blonde hair that was draped over her shoulders, hiding most of her face. After about a minute, a tall man with short black hair, who he assumed was Alex, walked out of the kitchen toward her and put his hands on her shoulders from behind.

Cailean tensed, waiting for him to do something. When he started to massage her shoulders he relaxed a little. She didn't look up at him and didn't seem to be talking, but Cailean could see her fingers tighten slightly on the cup she was holding on to. Alex suddenly leaned down and said something into her ear. She nodded without raising her head and he turned and went back toward the kitchen, leaving her alone to strangle her cup.

He had to figure out a way to get her out of there, or alternately, to get Alex out of the house.

Cailean stiffened when he heard a sound nearby and spun round to find a small cat picking its way through the flowers toward him. It stopped at his sudden movement, arching its back and hissing softly. He blew out a sigh of relief and stooped down, putting his hand out to the wary cat.

After three minutes of staying perfectly still, the cat decided that Cailean obviously meant no harm and sauntered over, allowing him the honour of scratching it between the ears.

Cailean had spotted a doggy door when he first circled the house and he picked up the cat and headed toward it, planning on shoving it through to cause a distraction.

The cat didn't like that idea at all and as he tried to push the squirming little beast through, it did its best impression of an octopus by grabbing onto every part of the frame it could find. Eventually Cailean had enough and just shoved it through roughly, holding the door closed against it as it tried to get back out.

Finding its escape route blocked, the cat let out a horrible yowl.

Cailean stayed crouched in front of the doggy door waiting to see who would come to investigate the stray that was screaming bloody murder in the house.

He heard a chair scrape against wood, then quick soft footsteps moving toward the door. Behind those he heard heavier steps and knew Alex was coming too.

"Oh baby, where did you come from?" asked Laney in a soothing voice.

The cat just yowled its indignation at being shoved through the door and hissed loudly.

"Don't Laney," said a deep male voice. "It might have rabies."

"Oh don't be silly," she scoffed. "The poor thing's just scared that's all."

"Well either way, be careful or it will scratch you. Here let me..."

Cailean heard the muffled sound of something soft hitting the floor, and the cat's yowling got even worse.

"I'll just wrap it up and put it outside."

"Well be gentle, I don't want the little thing to have a heart attack, he's scared enough as it is."

Cailean waited until the door had been unlocked and opened a crack before hurling himself through it, throwing Alex off his feet and into the wall behind him with a bone jarring thud."

Laney screamed and backed away, eyes flying from Alex to Cailean in terror, not knowing which one was the better of two evils.

"Laney get outside," he yelled, praying that hearing him say her name would make her realize she could trust him.

Alex growled in anger and then swore loudly as the cat scratched him deeply from his cheek to jaw in its desperate attempt to get away.

To Laney's credit, she didn't hesitate for even half a second before she was out the door and running.

Satisfied that she was safe for the moment, Cailean rammed his full weight against Alex who had just stood up. He yelled in anger as he went flying again. The two of them fought for a full five minutes before Cailean remembered that he had a dagger in his sporran. After another five minutes, he finally found the opportunity to pull it out. Alex stopped dead in his tracks when he realized what was under his chin.

Cailean forced him to back up and shoved him into a chair.

"You must be the famous MacLeod," Alex spat out angrily.

"And you must be the stupidest fae I've ever met," countered Cailean, drawing a growl of anger from the enraged faery.

"What are you going to do with me?"

"I want answers."

"I have none to give you," he ground out.

"Then you'll die," Cailean replied calmly, knowing he couldn't let him live and hope to get away alive.

Alex narrowed his eyes and looked at Cailean closely. "You would kill an unarmed man?"

"Nay," assured Cailean. "But you're a faery...there's a huge difference there."

Suddenly Alex didn't look too sure.

"What do you want to know?" he finally asked.

"Why'd you no' kill Tessa?"

"King Teluth told me not to...he wanted her alive."

Cailean chewed on that for a moment.

"And why'd you no' kill Laney?"

He growled, and after a few moments, Cailean was starting to think he wasn't going to answer.

"There was no need. She believed my story."

"What did you plan to do with her?"

"Marry her...eventually."

This shocked Cailean so much that he almost let go of the dagger.

"Why?" It was all he could think to ask.

"I've been alone for two thousand years. A wife seemed like a good change of pace."

"Are you trying to tell me you have feelings for her?" he asked incredulously.

"Are you insane?" Alex asked in disgust. "She's a human. It's simply in the best interest of my business. A man such as myself is perceived as more approachable and trustworthy when he has a wife and child."

Cailean growled through clenched teeth. "You canna get her pregnant, you're Unseelie!"

"I know that you idiot," he said in disgust. "We would adopt!"

Cailean forced the image of a poor innocent child being forced to accept an Unseelie as a father and be used by him in such a cruel way out of his head before he lost control.

"And then what? Live happily ever after?"

Alex smiled. "Even better than a man with a wife and child, is a man having to raise that poor child alone because of his wife's untimely death."

"You sick bastard," he spat at the same time he slid the dagger across Alex's jugular.

Alex yelled in pain and grabbed his neck, eyes wide with shock. Blood gushed out, staining his white shirt red in a matter of seconds. He looked at Cailean in disbelief before sliding slowly out of the chair and falling to the floor, dead.

Cailean looked at the fae lying face down in his own blood and wondered when he had gotten to the point that he could murder in cold blood without a moment of remorse. The realization made him shudder.

After a few moments, he turned and walked out, closing the door quietly behind him. He saw Laney peeking out from behind a car and took a deep breath and walked toward her.

Not quite sure what to make of her tall saviour, she eyed him warily from her crouch behind the car.

"'Tis ok Laney, I'm Cailean. Tessa sent me to rescue you."

She stood hesitantly. "Is he dead?"

"Aye."

"Is Tessa ok?"

"Aye."

"Are you taking me to her?"

"Aye."

"Do you say anything other than 'aye'?"

He grinned at her. "Aye."

She smiled through her tears despite the traumatic experience she had just been through and Cailean knew right away that she was much stronger than she appeared. He smiled reassuringly at her while motioning to the door.

"Jump in, I'll drive."

She looked alarmed. "Where are we going?"

"Back to Alex's house. 'Tis where the porthole is. Much faster than flying."

She looked surprised but didn't say anything as she got into Alex's car which was parked behind hers. Luckily the keys were still in the ignition.

*   *   *

"Colin," asked Tessa hesitantly. "Have you ever been married?"

She looked at him curiously with an almost vulnerable look on her face that he couldn't decipher.

He thought about Katie and his heart did a familiar flip. Although it had been about two hundred years since her death, he had never stopped loving her. He still remembered the little things, like the time she brought him breakfast in bed after one of his fae fights and managed to tip hot coffee onto his lap, scalding a most sensitive area. She was more upset about that incident than he was. He was just thankful she hadn't burned it off completely. It healed quickly of course.

One of his most favorite memories of her was the day their first child, Calum, had been born. She was lying on their bed with her hair plastered to her face after ten hours of intense labour, smiling at their little angel. She had looked up at him then, and in her eyes he saw such intense love that it took his breath away.

"Colin?"

Colin cleared his throat and looked at Tessa as she sat in the same chair Katie used to nurse their babies in. A memory flew by of Katie laughing because Isobel, who had just cut her first tooth, had bitten her while nursing. She had teased him about having a vampire baby.

"Yes luv, I was married once. Her name was Katie."

"Did you love her very much?"

He sighed at the memories. "More than my own life lass. She gave me three beautiful bairn and loved them each with a passion unlike any I've ever known."

"What were their names?"

"Calum was first. He was a strong, handsome lad who had the ladies trailing him for miles. Bit of a cad that one, but loyal to the end to his Marie, who he finally married, leaving all the other lasses depressed for months." He laughed at the memory. "Isobel was next. From the time she was three she had already decided that she would marry a fine man and have five bairn. And she did too. She was a strong willed lass with so much love to give. The last was Angus who was the worst troublemaker you could ever imagine," he said, remembering the time he had thrown a cat at his older brother, leaving him with deep scratches that took weeks to heal. "Despite that though, he was the most loyal lad you could have ever met. He would do anything for family or friends, even if it meant giving his own life for theirs."

He looked out of the window, lost in his memories, and Tessa was quiet for a moment.

"How did you deal with it...with losing them?"

Colin turned back to Tessa and smiled sadly. "I'm still trying luv. 'Tis hard to let go of those you've loved so dearly. They never truly die because they live on forever in your memories."

She looked over at him sadly, a tear in the corner of her eye.

"'Tis no' such a bad thing luv," he assured her, reaching over to wipe her tear away. "I consider myself one of the lucky ones. I was able to find and love a wonderful woman. I cherish all the

years I had with her and thank God everyday for giving her to me.
I also thank him for my bairn and the many, many grandbairn
along the way. I was very lucky in comparison to a mortal man. I
got to meet all of my descendants."

Tessa laughed softly. "Do you have any regrets?"

"No' a one lass. I got to live a dream that no other man ever
has...no' even Cailean."

"Was he never in love?"

Colin looked at her with an unusual expression. "I think that's
something you'll need to ask him luv."

She nodded and looked out the window at the moon.

*   *   *

"Tessa? Colin?"

"Cailean!" shouted Tessa, running for the door with Colin at
her heels.

"Laney!" she yelled when she caught site of her childhood
friend standing next to Cailean.

Laney ran to her and they both hugged and cried in each
other's arms.

"Oh God I thought you were dead!" cried Laney, squashing
Tessa so hard she could barely breathe.

"Laney...thank God you got away from that maniac."

Cailean and Colin looked on in amusement with grins on their
faces.

"I rescue her best friend and I doona even get a thank you,"
Cailean grumbled to Colin, doing his best impression of a pout.

Tessa turned from Laney and jumped into his arms, kissing
him thoroughly.

"Thank you," she said breathlessly when she finally pulled away.

"Wow! Do you have any more friends I can rescue?"

She laughed and swatted his chest, then introduced Laney to Colin who took her hand in his and kissed it gently.

"'Tis a pleasure to meet you lass."

Laney took in the tall, muscular Scot with his long hair and turned to Tessa with a helpless face, causing her to roll her eyes and drag her off to the kitchen for some comfort food.

"Good Lord woman, we just rescue you from one guy and you promptly fall for another."

"Is it my fault that Scotsmen and faeries are so gorgeous?" she demanded with her hands on her hips.

Tessa giggled and pushed her down in a chair before raiding the freezer for butterscotch ice cream. She got two bowls out of the cupboard and dished out a very unhealthy portion for each of them, topping it with chocolate syrup.

As they sat gorging on ice cream, Laney filled Tessa in on what had happened from the time she got out of the bathroom and found them gone, to when Cailean rescued her. Tessa was quite sure she embellished a little to make the story sound even more exciting, and laughed at her friend's account of the cat clawing Alex's perfect face.

Tessa got serious. "So what happened to him?"

Laney put her last bite of ice cream in her mouth before answering quietly. "Cailean said he's dead. I don't actually know any details." She shook her head. "I didn't see what happened."

Tessa looked down at her empty bowl, unsure of what to say.

Laney put her hand on Tessa's and she looked up at her. "I'm not sorry Tess. Cailean told me that he had planned on marrying me, adopting a poor innocent baby, then killing me. All to gain sympathy and trust from his business clients."

Tessa frowned angrily. "That asshole!"

"That's exactly what I said."

Tessa got up and went around the table, pulling Laney into a tight squeeze. "Oh Laney, I don't know what I would have done without you."

"I felt exactly the same way when I thought I'd lost you Tess," she sniffed, squeezing back.

"Let's promise never to die on each other ok?"

Laney laughed at her friend but agreed. "You got it sweetie."

*   *   *

"Well if you lasses are done with your comfort food, 'tis high time we all got to bed," said Cailean, walking into the kitchen with Colin following on his heels.

"Aye," agreed Colin with a grin. "Laney, I'll show you to your room lass."

Laney glanced at Tessa with a grin. "Lead on."

Tessa rolled her eyes at her friend and turned to Cailean. "She's hopeless around gorgeous men," she explained tiredly.

"Oh so you think Colin's gorgeous?" he asked in mock anger.

She grinned up at him. "He's pretty cute, but nothing compared to you."

"Ah you're lucky you came to your senses lass," he teased as he pulled her firmly against him, bending down to kiss her.

"Oh, and what would you have done if I hadn't?" she asked curiously, marvelling at the feel of his already rigid shaft pressed hard against her.

He looked down at her wickedly and lifted her against him, pressing her backward into the wall, his manhood nestled snugly against her thighs. She gasped in surprise and looked up at him curiously, no doubt wondering if he meant to take her right there in the kitchen.

He chuckled softly at the look she gave him and thrust against her. He felt her push her hips against his and growled with desire. He had planned on teasing her but the fact that she was just as willing as he was, in the middle of the kitchen where they could both get caught by any number of people, made him rethink his plans. The temptation and risk was intoxicating. He bent his head and captured her mouth. Her tongue was still cold from ice cream and she tasted like chocolate.

He moaned in approval and thrust against her again, trembling from the intensity of his desire. His breathing sounded harsh to his own ears as his heart hammered mercilessly against his chest and his shaft pressed against the blazing heat in the junction of her thighs.

Tessa leaned in and licked him and he inhaled raggedly at the feel of her now warm tongue against his neck, sliding up toward his ear. A shiver ran through him and he pulled her harder against him, softness against muscle.

He backed off slightly and tugged her pants off, then her underwear.

After he had gotten her sufficiently undressed, he removed his sporran and undid his own pants, pulling it down partway before she suddenly dropped down to her knees, capturing him in her mouth before he could stop her.

He leaned his head back against the wall, gritting his teeth as he fought for control. He knew he should stop her, pull her back up, but the smooth heat of her mouth gliding up and down his shaft was just too intense. He would just let her...for a minute. He groaned in pleasure when he felt her tongue flick against the head of his painfully aroused shaft and his hands splayed against the wall, keeping him balanced as she drove him into her mouth over and over, ripping the breath from his lungs.

He shuddered as he felt the familiar spasm, warning him that he was about to come, and forced himself to push away from the wall, grabbing her arms and pulling her up against him, attacking her mouth with ferocious need.

She moaned in surrender and wrapped her arms around his neck as he pressed against her once again. This time there were no barriers and he rubbed the head of his cock back and forth against her slick folds. She held on tightly, gasping with each stroke.

Somehow he managed to unbutton her shirt and maneuver her so that he could wrap his mouth around her breast, sucking and flicking her nipple with his tongue, making her squirm in pleasure. He devoted lavish attention to her breasts, squeezing them and fondling until she was nearly delirious with need and on the brink of orgasm. He slid her nipples along the soft stubble of his cheek and she jerked her hips against his, slowly destroying his willpower.

"Please Cailean...I want you so badly," she begged.

"How badly lass?" he asked as he pushed his cock slightly inside her, allowing no more.

She moaned and tried to push down on him but his hands on her hips prevented her. Instead, she started moving back and forth against him, making his breath catch from the pleasure of it, knowing she was bringing herself closer and closer to orgasm.

His breathing grew ragged as she continued moving, sliding his cock along her folds over and over again.

Unable to hold back any longer, he plunged into her and cried out in pleasure.

"Yes," she whispered, and he kissed her savagely, pushing into her again and again with his hand against the small of her back to protect her from the wall behind.

His body strained from the effort it was taking to stay standing while his world spun around him. He could think of naught but the woman in his arms, her legs wrapped tightly around his, matching his rhythm as he thrust into her.

"Cailean," she cried, arching her neck.

He drove into her hard and fast, until he was almost mindless with need. He heard her cry out and felt her spasming around him as she came. He covered her mouth with his, catching her cries of pleasure against his tongue.

"Och, I love you lass," he groaned as his own orgasm washed over him, almost causing his knees to buckle with the force of it. He pressed her hard against the wall in his attempt to stay standing and his seed flowed out of him in waves as his husky voice whispered into her ear. Although he knew she wouldn't understand the words he said in Gaelic, she suddenly came again, causing him to moan in pleasure as he felt her pulsing along with him. Once again he felt that familiar surge of power that came with making love to her and marvelled at the intensity of it.

They stayed that way, propped against the wall, breathing hard. Her head was tilted back the wall and she looked so beautiful, so wonderfully erotic in that moment that he vowed he would never let her go. Somehow he would convince Finvarra to make her immortal too. He refused to watch this woman die...refused to live on without her in his arms every day. His heart swelled with the love he felt for her.

She opened her eyes and looked up at him with a shy smile. "That was amazing," she gasped. "And I love you too Cailean MacLeod."

He could see the love reflected in her eyes and it made him even more determined to force Finvarra to accept him demands. If her life was destined to end...he would damn well make sure Finvarra understood that his would too.

~20~

"**W**hat do you mean you'll no' live without her...you mean you canna, right?" asked Colin in surprise after hearing Cailean's vow.

"Both Colin," he answered in a clipped voice. "Unless Finvarra agrees to make Tessa immortal, I'll no longer be his pawn."

Colin looked long and hard at his brother, weighing his next words carefully. "So you'd would let the entire world suffer?"

Cailean smashed a glass against the kitchen wall with a savage curse and stormed out of the castle.

Colin sighed and resumed his seat at the kitchen table, putting his head in his hands. He had seen the raw pain in his brother's eyes and knew that the day Tessa's life ended...he would lose his brother forever.

He poured milk into his cup, splashing some on the table in the process.

"You really should watch where you pour that," said Laney from behind him. In his distraction he hadn't even heard her walk in.

Colin turned and smiled at the blonde haired woman, pushing out a chair for her with his foot and motioning for her to sit.

Laney dropped into the offered chair and looked at him intently. "Why do you look so sad?" she asked, reaching out to pour herself some milk.

Colin sighed and rubbed his eyes tiredly. "My brother refuses to live without Tessa."

Laney frowned and looked up from the bread she was spreading honey on. "And that's a bad thing?"

"'Tis when she's no' immortal and he is."

"Ohhh," said Laney, catching on to the dilemma. "How can he refuse to live without her then?"

"There are ways," Colin assured her, looking miserable.

"He would end his life?" she asked, her eyes round.

"Aye, as far as he's concerned, his life will mean nothing without her."

"Oh," she said softly. "That's so romantic."

Colin looked up at her with one eyebrow raised. "Romantic? Are you daft lass?"

Laney smiled self-consciously at him, playing with her bread. "Well, it's like Romeo and Juliet...both refusing to live without the other."

"Ahhh Shakespeare," sighed Colin, shaking his head. "The man was a hopeless romantic who loved a good tragedy."

"Did you know him?" she asked, eyes wide with hope.

"Alas no, he died well before my time. But his work was well known among the Scots."

Laney smiled. "Well I still say it's romantic."

Colin shook his head at the woman and reached over to refill her milk. "So 'tis true what Tessa says about you then?" he asked, mysteriously.

"What did she say?" She looked at him, horrified.

"That you're a hopeless romantic."

"Oh...well," she fussed with the edge of her napkin. "I just think life is boring without love."

Colin pondered her worlds carefully. How long had it been since he'd felt love? Since Katie died? Almost two hundred years. He could hardly believe it had been that long.

"What about you Colin? Are you in love with anyone?"

He laughed humourlessly. "Nay lass, I'm sure I've forgotten how to love by now."

"You can't just forget how to love. It comes naturally. You'll see, one day it will hit you again like a stone. It will make you fly off your feet and land on your butt in surprise."

Colin roared with laughter at her description. The lass definitely had a unique way of looking at things. He'd never heard anyone describe falling in love quite like she had, or with as much enthusiasm.

She looked at him with a grin and drank the rest of her milk, leaving a white moustache above her lip. He grinned at it.

Tessa walked into the kitchen at that moment. "Hey Laney, Colin. You have a milk moustache sweetie," she said, grinning at Laney.

Laney wiped at it quickly with her hand, looking accusingly at Colin. "You could have told me."

He just grinned and stood, offering Tessa his chair. "I need to talk to Cailean. If you lasses will excuse me."

After pushing Tessa's chair in, he turned and walked off in search of his brother.

*   *   *

"So?"

Laney looked at Tessa, confused. "So what?"

"Don't so what me Laney Ferrel! Have you fallen completely head over heels with Colin already?"

"Tessa!" she complained loudly. "I do not fall in love with every man that walks by."

Tessa didn't speak, just continued to stare at Laney knowingly.

Laney sighed and looked back at Tessa, eyes narrowed. "I think he's cute ok...that's all. Besides, I think I've had enough of gorgeous men for the time being."

"Uh huh," sighed Tessa, rolling her eyes as she reached for a cinnamon bun that was dripping in white icing. "You're hopeless sweetie," she said affectionately as she tucked a piece of the soft bun into her mouth. "Mmmm oh that's good." She opened her eyes to find Laney grinning at her.

"As good as last night?"

Tessa almost choked on the bun and looked at Laney with wide eyes. "How did you know about last night?" she demanded.

"I didn't," she admitted, then added slyly with a grin, "but I do now."

Tessa threw a piece of bun at her, causing Laney to squeal in delight as she took that for confirmation. "Soooo? What did you do?"

"None of your business!" said Tessa, amused at Laney's trickery.

"Fine," she sighed, pretending to be upset. "But you have to realize that I depend on you for excitement in my life."

"Oh good God Laney...you have enough excitement in your life to give me a heart attack."

They both laughed and sat talking for another half hour before Cailean and Colin came inside. Cailean ran over to Tessa and pulled her out of the chair.

"You and Laney have to get to safety. They're here."

Laney looked around, scared and confused. "What? Who's here? Where are we going?"

"No," cried Tessa, grabbing Cailean's arm as he pulled her out of the kitchen. "I'm not going to lose you Cailean."

He looked down at her and abruptly pulled her to him, kissing her as if it would be the last time they would taste each other. At that moment her entire world felt complete and she knew that if she let him go, let him fight, that she would never see him again. Her heart broke as he kissed her with so much passion that it threatened to drown her. His lips moved over hers possessively, taking, giving. She suddenly realized that she needed him. It wasn't just that she wanted him or had to have him in her life, she absolutely needed him in order to survive. Her life was worthless if he wasn't in it.

He pulled back. "Tessa love, I will return," he promised in a husky voice. "Have faith lass."

"Please don't go," she begged, panicking.

Thunder crashed so loudly overhead that she jumped violently, her panic increasing tenfold.

"I have to go lass. If I doona, there'll no' be a world left for us."

She let him go and put her hands over her mouth, shaking her head, tears rolling down her cheeks. He looked down at her with raw pain on his face. She wondered if he was thinking that this moment might be the last time they would ever see each other again. She almost crumpled to the floor, the agony too real. He reached toward her one more time and kissed her gently. It felt like a kiss goodbye and she trembled in fear, unable to voice her terror.

She felt a hand around her shoulder and someone tugging at her. Cailean was forcing her to move from behind and Colin was dragging her down a flight of stairs into a basement of sorts. Just as she was starting to panic, the room was lit in a dull yellow light, showing what almost resembled a bomb shelter. There were cans and dried foods stacked on shelves along the length of the room and shelf after shelf of bottled water.

"You and Laney will stay here," Cailean ordered. "When 'tis over we will come back and get you. 'Till then you'll be locked in."

"No!" shouted Tessa in horror. No way to get to him if he needed her. No way out if he didn't...if he didn't return.

Colin was in the corner, he was leaning over, talking to Laney. She nodded at something he said and turned to look at Tessa in concern. She felt as if she had suddenly been thrust into the rabbit hole of Alice's wonderland. Nothing made sense. Above her she could hear the crashing of thunder and feel the trembling of the stones that were holding the castle together. How could Cailean hope to survive such fury? How could he think himself strong enough to fight fantasy creatures and win? What kind of powers did they have, these creatures? Was he going into this with a hope and a prayer?

She realized that he was prying her hand off of his shirt and grabbed even tighter. "You can't lock us in!"

He looked down at her sadly. "I must Tessa. If I'm distracted by worrying about you running about, getting killed by one of those monsters, I'll surely be killed myself."

She gasped and grabbed her hand away from his shirt as if burned. Laney came to her and pulled her into a hug, falling to her knees with her, doing her best to comfort her while she cried.

Cailean pulled the door shut behind him and Tessa cried even harder, knowing she would never see the man she loved again. Laney held her fiercely, tears in her eyes as she watched her best friend break apart.

*   *   *

Cailean leaned his head against the heavy wooden door while Colin locked it. His heart broke into a million pieces as he listened to Tessa's own heart breaking. If there is a god, he prayed silently, protect her.

He felt Colin's hand on his shoulder, firm and reassuring. "We must go Cailean. The faster we get this done, the faster you'll make it back to her. Let's no' prolong this any more than we have to. I gave Laney the spare key...just incase."

Cailean took a deep breath and turned to follow his brother up the stairs.

As they neared the front door another crash of thunder echoed through the castle and the brothers felt residual tremors run through them. The previous storm hadn't been as strong, and just standing inside, they could feel the power of the wind slamming against the castle.

Taking a deep breath, Colin pulled the heavy wooden door open and rain pelted through the doorway, soaking him instantly. A huge tremor suddenly shook the ground, knocking them both off their feet. Getting up quickly, they forced their way out into the gale force winds and looked through the driving rain.

After a minute Colin yelled out and pointed to their right. Cailean followed his gaze and nodded. They pushed away toward the porthole, keeping as close to the ground as possible to avoid the debris that was flying around.

As they neared the shimmering light, they noticed a group of fae in the porthole's entrance, staring at them menacingly; all holding daggers. The leader appeared to be a woman.

"Kynleigh!" Colin shouted to Cailean. He nodded.

Colin's long hair was plastered to his head and he swiped it away from his face before he moved forward toward the beautiful but deadly fae. She held her hand up, warning him to stop.

"What are you doing Kynleigh?" demanded Colin, standing five feet away from the angry fae, struggling to stay upright in the wind.

"Avenging the king's death!" she growled.

Both brothers looked at each other with frowns. Did Finvarra actually kill Teluth?

"He did!" she confirmed, reading their minds. "We couldn't stop the bleeding."

There was pain in her words. Anger. For a moment Cailean felt sympathy for the woman, but it was quickly extinguished.

"Now I will continue what he started!"

"Kynleigh, this is no' you. You dinna want it to end this way," yelled Colin over the storm, praying the woman would see reason before it was too late.

She looked angrily at the younger MacLeod, a tear escaping and rolling down her flawless cheek. "You have no idea who I am human! Don't pretend to know me, to know what I want."

"I'm no' pretending Kynleigh. You told me yourself that you dinna want to see my world end, that you dinna want the violence. Who will be there to see your revenge if everyone is dead? The hole you just put between our worlds will kill us all if you doona end it now," he warned. The edges of the porthole throbbed.

"Finvarra dinna want it to end this way either. He dinna want to kill his own brother. Teluth forced his hand, we were there, we saw what happened."

Both brothers saw the shock on Kynleigh's face at this admission. Her mouth dropped open and she looked from one brother to the next as if hoping one would deny what was just said, but neither did. She shook her head slightly. "You're lying!" she screamed.

Colin reached out and grabbed her arm, refusing to let go as she tried to pull away from him. "Then read my mind Kynleigh...you know I'm telling you the truth," he yelled.

"No!" she screamed, still trying to pull away. "Let me go!"

The warriors who had been standing beside her suddenly grabbed Colin and yanked him off of their leader, throwing him a good ten feet. He crashed to the ground with a grunt and lay there looking up at her. "You know I'm no' lying," he yelled again. "You could feel the truth in what I said. Admit it Kynleigh!"

The warriors all converged on Colin and Cailean, stabbing at them with their daggers. They fought off the fae with their own daggers, managing to kill seven of them before Kynleigh held her hand up and yelled for them to stop. The warriors looked at her uncertainly but eased back, keeping their eyes on the brothers for any sign of aggression.

The powerful woman just stood staring at Colin, tears rolling down her face.

"Kynleigh, 'tis all up to you now. You have the power to end this. Please..."

Cailean stood tensely, waiting for Kynleigh to decide their fate. His left arm was burning where the warrior's dagger sliced into it and he tried not to wince at the pain. From behind Colin, he saw him reach up and wipe his cheek. His hand came away with blood and he swayed slightly. Cailean became alarmed.

"Please Kynleigh..." he begged again, softer this time, weaker.

"Make up your mind you stupid fae!" yelled Cailean. "Your lover chose his own death, he knew he was no match for his brother, yet he insisted on battling him. He even tried to kill Colin in the process. You canna avenge his honour...he died without any! Decide now! Would you kill an entire world now because of his lies or will you stand up for what you believe is right. The future of our worlds rest on your decision!"

He lunged forward just as Colin dropped to his knees and caught him before he hit the ground. As he laid him down, he saw a black dagger sticking out of his chest, in almost exactly the same spot he had been cut before. Blood coated his shirt and his face was white and unresponsive.

Colin looked up accusingly at Kynleigh. "If you wanted an eye for an eye you should have gone after the one who was responsible for Teluth's death!" he bellowed in anger, not daring to believe that his brother once again lay dying in his arms.

He saw Kynleigh's face twist in regret as she looked down at Colin's unconscious form. Her head suddenly jerked up to look behind him and any regret he had seen disappeared completely as she moved aside to allow her warriors through. Within seconds, hundreds of fae were pouring through the porthole. Cailean looked behind him and saw king Finvarra approaching with his own army.

Everything turned to chaos at that single moment that the Seelie and Unseelie met in battle. There were fae as far as the eye could see, surrounding the castle like a carpet, some with daggers, most without.

Cailean fought through the angry fae as he dragged Colin to the safety of the castle. When he reached the doorway, he laid Colin down and pressed his hand to his chest to stop the bleeding as he looked out over the battle. Fae after fae were dropping like flies as the Unseelie's daggers found their mark. Screams of pain flowed through the air as more and more blood was spilled. Cailean looked down at his brother helplessly, knowing he would have to leave him and fight if their world was to stand any chance at all.

Colin looked up at Cailean weakly and whispered, "Go Cailean. My life will be of no use if there is no world left to live in."

Cailean closed his eyes in pain, knowing he was right.

304

"I love you brother," said Colin softly.

Cailean held onto his hand and lay his forehead against Colin's. "Always."

Before he could change his mind, he let go of Colin's hand and turned to face the battle. Anger burned inside him as he sought out Kynleigh. He would make her pay.

Growling, he shoved forward, slamming the Unseelie aside in his quest for vengeance. Finding a dagger on the ground, he picked it up and continued pushing his way through the battle, slicing through fae as he went.

Spying Kynleigh fifteen feet away, he continued battling the Unseelie as he moved forward. He felt a burning across his arm as a dagger found its mark but continued on, ignoring the pain.

As he approached Kynleigh, she turned around and looked at him with so much pain masking her face that it brought him up short. For a moment he fought with himself, with the urge to run her through with the dagger in retribution for the pain she had caused.

Kynleigh spread her arms to either side, the dagger dropping from her fingers in surrender.

"Do what you will MacLeod, I deserve no better."

With those words, the powerful fae closed her eyes, prepared for death.

For what seemed like forever, Cailean stood looking at the fae while the battle raged around him. Screams of agony filled the air but he stood, deaf to everything but the sound of the fae's shaky breathing.

Finally he bowed his head and let out a sigh. "I'll no' kill you Kynleigh. A worse punishment for you is to live with what you've done. That will be my revenge."

The beautiful fae opened her eyes and looked at Cailean for a moment before nodding softly. "As you choose, human."

Without saying a word, Kynleigh looked around and her warriors suddenly stopped fighting, raising their hands in surrender.

The war was over.

The rain and thunder stopped instantly as if a button had been pushed. It was eerily quiet.

The Unseelie turned as one and started filing through the porthole, some limping, others being carried. When they had all disappeared, Kynleigh turned to look at Cailean one last time before moving through the porthole herself.

Finvarra came up behind Cailean while the Seelie gathered their injured and made their own way to another porthole.

"Go to your brother Cailean, the war is over."

Without saying a word, Cailean turned and headed back to the castle. Each step was agony as he wondered what he would find. His legs felt like lead.

He pushed the castle door open and found Colin where he had left him, lying on his back, eyes closed. Pain crashed down on him as he looked at the gash in his brother's chest. He dropped to his knees beside Colin and closed his eyes.

"You dinna think I'd die that easily, did you brother? Where's your faith man?"

"Colin!" yelled his brother in joy, jostling him as he pulled him into a bear hug.

Colin gasped in pain. "Ah shit Cailean...just because I'm alive doesn't mean I'm no' in pain!"

"Och Christ sorry," he shook his head, looking at his brother in amazement.

He carefully helped Colin to stand and half carried him across the room, laying him on the couch gently. He yelled for the maids who had been hiding, and ran to call the doctor.

By the time he got back to Colin, three maids were already fussing over him.

Seeing his brother's grin, he shook his head in amusement. It never ceased to amaze him how fast the women came running.

Colin reached into his pocket and withdrew a key, holding it up for Cailean. He walked over and took it before heading down the stairs to release Tessa and Laney.

As soon as he fit the key into the lock he heard Tessa yell, "Cailean?"

"Aye lass, 'tis all over now," he assured her as he pulled the door open to see her standing with tears streaming down her face. Happy tears this time.

She jumped into his arms, surprising him. He felt her terror, her anger, and her love all mixed together in a single kiss and kissed her back roughly, groaning, pulling her tightly to him.

From behind Tessa he heard a polite 'ahem' and pulled away reluctantly from the kiss. "Ummm if I could just squeeze by..." said Laney, her face red as she tried to get through the narrow space between Cailean and the doorframe.

Cailean laughed loudly and put Tessa down, motioning to the stairs. "Shall we lasses?"

Laney took the lead, probably to make sure she wasn't trapped again incase they decided to have another go at each other. Cailean followed them, never taking his eyes off of Tessa.

"I love you," she mouthed to him.

"I love you too lass," he whispered back.

They reached the main floor and Laney gasped. "Oh my God Colin, what happened?"

Tessa's face lost its smile and she too went over to him in concern.

Colin looked over at Cailean and grinned, obviously very happy about all the attention he was receiving.

"Alright, alright...the lad will start getting hurt on purpose if you lasses keep carrying on this way."

Colin laughed softly. "Doona listen to him, he's just jealous."

Cailean shook his head grinning on his way to the door to see who was knocking.

Dr. Bentley entered the castle and looked over at Colin, shaking his head. "You know, I could make a living off treating you MacLeods alone."

"Well if things turn out the way we hope, we may no' be needing you as often from now on."

The doctor looked at him with one eyebrow raised, then shook his head smiling as he walked toward Colin.

"Well Mr. MacLeod," he said, looking at his patient in amusement. "Did you no' think it hurt enough last time? Or is it the lasses you're after?"

Colin just grinned at the doctor. "It worked last time...why mess with a good thing?"

The doctor bellowed with laughter and shoed the women aside so that he could get to his patient.

Cailean took Tessa's hand and led her outside. The air smelled of wet grass and rain, and the sun was shining brightly. It was hard to believe that just twenty minutes before, a hurricane ravaged the countryside.

He walked silently for a while, revelling in the feel of Tessa's small, delicate hand in his. He hadn't dared to believe that one day he might find someone he would fall in love with so completely. Had in fact avoided it at all costs. Now he couldn't even remember why, so complete was that love that he felt he'd die without it.

When they reached the water, he stopped and turned her around to face him. "Lass," he started hesitantly. "There's something I want to ask you." He looked down at her smiling face, taking a mental picture of how beautiful she was as she looked up at him expectantly, trusting him completely. The birds started singing at that moment, and for some reason everything seemed all right in the world. It was as if the past few weeks hadn't happened. As if he hadn't faced the possibility of life without his brother, without Tessa.

A soft breeze caressed Tessa's face, blowing her hair softly against her cheek. He reached down and took the stray strand of hair in his fingers, marvelling at its softness. He finally understood how lucky he was to be immortal. Realized that if he had just been a normal man, he would never have lived to meet this remarkable woman. Never known a love so strong that a single glance from her could take the breath from his lungs. He was finally, truly and completely happy.

His heart pounded as he got down on one knee in the wet grass and looked up at her surprised face in adoration. Tears threatened in her wide eyes.

"Tessa love, will you marry me and spend the rest of your life with me?"

Her tears started in earnest then and she dropped down on her knees with him and held him tightly, whispering the answer he had been praying he'd hear.

"Yes."

*   *   *

Tessa felt one strong arm wrap around her and the other tilt her chin up so that she was looking at him. In his eyes she saw the kind of love people die for and knew how lucky she was to find this man. He made her whole world right in every way and she could never imagine a life without him. He was hers forever. She could hardly breathe at the thought of being married to such a wonderful man.

She shook slightly as he leaned his head down to claim her mouth. The feel of his firm lips against hers made her melt immediately and she opened up to him, sliding her tongue against his, feeling him tremble at the touch.

Electricity shot through her as their kiss deepened and he pulled her more firmly against him, moaning. Needing to feel him, to have him so close that there would be nothing between them, she slid her hands behind his head and grabbed his hair, pulling him more firmly against her. For one moment she opened her eyes, needing to see him, and then let out a shriek of terror when she caught a glimpse of someone standing behind him.

Cailean whipped her away from him and spun around, ready for battle. Almost immediately he sagged in relief, dropping his arms with a heavy sigh.

"Christ Finvarra, are you trying to see if an immortal can have a heart attack?"

The king laughed loudly, shaking his head in amusement.

"I hear congratulations are in order."

"What? How?"

"I have my sources," said the handsome fae mysteriously.

Cailean looked over at Tessa and rolled his eyes.

"My dear," said Finvarra, looking at Tessa. "Would you allow me to bestow a wedding gift upon you?"

What a strange way of asking, she thought before nodding uncertainly.

King Finvarra looked at Cailean with a smile. "I heard what you said to Kynleigh, Cailean. We are forever in your debt. As powerful and intelligent as we are, challenging her morals wouldn't have been something we would have thought to do. You and Colin have managed to save not only your own world, but the Seelie as well. Because of this, I bestow the gift of immortality upon your fiancé and any children you may have." He stopped his speech and turned from Cailean to Tessa and back again. "That is...if you want it."

"Yes," yelled Tessa before Cailean could even think of a response.

He looked over at her with a small smile. "You would choose to spend eternity with me?" he asked, a little awed.

"Of course Cailean. I love you so much. I couldn't stand knowing I would die and never see you again."

He released a breath he hadn't realized he'd been holding and grabbed her tightly, not wanting to ever let her go.

King Finvarra cleared his throat, causing them both to look up.

He reached out and touched her wrist.

When he removed his hand, a small, black figure eight was left behind.

"It is the mark of immortality."

He then reached down to put his hand on her flat stomach, startling her. "I also bestow the gift of courage onto your sons. They will be strong men...with giving hearts."

Tessa looked at Cailean in shock. "Sons? I'm pregnant? Twins?"

Finvarra smiled at her then inhaled deeply. "Ahh I do so love the smell of wet grass after a storm."

Without another word, he disappeared into thin air, chuckling as he went.

Cailean looked at Tessa's stunned face and laughed with joy, lifting her up and spinning her around before suddenly putting her down again with a look of concern on his face. "Are you ok?"

She looked up at her soon-to-be husband and tears of joy rolled down her cheeks. Well at least she had a good reason for all the crying she had been doing lately. "I love you so much Cailean MacLeod."

He leaned down to kiss her gently. "I am truly the happiest man in the world," he said softly. "You are my life Tessa MacLeod."

She thrilled at the name and held on to him, promising herself that nothing would ever come between them. They would be together forever, she and her immortal highlander...and their sons of course. She put a hand on her stomach and smiled happily, wondering what kind of men her babies would grow up to be.

EPILOGUE

*T*essa MacLeod looked down at her beautiful son, Teron,

sleeping soundly in her arms. He had black hair like his father and

the blue eyes of a newborn. She gently brushed his hair off of his

forehead and wondered what colour his eyes would change to as he

grew.

His tiny mouth opened in a yawn and his small fist touched

her chest, seeking comfort in her warmth. She saw the small figure

eight on the inside of his wrist and sighed happily. Her child would

live forever. Such a gift is more than any mother could hope for.

Finvarra had come the day before, somehow getting the news

of the boys' birth, to drop off a gift for them. Two chains, one

silver and one gold, both with infinity symbols on them, like the

one on their wrists.

A permanent rift had opened up between the worlds because

of Kynleigh's aborted attempt to start a war. Guards were now

posted on the fae side, preventing others from passing through

without permission. For the most part, the Unseelie had ceased to cause any more trouble under their new leader. There was always, of course, the rogue fae who thought Teluth's plan was the right one. They were quickly disabused of that notion and punished accordingly by Kynleigh herself.

Tessa looked up from her precious little boy to see her handsome husband walk in holding Eridon carefully in his arms. He was the splitting image of his brother in every way. The chains that they already wore were the only way Tessa and Cailean could tell the boys apart. Apparently Finvarra had also known they would be completely identical.

"I think this wee lad is hungry," said Cailean softly, still nervous about holding something so fragile, despite the fact that his sons were immortal.

He leaned over and Tessa placed Teron in one of his arms before taking Eridon from the other. She stroked his soft cheek and bent to kiss his forehead. He smelled so wonderful.

They were truly the most beautiful babies she had ever seen. She still couldn't believe she and Cailean were responsible for their tiny lives.

Eridon opened his blue eyes and looked at his mother for a second before opening his mouth, searching for food.

She smiled happily and let him latch on to her already sore breast, amazed that even at one day old, he was able to show her what he wanted.

Looking up at Cailean she saw him smile down at his other son, running his big hand gently over Teron's soft hair. Her heart swelled with joy as she realized how complete her life was.

*   *   *

Cailean held his son carefully as he went down the stairs. He had never dreamed he could love anyone as much as he loved Tessa, but his sons proved to him that love came in all different forms. When he reached the bottom of the staircase he looked down at Teron and shook his head in amazement. He was so tiny and fragile. His thumb was barely bigger than the finger nail on Cailean's little finger. He was in such perfect proportion. An incredibly tiny person.

The moment he had seen his son for the first time he'd felt overwhelming panic. How was he supposed to protect such a tiny being? Then Eridon came out and he nearly panicked in truth as he realized he now had two tiny beings to protect along with their mother.

It had taken him most of the night to calm down and realize that he wasn't alone. Their uncle would also be there to help protect his nephews and Tessa. That made him feel a little better, but he supposed he would have to actually let Colin hold his nephews at some point. He felt like a mother hen, not wanting to let his sons out of his sight for even a second.

"Well?" asked Colin, walking up to his brother. "Have you decided you can trust me to hold my nephew yet?"

Cailean looked at Colin and then back at Teron. Now or never.

Very carefully he placed his precious son into his uncles waiting arms and watched in amazement as a look of pure love stole over his face. "Wow, he's such a wee thing," said Colin in awe. "And so soft."

"Oh my God, I can't believe he let you hold him before me," came Laney's offended voice from behind him.

"Told you I had more clout," teased Colin with a grin, never once looking up from Teron's little face.

She was just about to argue when Teron yawned and stretched his little fists in the air. "Awwww," said Laney helplessly, argument completely forgotten as she held out her finger and watched Teron wrap incredibly small fingers around it.

Cailean shook his head and laughed. Only a day old and his son already knew how to get a woman's attention.

As he looked at his son being fussed over, he felt his heart swell with pride and happiness, realizing for the first time how much love flowed through the walls of Dunvegan Castle. He was truly the luckiest man on earth.

Kristy Pantin